The Jaubert Ring

The Jaubert Ring

WILLO DAVIS ROBERTS

PUBLISHED FOR THE CRIME CLUB BY

DOUBLEDAY & COMPANY, INC.

GARDEN CITY, NEW YORK

1976

All of the characters in this book
are fictitious, and any resemblance
to actual persons, living or dead,
is purely coincidental.

ISBN: 0-385-11591-1
Library of Congress Catalog Card Number 75–40742
Copyright © 1976 by Willo Davis Roberts
All Rights Reserved
Printed in the United States of America
First Edition

The house was cool and still in the Virginia dawn. It was a time of day I had always enjoyed, but there would be no joy in this day.

I heard Phoebe moving in the kitchen, starting the fire to cook the breakfast grits. The thought of food stirred a twinge of nausea. For a moment I nearly cried out to her to forget the grits, and then reason prevailed. Even if no one ate, Phoebe needed something to do.

The shadows lessened across the room where I sat motionless in my rocker, allowing the coffin to emerge from the gloom. There had been a candle burning at the foot of it, but it had gone out some time ago.

I sighed and rubbed at my aching neck, and then the sound of horses on the road brought me out of the chair. It was too early for callers, unless . . .

Three horsemen were coming up the lane toward the house. None of them was Francis; the accelerated pulses slowed when I realized that. One of them was Francis' employer, though, Mr. Courtney, from the bank. Mr. Dunning, the constable, was with him; the third man was a stranger.

Our rising smoke would have assured them that the household was astir; yet the earliness of the hour, and the fact that I had sat beside Aunt Rachael's body through a long and lonely night, no doubt contributed to the surge of alarm I felt. My vague foreboding came to fruition when Phoebe ushered the men into the sewing room a moment later.

It was not the place I would have chosen to receive them, since only yesterday morning we had been working there, Dorothea and I, and our stitchery had been abandoned without ceremony when Rachael collapsed. Still, the parlor where the casket stood was even less appropriate for their reception.

I swept into the room, head held high, as if I unconsciously braced myself for further catastrophe. I knew as soon as I saw their faces that I would find it.

The three men stood uneasily in the middle of the small room, twisting their hats in their hands. Mr. Dunning cleared his throat as if to speak, then glanced in deference to the banker.

"Saunielle," Mr. Courtney said, stepping forward as if reluctantly.

"I hope you will excuse us for coming so early, but the matter seemed urgent. You know Mr. Dunning, of course, and this is Mr. Wooster, the bank examiner. He has been kind enough to come with us on an errand which we all deeply regret . . ."

"I told you yesterday, Mr. Courtney, that if Francis was involved in . . . in anything regarding bank funds . . . I know nothing about it."

"Yes. Yes, of course. I'm sure that is true. Mr. Wooster has, as you know, been making a routine examination of our accounts, and there is no question that a considerable sum is missing. However, we now have reason to believe . . ." He cleared his throat, his kindly face looking overheated. "We may have jumped rather too rapidly to conclusions when we learned that young Francis had . . . ah . . . vanished from his rooming house."

Ever so briefly, my heart leapt. But their faces precluded my expectation of good news. I waited, wishing the blood would not hammer so in my breast, resisting the urge to quiet it with a hand pressed there.

"I think . . . perhaps Miss Hunter would like to sit down," Dunning suggested.

That was sufficiently ominous so that I brought out a hand to touch the back of a chair; that was all. "Please. Tell me what you came to say."

There was a general shuffling of feet and further twisting of hats in hands, certainly not a favorable omen. My apprehension grew.

"You were acquainted, I think, with another teller in the bank, a Mr. Lionel Erquart. He served the window next to Francis Verland's."

"Yes," I agreed, thoroughly mystified. "That is to say, Francis had introduced us."

Courtney made sounds that were impossible to interpret. Had it not been for his obviously genuine distress, I would have urged him more strongly to delay no further in conveying whatever he had come to convey. Perhaps, I remember thinking, I ought to sit down, but I made no move to do so. Indeed, my fingers were curled painfully around the chair back by this time.

"It has come to our attention . . . that is to say . . ." To my horror the banker's eyes filled with tears and it seemed that his throat closed, making speech beyond him. I glanced in alarm at the others. The bank examiner was rather red in the face. It was Constable Dunning who had to take it from there.

"It seems that Mr. Erquart, too, is missing from his lodgings. Mr. Wooster may have been a bit hasty in jumping to the conclusion that the shortage in the bank's accounts must be laid at Francis Verland's door. It now seems quite possible that Mr. Erquart may have skipped off with the money, not Mr. Verland."

The constriction in my chest was extremely painful. Had the chair been in a position where I might easily have slipped into it, I would have done so. As it was, I continued to cling to its back while a wave of vertigo rose and subsided.

"Then Francis . . . have you found Francis?" Even as I asked, I knew that if they had found him, and he'd been able to come himself, he would have done so.

For a series of seconds none of the men spoke. And then Dunning pulled something out of his pocket and extended it toward me, palm open to reveal it.

"Do you recognize this, Miss Hunter?"

Perhaps it was that I had not slept the previous night, or perhaps the entire preceding forty-eight hours was overwhelming me. At any rate, I felt lightheaded and curiously detached.

"Yes. It is a ring that came to me from my mother's family . . . the Jaubert ring. I had . . . had given it to . . . Mr. Verland." My words seemed to come from a long way off. "Where did you get it?"

"I'm sorry, miss," Dunning said, his face grave. "We recovered it this morning, on the body of a young man who was found in the river. He . . . excuse me, but he was not a pretty sight after several days in the water, and it was impossible to identify him with any certainty. Except for the fact that he wearing this ring, miss."

I recall thinking, quite calmly, I was sure, *Francis is dead.* And I was astonished that I should accept this second death in a matter of hours so matter-of-factly.

And then I, who had never fainted in my life, slid quietly down the back of the chair into a limp heap on the floor before any of them could reach me.

◇◇◇◇◇◇

Ever since I had come to Aunt Rachael's house five years ago, at the age of twelve, my life had been a simple one of housework and gardening and the sewing that earned us our livelihood. There were no luxuries here such as I had known with my own parents, and our entertainments were simple. Mostly we took turns reading, except for my cousin Dodie, who read badly, while the others sewed or knitted during the evenings. And from the time I was fourteen, I sang in the church choir.

This was my only escape from the house, and I took advantage of it. I was blessed with my mother's voice and love for music; it wasn't long before I was being asked to sing solos, which pleased me. Since the pastor himself asked that I be allowed to sing, Rachael could not say no, and so every Wednesday evening I would go along to choir practice.

During the winter months, the minister saw me home. In the summer, however, when the daylight lingered until nearly nine o'clock, I was allowed to walk home by myself. And that was how I met Francis.

I knew who he was, of course. In a village the size of ours it could not have been otherwise. He was a teller in the bank where I sometimes went on an errand for Aunt Rachael. He was older than I, and I had been well aware of him for a long time before he noticed me.

Francis was very tall and slender and elegant in his business suit as he stood behind the barred window at the bank. He had dark hair and eyes a lighter brown than my own, and he had a small diamond stickpin in his tie. I thought him inordinately good-looking; even Dodie had to admit that he was one of the handsomest men in town.

The first time he looked at me . . . *really* looked at me . . . he was with a group of young men. He didn't say anything, but I met his eyes and knew that he *saw* me.

I walked on quickly, but with heat surging through me that could not be accounted for by the summer evening. Two days later, when I had one of the rare bank drafts from Papa to cash, he counted out the money and then for the first time made a personal remark.

"I noticed you going to church the other night."

"Yes. I always go to choir practice on Wednesdays."

"I've heard that you sing solos sometimes. I must come and hear you one of these days," he said.

I may have blushed slightly. No young man had ever addressed me thus before. My answer was certainly as prim as even Aunt Rachael could have asked. "I'm sure Pastor Gordon would be most gratified if you were to attend services," I told him, and he laughed.

I walked all the way home in a daze of imaginative indulgence. And on Sunday morning there he was, in a high starched collar and his diamond stickpin, in the second pew.

That was the beginning. Aunt Rachael was not to know, of course, that Francis Verland came to church because I was there, but *I* knew it. I was careful not to mention his name, ever. Rachael had a sharp eye where her charges were concerned.

The following week, Francis showed up for choir practice. Pastor Gordon was delighted to learn that the young man had a fine, clear tenor voice, and the next thing I knew, we were practicing for a duet.

We were most discreet. No doubt Francis knew as well as I did that my aunt would not be pleased by our growing attachment. Nor would his family, I suspected, although I had never met them. They lived in a finer house than ours, and I sometimes sewed his mother's underwear.

It happened to be me who picked up the long-awaited letter from Papa when it came in that summer of 1895. I had walked into the village during the afternoon to pick up some thread, for the cat had gotten hold of our last spool of black, and the Widow Hedgely must have her new dress at once.

The thread was forgotten when I was handed the envelope. From Papa in San Francisco! I opened it on the spot, and as I read joy flowed through me.

"My darling Saunielle," he had written. "No long letter this time, for there are many things to do. But at last I can tell you. Our lengthy separation will soon be over. There will be money aplenty, money for a house and a carriage and money to bring you to California! Think of that! We will be together again, and I will be able to buy you all the things your lovely Mama would have wanted you to have! Very soon . . . the next time you hear from me, no doubt . . . you will receive funds to pay your fare to San Francisco! Don't worry about clothes, you can buy all you need once you are here. I will send money to Rachael, too, in payment for all that she has done for you. Until then, I remain your affectionate Papa, Edward Marshall Hunter."

Dizzy with happiness, I had to restrain myself from dashing wildly across the street to the bank. Instead, I managed to remember my thread, spoke politely to the ladies in the store around me, and walked . . . no, floated . . . out into the summer sunshine.

Francis was at his post in the bank, and there were no other customers close at hand.

"Good afternoon, Miss Hunter," he said formally, for the benefit of Mr. Courtney, who was passing behind him. Then he grinned at me and lowered his voice. "You are positively sparkling today. Have you had good news? Your Aunt Rachael is going out of town for a month?"

I laughed. "Not likely. But I did get this. Look!"

I passed the letter to him, and he read it with rising eyebrows. "Well! That certainly is exciting. Only I don't like the idea of you going off to California, not by a long shot, I don't!"

"Don't you?" I asked archly. "Well, the money hasn't come yet. But oh, seriously, Francis, isn't it marvelous?"

"I'm being serious, you know, Saunielle. I really don't want you to go off to the other side of the world, practically."

I felt quite daring, with this letter to be tucked into my pocket. "There are banks in California, too, aren't there? Maybe *you'd* like it out there."

He looked at me for long moments, and then he said very softly, "Maybe I would, at that. Saunielle, I've got to talk to you. May I walk you home tomorrow night?"

"But we've never . . . Aunt Rachael . . ."

"Aunt Rachael be damned! Saunielle . . . all right, I know we have to consider her. Tell her we needed extra practice for our duet Sunday or something . . ."

"We aren't singing a duet on Sunday."

"Well, she doesn't know that. You can tell her we didn't sing it after all because we didn't get it just right, or something. I'm determined to talk to you without half a dozen people listening in."

I couldn't help smiling. "All right. Tomorrow night."

It was a mile home and I scarcely remember walking it. I was torn between dreams of joining Papa at last in California and of walking home with Francis at my side, and by the time I'd reached the front gate the two dreams had merged, so that Francis had found a position in San Francisco and was courting me at my father's palatial mansion.

Aunt Rachael was in the kitchen, scolding Phoebe about something. Dodie was there, too, head diligently bent over her needlework as I came in.

Rachael broke off her tirade against poor Phoebe to stare at me sharply. "What took you so long?"

"I didn't think I was very long. In fact, I was so excited I ran part way home. I have a letter from Papa!"

"What will people think, a girl of your age running?" She accepted the letter I passed over to her, but her expression didn't change as she read it. If anything, the lines around her mouth deepened.

Unable to restrain myself, I turned to my cousin. "Papa's come into some money, Dodie. He's going to send for me to go to California."

Dodie was a thin girl with nearly colorless gray eyes and mouse-colored hair which she wore twisted into a knot on the back of her neck. Her features were good, and her skin was pale and clear, but she did nothing to make the most of them.

Her eyes widened now as she forgot the corset cover she was stitching. "When are you going, Saunielle? Right away?"

Rachael folded the letter and passed it back to me. "Not this week, from the sound of it. Nor next. She'll be lucky if she goes at all. You'll note he says he *expects* to get the money, not that he already has it. I'm afraid Edward is a good one for counting chickens before they're hatched, and if I were you I wouldn't pack my bags yet, miss. Did you get the thread? Mrs. Hedgely's dress is waiting and if you don't get it finished before dark you'll find it hard going. We're running low on oil and I don't want to burn more than one lamp."

My spirits refused to be suppressed, however. I didn't believe Papa would have written such a letter unless he'd been *sure*. As I plied the needle for the rest of the afternoon, I was totally detached from the black bombazine. I was already on my way to California.

The following night Francis walked me home from choir practice. We dawdled along the way until it was full dark, though I knew I risked Aunt Rachael's anger by doing so. And under cover of the darkness, he not only held my hand but kissed me on the mouth.

Mama had adored romantic novels, and I knew all about the strange and wonderful sensations brought on by being kissed. I was delighted to find that for once something hadn't been overrated; being kissed was the most pleasant thing that had ever happened to me.

"Saunielle, I can't let you go off to California," Francis whispered against my cheek.

"I must go in. Aunt Rachael will be setting off to find me," I whispered back. "Good night, Francis!"

But he caught my hand, and held me fast, and kissed me again, until I was literally dizzy from it.

"Saunielle! Are you out there?"

I drew away from him in a panic, not even waiting for him to blend into the deeper shadows under the trees that lined the road. "I'm coming, Aunt Rachael," I replied, and moved into the circle of light from the lamp she held.

"What on earth kept you?" She leaned closer to me, lifting a hand to my face. "You're flushed and warm. Are you ill?"

"Well, I do feel strange," I admitted truthfully. "I've never felt quite like this before."

"Do you have a headache?"

"No, not exactly. I'm only rather . . . giddy."

"You'd best get up to bed. I hope you aren't ailing. I have to leave in the morning, Dorothea and I are going over to Petersburg to your Aunt Theodora's. Her three have all been down with fevers, and now she's collapsed herself. I'd take you along to help, too, but those things of Mrs. Harrison's must be finished."

She led the way into the house, giving me instructions, calling out to Phoebe that if I seemed worse in the morning she was to send for the doctor at once and that until it was clear whether or not I was ill, Phoebe and Aunt Pity were to keep their distance from me.

I went up to bed in a state of exhilaration. With Rachael and Dodie gone, probably for several days or perhaps even a week, there would surely be opportunities to see Francis alone. Pity would ostensibly be my chaperone, but I had no worries about outwitting poor old Pity.

Convinced that I had fallen head over heels in love, I crawled between the sheets, to lie in a delicious state of euphoria, reliving my moments with Francis.

◇◇◇◇◇◇

Conspiring to be alone with my young man proved to be only too easy. Pity, unsuspecting, went about her own tasks, and in any event usually went to bed early.

Phoebe, of course, was aware that something was afoot. But I didn't worry about Phoebe giving me away. Phoebe, at fifteen, was a born romantic.

And so it was that four days after Aunt Rachael had gone to Petersburg, during our third surreptitious rendezvous, Francis met me with a quick embrace and then released me to speak with great earnestness.

"Saunielle, I've made up my mind. I can't possibly let you go off and leave me. I can't even bear to be away from you for a day! I want to marry you!"

My breath caught painfully in my chest, yet it was not a pain I would have passed by. "But Aunt Rachael will never permit it, I know she won't!"

"Then we won't tell her. She's still in Petersburg, and judging by the message she sent with Pastor Gordon today she won't be back until at least next Thursday. We can get married before then and she'll never know the difference. Then when your father sends for you to go to California we can go together; it'll be too late for anyone to stop us."

"Get married secretly?" I was aghast, yet excited at the same time. "Pastor Gordon would never do it, he'd know how Aunt Rachael would feel . . ."

"Not Pastor Gordon. I've rented a trap, Saunielle, and if we cross into Prince Edward County there's a justice of the peace there who'll marry us and no one will be the wiser. You've only to fudge a little about your age . . . what's six months? Will you do it? Tonight?"

Tonight? I nearly smothered, contemplating it. "I . . . Francis, I'll have to think . . ."

"There isn't much time for thinking. I've got the trap now, and your formidable aunt is gone . . . You *do* love me, don't you?"

"You know I do," I said, melting. "Only I'll have to tell Aunt Pity something, she'll know I've been gone . . ."

"Tell her you're going to help a friend who's ill. Your Dubonnet cousins, there are dozens of them, and it'll be months before any of them see the family here. By then we'll be on our way to California," Francis urged. Francis, it seemed, had thought of everything.

And so I packed a valise, lingering at the last moment over my valuables and putting them in, too. I was coming back, of course.

But just in case something happened and I didn't, well, I wanted to have the miniature of Mama with her sweet, gay face, and her pearls, and the ring that had belonged to her father. They went into the bag with my change of clothing, and I was off to join Francis, leaving only a brief note to Phoebe.

A few hours later, I was married to Francis Verland.

The justice of the peace was a bumbling old man who accepted my age as I stated it, asked for no proof of anything, and whisked us through the ceremony in a trice. Only when he asked for the ring did I realize that Francis had not, after all, thought of quite everything.

"Oh, God. I forgot to get a ring! Do we have to have a ring? Isn't it legal without it?"

"Well," said the old man, "it's customary, I'm sure. Let me see . . ."

"I have a ring," I said quickly. "It belonged to my grandfather. It's a man's ring, and much too large, but perhaps it would serve . . ."

And so Francis accepted the Jaubert ring, and it was placed on my finger, and we were pronounced man and wife.

Our honeymoon lasted two precious days, in a small country inn. Francis was a delight in every way; tender, passionate, exciting.

I could not continue to wear the ring, of course.

"I'll get you another," Francis promised me with a kiss. "A real wedding ring. But you'd better not wear it until we're ready to leave for California. No sense in stirring up your aunt before it's necessary."

He examined the ring when I took it off. "It's rather a strange thing, isn't it? Why did your mother have it? She can't ever have worn it, it's much too heavy for a woman's hand."

"I think it was just a memento of her father. I don't really know the circumstances of their parting; I think there was some sort of unhappiness, because they were estranged before she came to America with her brother for a visit. Her brother went back to France, but Mama never did. She wrote to her father a few times, I know, but he never replied. Put it on," I suggested impulsively.

He looked at me questioningly, then slipped it onto his finger. It was a massive ring of gold with a square-cut black stone on which an E and a J were intricately entwined. Francis extended his hand, surveying it through an imaginary monocle. "Gives me a certain dash, wouldn't you say?"

We laughed, and kissed, and I told him that I wanted him to keep it, that it was time someone wore it and enjoyed it.

When we came home, Francis left me off at the house very early in the morning, before the others were up. I was relieved to find that there was no sign of the wagon, which meant that Dodie and Aunt Rachael had not yet returned.

Phoebe came down to find me starting breakfast. "Oh, you're back, miss. How are the cousins?"

"Fine, now," I said, poking kindling into the stove so as not to have to look directly at her. "I think it was all a pig in a poke, anyway. But I stayed until I was sure Aunt Sophie had settled down. Have you heard from Aunt Rachael?" I wanted to ask her not to mention my absence when the others came home, but I knew that would be a mistake. There would be no reason not to mention a genuine mercy visit.

Aunt Pity had scarcely noticed I was gone. She'd had one of her "spells" and spent most of the two days in her room, where Phoebe fed her from a tray. She made no comment on my journey, and by the time Rachael returned had forgotten it, and Phoebe apparently considered it unworthy of mention.

The night before my aunt and cousin came home, Francis and I spent several hours out in the orchard, talking and kissing under the apple trees. I remember when he said good night, and our hands were clasped tightly for a lingering moment, the ring cut into the back of my hand.

That was the last time, until Mr. Dunning gave it back to me, that I saw the Jaubert ring.

❖❖❖❖ 2 ❖❖❖❖

Once there had been a hundred slaves to work the tobacco fields at Hunter's Hill. It was not the largest plantation in Virginia, nor was it the grandest. Yet it was, I was sure, among the loveliest. The house stood three stories high, its mellow pink brick and white pillars welcoming the carriages and the elegantly dressed ladies and gentlemen who came there to balls and dinners and house parties. A staff of a dozen more slaves had waxed and polished and maintained the household under the direction of my grandmother.

The lawns and gardens were the most attractive in the county. There was a library to rival the one at the university at Charlottesville where my father had been at school at the outbreak of the war. It was the contents of that library that I coveted when I gazed from my window at Hunter's Hill.

I had never seen it, the library nor anything else inside the mansion, for it was lost to our family, along with everything else they owned, when the Confederacy at last gave up the terrible struggle.

But Papa and Aunt Rachael had grown up there, and I had listened all my life to their stories.

Rachael talked of little else. Whether supervising Dodie and me with our sewing, Phoebe in the kitchen, or between her own hours spent at the piano instructing the young people of the county, if Rachael talked at all it was of Hunter's Hill. Aunt Pity once remarked that the plantation was an obsession with Rachael; we'd all have been better off had we been banished somewhere out of sight of the place.

This may have been true, for the loss of her home, the home she had adored, had made a bitter and resentful woman of Rachael Hunter Calhoon.

Edward, my father, had as many reasons as his sister to mourn the loss of his home. It was he, as the only surviving son, who would have taken over its management had there been a different outcome to the war. It was he who loved the land itself, the growing tobacco, the drying sheds, the blacks who worked in the fields. And his beloved library; when he talked it was without Rachael's bitterness, but he missed his books.

It had not been an unhappy childhood for me, for the War Between the States had ended thirteen years before my birth in 1878. By that time Papa was teaching in the village and we lived in a rented but perfectly respectable house on the opposite side of town from his old home.

Since my mother, Angélique, found Aunt Rachael "tiresome," we seldom visited much during those early years of my life, except for holidays. Dodie was three years older than I, and I thought her rather dull, too, since she was not much interested in clothes or books or even dolls or horses. Mama was very pretty and very lively; she was always "up to something," as Papa used to say, and we often had visitors in and plenty of music when Mama played the piano and everyone else sang.

I learned to read at the age of four, and was well into piano lessons by six. Our household was not one of those where children are seen but not heard. I was allowed to contribute my own small opinions, even when there was company, frequently being bewildered by the amusement these opinions engendered. Neither of the two brothers who were born into the family lived past infancy; I had little recollection of them at all. I grew up a rather indulged, though certainly well disciplined, "only child."

And then when I was nearly twelve, Mama took sick. At first I didn't notice the change too much, for though the parties and the guests became fewer, Mama herself spent more time with Papa and me, reading together or on weekend outings.

The first time I heard the word "tumor" was from Aunt Rachael. I had been left at her house for a few days while my parents traveled to Richmond. I didn't even know they had gone to consult a doctor until I overheard Rachael speaking to Pity. I remember standing rigidly behind the kitchen door when my mother's name was mentioned.

"Well, Angélique's always put a lot of stock in her looks," Rachael observed. "Not likely it will do her much good now."

"Sometimes," Pity suggested, "it's possible to remove a tumor, and the patient recovers."

Rachael gave a short bark of laughter. "Can you see her allowing anyone to cut into her precious skin? No, if cutting would cure it Dr. Lemming would have done it before this; he's no stranger to surgery, didn't he take off Johnny's leg, neat as you please? It's too late for that. I tried to tell Edward that, but my brother has never listened to me before, why should he do it now? There's a look about her face, I've seen it before, on old Mrs. Shindley, and Carter Stanton. Both of them died of the tumors, and you mark my words, Angélique is past help."

Terrified, I stood there in the darkened passageway, tears running down my face, until Dodie found me and led me outside.

Significantly, she didn't ask why I was crying. Her plain, thin face was sober.

"What's a tumor?" I wanted to know, and Dodie told me.

"But if it's inside, how can they know? How can they tell?"

Dodie didn't know that, but she was sure there was some special way the doctor could tell what went on inside of one.

I didn't ask for my cousin's confirmation of the fact that my mother would die. I didn't want to hear it; I didn't want to know.

But I did know, of course. I saw it immediately in Mama's face when she came home from Richmond, and wondered how I could have been so blind I hadn't seen it before. It was there in her face, in her lovely dark eyes.

It was there in Papa's face, too. He suffered every bit as much as she did, perhaps more, for in time Dr. Lemming gave her a bottle of stuff that I was bidden never to touch, and after she'd taken a spoonful of it the lines would ease in her face and sometimes she'd sleep deeply for hours.

She died four days after my twelfth birthday and life would never be the same for me again.

Perhaps Papa's drinking began before she died, although I wasn't aware of it. There had always been spirits in the house, to be brought out to serve to company. Now, however, in my loneliness I was shut away from him. His speech would be slurred, his attention wandering, and there were times when he would lock himself in his study and not open the door when I called to him.

Mattie still came in daily to "do" for us, but somehow, without Mama there to supervise, the house began to deteriorate. Rachael, inspecting, flicked a white glove over the piano and exclaimed in horror.

"Edward, this is not way to raise a daughter! It isn't fitting for a young girl to be alone in the house with a man who is often so drunk he doesn't even know she's there."

"We're all right," Papa said, and momentarily quieted my apprehensions that our status would be changed. For all that it was an unhappy household, I thought it better than to have Aunt Rachael in charge of it.

I never learned why my father lost his position at the school. I only knew that one day he did not go off to work, and he never did again. Eventually the bill collectors and the landlord between them managed to evict us, and the day came when Rachael, grim and silent, came with her wagon to salvage what goods she could before they were set out into the street.

Among the items salvaged was Mama's piano. "I shall use it, to give lessons," Rachael said, and he didn't argue with her.

When she would have disposed of Mama's pearl necklace, and the ring that had come to her from her family, however, he was adamant. "They are for Saunielle. Angélique wanted her to have them. They are not to be sold."

And so we were moved to Rachael's house, where it must have pained Papa to be able to view his old home every day and know that it was lost to him forever, as was his darling Angélique. Papa himself stayed with us only a short time; one day he kissed me goodby and said that he was going West to try to find a better life for us both.

It took him a long time to find it. His letters were infrequent, although loving and lengthy when he did write. With each one, I hoped that he would send for me, that I might escape from the dreary life I lived with Rachael and Pity and Dodie.

From twelve to seventeen, five long years I spent with them. I was a good seamstress, and every day I joined Dodie after our lessons with my aunt (for I dropped out of the public school, which Rachael thought unsuitable for young ladies in our position, although I couldn't for the life of me determine just what "our position" was), in sewing for the ladies of the county. Sometimes, when Rachael's hands were stiff and painful in the wintertime, she would allow me to conduct the piano lessons, as well.

Until Francis came into it, my life had been rather dull. And now Francis was gone, Aunt Rachael was dead, and we were all of us on our own . . .

"Miss Nell. Miss Nell, are you all right?"

Reluctantly, I opened my eyes. Phoebe hovered over me, her pale, freckled face showing concern, her carroty hair forming a flaming halo in the morning sunlight. Aunt Pity was peering over her shoulder.

I was sprawled ungracefully on the settle, amid the lingerie I had been sewing yesterday, and I pushed myself into a sitting position.

"Of all times to come calling," Pity said crossly. "The poor thing didn't sleep at all last night, sitting in there beside poor Rachael; why did you let them in, Phoebe?"

"I'm all right, Aunt Pity. Of course she had to let them in. It's only that I've gone too long without eating or sleeping. Is there coffee? I think I'd like a cup."

"Just the thing! I'll get it," Pity offered, and trotted off, a tiny, frail old woman who had not yet combed her white hair and who had buttoned her dress crookedly so that it would have to be redone.

Phoebe continued to look down at me. "It was about *him,* wasn't it?"

"Him? I don't know what you're talking about." The men were gone, and I was glad of that . . . how mortifying, to faint in front of them! But the ring . . . what had happened to the Jaubert ring? And then I felt its rigid contours in my apron pocket, where my fingers closed convulsively around it.

"That Mr. Verland. That's what they told you, wasn't it? He's dead, isn't he?"

Such a short time ago, I had felt so young and so happy and so hopeful for the future. Now I felt old, older than Pity, as dead as the woman who lay in the coffin in the next room.

I sighed, knowing it was of little use to pretend to Phoebe. "Yes. He's dead."

Tears filled her blue eyes, and she made as if to touch me, but I shook my head.

"Please don't, Phoebe. Could I have the coffee?"

And so no more was said. I don't know what Mr. Courtney told Pity as he was leaving, but she asked no questions about their visit. We ate our breakfast and tidied the kitchen, and after a time the people began to come. Most of them brought funeral meats, far more than we could expect to eat, I thought in a mercifully detached fashion.

We buried Rachael, and in my heart I also buried Francis. There would be a funeral service for him, of course, when his family claimed his body, but I would not attend it. No one knew we had been married, and there seemed nothing to be gained by telling anyone now. It would only be considered scandalous behavior on my part, and would avail me nothing so far as I could see.

A telegram had gone off to Papa. We waited for his reply, and while we waited, we put the house in order and began to dispose of our belongings. There was no question of staying in the house, whether or not Papa sent for me. We had barely made ends meet when Aunt Rachael was alive to help with the sewing and to give music lessons and to work in the gardens that provided a major share of our food.

Mr. Courtney paid us five dollars for the piano, but was courteous enough to assure us that there was no need for him to collect it until we had actually moved out of the house. The New Jersey industrialist who now owned Hunter's Hill sent word that he could offer us seven hundred and fifty dollars for the house. This seemed a considerable sum, and Mr. Courtney confirmed that it was a fair one, but there was one thing we hadn't known about: Aunt Rachael had mortgaged the place that was all she had been able to salvage from the family holdings after the War Between the States.

We knew little or nothing about mortgages; I had to ask him to explain, which he did gently.

"It means that Rachael borrowed money against the value of the house. She was paying it back gradually, a little out of each of the drafts that your father sent her. So you see, my dear, when the house is sold not all the money will revert to you and Dodie, as the heirs. Five hundred and ten dollars of it is owing to the bank."

What had seemed a comfortable sum shrank, in a matter of minutes, to an amount small enough to be frightening. However, since it was summer and our garden was still producing, we were in no immediate need of anything. We would be able to settle the remaining small debts, and no doubt Papa would soon be sending along the money for me to go to California. In my own grief and preoccupation, I had not yet given much thought to what the others would do, when Phoebe approached me somewhat diffidently.

"Miss Nell, there ain't . . . isn't going to be much money left, is there?"

"Not much," I admitted. I inhaled deeply, feeling the stays cut into my flesh, which had felt bruised ever since my long vigil beside the coffin. "But Papa will send something soon, and there'll be a little left for Dodie and Aunt Pity to establish themselves in a small place in the village."

"Miss Nell . . ." She looked me straight in the face, her eyelids reddened from weeping. "Will you take me with you?"

She must have seen the answer forming in my face, for she didn't give me a chance to reply. "Please, miss! You'll need me, once you get out there! And I've nowhere to go, my gram's all the family I got left and she's older than Miss Pity and in poor health! She don't want me, even if she had the means to keep me. And there's no posi-

tions to be had, not here in the village, there isn't, I've asked and
asked!"

I knew as well as she did how precarious was Phoebe's future if I
left her here. Yet unless Papa sent enough money for both of us to
join him, what could I do?

"I don't know what will be possible, Phoebe," I said gently.

Her eyes glazed somewhat, but the hope did not completely die
out of them. "I know you'll do what you can, miss. And no doubt
Mr. Hunter will send you the money as soon as he knows what's
happened. The letter said he was very rich, didn't it?"

"It said he hoped to have a good deal of money very soon. There's
no telling if he actually got it. We haven't heard anything from him
since that was written almost a month ago."

"I would dearly like to go to California," Phoebe said, and managed a watery smile before she went back to the kitchen.

The day was hot, and I'd been sorting through various belongings
that might be sold, since Dodie could not bring herself to take on
this task. I turned to go up the stairs to freshen up, and met Aunt Pity
coming down.

Aunt Pity wasn't actually related to me; she had been the aunt of
Rachael's husband, dead these many years. Like me, she was an
orphan taken in from the storm by Rachael Calhoon simply because
she had nowhere else to go.

Her fingers struggled with the buttons of her dress and one of
them came off and rolled along the passageway.

"Drat! Do this button for me, will you, dear, my fingers are so stiff
this morning." While I performed this task, she smiled brightly at
me.

"You're such a good child, Saunielle. I suppose you haven't heard
any more from Edward about going to California?"

"No. But we sent him a telegram after Aunt Rachael died, so it
won't be long now."

She nodded, her hair pulling loose from the careless knot at the
back of her neck. Pity had been a very pretty young woman, and she
was still attractive at seventy, but her eyesight was poor and she was
becoming untidy.

"Yes, yes. You know, my dear, I've decided to go with you.
There's really nothing to keep me here in Virginia. No relatives left
except poor Dodie. I know there isn't a great deal of money, but
I have twelve dollars. That will help."

Twelve dollars! I hadn't yet inquired into the fare to San
Francisco, but I doubted that twelve dollars would make much
difference, one way or the other. Still, why crush her hopes until I
knew what would be feasible?

"Phoebe wants to go, too," I said dryly.

"Phoebe? Pah, what good would she be? Or Dorothea, either . . . has she said what *she* plans to do?"

I couldn't imagine my cousin Dodie, for all that she was twenty to my seventeen, making any plans on her own behalf. "Perhaps she can find a room with Mrs. Bell, and continue to take in sewing . . ."

Pity made a rude sound. "Do you really think, slow as she is, that she'd be able to earn enough to keep from starving to death? And she doesn't have your neatness, either. You know how Rachael always insisted you do the delicate work and the top-stitching. My guess is Dodie will be begging to go, too. Maybe she could find a husband in California. I understand there's a dreadful shortage of women out there. One of those men might want Dodie." She passed on toward the kitchen, leaving me to climb the stairs.

I was tired. So tired. I poured tepid water into the bowl and began to undress, wishing that I might crawl into bed and sleep until Papa's next letter came.

The fasteners on my corset caught, and when I gave an impatient tug the material ripped with a dismaying sound.

Well, it was off, but it looked as if I'd finished it, once and for all. I stared in exasperation at the remains, than flung them across the bed. To the devil with the thing, I'd manage without it today.

I washed quickly, then dusted myself with the powder my mother had had sent many years ago from her home in France. It had a light, delicate scent that I loved, for it always reminded me of her. There was very little of it left. Francis had liked it as much as I did.

Francis . . .

I had deliberately kept my thoughts away from Francis. Or had I? Did there lurk some small hope that it was all a mistake, that Francis would appear on my doorstep and take me in his arms and comfort me, that he would explain where he had been and why he had nothing to do with the funds that were missing from Mr. Courtney's bank?

I found fresh underclothes and put them on, hoping no one would notice the lack of a foundation garment, since the damaged one was the only corset I owned. Luckily my waist was naturally slim and it took only a minimal amount of squeezing to fasten the black dress I would wear for Rachael's funeral.

The mirror over my dressing table was one that had come from the manor house at the Hill. It was in excellent condition except for a crack that divided it diagonally, running from north to south. I remembered Rachael's tightened lips when she had discovered it, and I had had to confess to having thrown a shoe at Dodie, who had ducked.

That had been several years ago, and I had long since become accustomed to viewing my face in two segments. I surveyed it now, brushing back my dark hair and securing it in a simple fashion at the nape of my neck.

I was somewhat too thin, and there was no vivacity such as Mama had displayed, but I thought, hopefully, that I looked a good deal like her. The clear skin, dark eyes, and hair so brown as to be almost black were a direct heritage from the Jaubert side of the family, the French relatives I had never seen.

A knock on the door brought me around, reaching for one of the dresses I hoped I could leave behind when I went to California. Everything I had was so old, so shabby . . .

"Saunielle?" Dodie poked her head around the edge of the door. "May I come in?"

I waved her toward the edge of the bed, not wanting to look at her. Rachael's bitterness at what the war had done to her way of life had cut her off from what might have been warm relationships with anyone, including her daughter. Yet Dodie had depended upon her, and now Dodie was alone. I knew what she would say before she said it, although it took her longer to get around to it than it had the others.

"Saunielle . . . Aunt Pity says she's going with you, to California. Do . . . do you think I might go, too? Do you think Uncle Edward would allow me to join you? If I don't . . ." She faltered, then gathered her courage for a final burst of words. "I'd have to go stay with Aunt Theodora's family in Petersburg, and I should hate that above everything! She has three daughters who are almost as plain as I am, and she's desperate to find them husbands, and they don't like me, any of them! I'm not likely ever to marry, I'd have to be the spinster cousin in that house forever, and I truly don't think I could bear it, Saunielle!"

So there they were, all three of them, depending on me to get them to the magical land of California. I didn't think Papa would object to providing for them, if he had the funds he'd expected to have, but I hadn't indicated in my telegram that I anticipated needing fare for four of us.

She touched my sleeve, and there was nothing for it but to look into her face. Moisture glimmered in her eyes, and her lips trembled, and I said the only thing I could have said under the circumstances. "If it's possible, we'll all go, Dodie."

It couldn't have been completely reassuring, but she smiled in gratitude and began to talk about selling the rest of our meager possessions, speculating upon how much they could be expected to bring.

I did not intend to tell anyone about my marriage to Francis, but it did occur to me that he must have had in his effects the marriage certificate, and that it might be awkward should it turn up now. I approached Mr. Dunning about it the first time I went into the village, obliquely, of course.

"Were there any papers in Mr. Verland's room, sir? Personal papers, I mean." I blushed scarlet, for unless I confessed that I had been his wife, what business was it of mine what personal papers he had?

Mr. Dunning scratched his head. "Nothing at all, miss. That's one reason why they thought he'd done the . . . well, there wasn't much of anything in his rooms, you see."

"Nor . . . nor on . . . his body?" I spoke around an enormous and painful lump.

"No. Nothing but the ring, the one we recognized as belonging to you since we'd seen your mother wear it, years ago, on a chain around her neck. I hope nothing's amiss."

"No. No, of course not. Thank you, Mr. Dunning," I said, but the sense of disquietude persisted long after I had left him.

❖❖❖ 3 ❖❖❖

We waited a week, and then two. At that time I sent another, more urgent, telegram to the address Papa had given in San Francisco. At the end of the third week there was still no reply, and my uneasiness had grown to alarming proportions. The present owner of Hunter's Hill indicated that he was in need of the house, if we were to relinquish it to him; otherwise, he would have to seek other quarters for his overseer. A few of the merchants in the village began to hint delicately, but with an underlying determination, that they would be appreciative of their money.

To say that we were a nervous lot would be a distinct understatement. I had followed my telegram with a detailed letter outlining our plight, a letter the stationmaster assured me must surely be delivered within a week, since the trains could travel the distance in that period of time.

A full month had passed. The heat was oppressive and I slept poorly, often waking with my shift clinging damply to my body and a queasiness in my stomach as a result of my increasing apprehension about what we should do.

And at last the day came when the New Jersey industrialist issued an ultimatum: did we want to sell the house to him, or did we not? If so, he must have possession within three days.

They stared at me, Dodie and Phoebe and Pity, when I read the missive in tones as dry as my mouth was.

Dodie made the sort of sound she had made as a child when she expected to be struck for something she had inadvertently done wrong. "Saunielle, what are we going to do?"

It was up to me. They would not, or could not, help me make the decision. Their eyes fastened on me hungrily, helplessly.

I drew in a deep breath. "We are going to go to California," I said. "I don't know why Papa hasn't replied, but we'll surely find him once we get there. The letters must have gone astray. Perhaps he made a mistake in the address he gave."

We sent the servant back to Hunter's Hill with the message that the house would be vacated within three days. I would have liked to add that the sooner I saw the money for it, the better I would like it, but I wasn't that courageous. I couldn't risk antagonizing the man and perhaps ruining the sale.

We then set about our arrangements, and very quickly made a disquieting discovery. There was no way, on the money we could expect to have after the debts were settled, that we could purchase four railway fares to California.

Each of the three eyed me fearfully, waiting for me to say which of them should be left behind. For a moment, I'm ashamed to say, I was filled with resentment toward them, that they had made themselves my responsibility, that they had piled the guilt on my head if I had to hurt one of them.

"I don't know what to do," I said slowly. "Perhaps we'll still hear from Papa . . ."

"It's cheaper to go by ship," Pity said unexpectedly. "I've heard that. It's considerably cheaper to go by ship."

"Ship?" Dodie's gentle smile broke through her anxiety. "I remember Miss Haines telling me about a voyage she took, on a ship. It was called *The Pilgrim,* and all the floors . . . or do they call them decks? . . . were carpeted as beautifully as those at Hunter's Hill, and there were a thousand of Mr. Edison's incandescent lights from stem to stern. She said it was lovely. She told me all about it while I was making her mourning clothes last spring."

"Ship," I repeated slowly, unimpressed by Dodie's second-hand reminiscences. It wasn't likely we could afford passage on any such vessel as Miss Haines had taken. "Yes, a ship might be the answer, although it must take a great deal longer. And Papa will certainly be sending money before long. Only it would be expensive to stay here, in lodgings, waiting . . ." I didn't say that if we ate any more deeply into our resources, there wouldn't be enough to travel anywhere. "I suppose Norfolk would be the place to make such arrangements. If only it weren't so far to go, without knowing . . ."

"The Widow Hedgely," Pity said suddenly.

We turned and looked at her. Sometimes her remarks were odd, but for the most part they made sense when one got to the bottom of them.

"She has a cousin who has something to do with ships. He sends goods out on them or something, I think she said. And he's in Norfolk. Perhaps he could find us a ship that's going to California."

"But what if we got all the way there and found we couldn't afford a ship, either," Dodie said slowly. "Then we'd be in worse shape than we are now, sitting here at home."

"Home will only be home for another three days," I reminded her.

"I know." Phoebe leaned forward, her earnest young face liberally sprinkled with freckles, her color high. "If Widow Hedgely will give us the man's address . . . her cousin, I mean . . . we can send a telegram and ask him to arrange for passage. We can tell him how much money is available, and . . ."

"No," I interjected. "If we do that, he'll come up with fares totaling all we have. We would do better to stress our need for economy and hope that will allow something left over."

For a moment we stood looking at each other, and then Phoebe grasped my hand and squeezed it and everyone was smiling. The decision had been made, and we all felt the better for it. Except that, deep down inside, I was not at all sure the decision had been the best one.

◇◇◇◇◇◇

The sounds and scents were both exciting and frightening. There was the smell of the sea, of course, but overpowering that was the odor of oil and fish and a dozen other things I couldn't have named. Vessels of all sizes and descriptions sent masts and rigging towering into the sky. Several of them were being loaded, and men hurried in every direction for all the world like a colony of ants, except that the men seemed less well organized. Voices shouted orders and oaths and our progress was slow because of the congestion of horses and vehicles.

The buildings that fronted the wharves were mostly lighted, though it was long past normal business hours. An ironmonger, a sail-maker, everything to do with ships and sailing were to be found here, as well as the bars where off-duty sailors sought drink and companionship.

If I had been reluctant to pay out the price of a conveyance, I begrudged it no longer. Imagine four females trying to navigate this area alone!

The Widow Hedgely's cousin had met us as promised; we had handed over the agreed price, and he'd provided, in return, our proof of passage. He was a gruff, short-spoken man in his middle fifties, none too clean about the collar, as Pity observed subsequently, but he seemed to know what he was talking about.

"The *Gray Gull,* she is, out of Newport. Not so fancy as some, but the price is right, eh? You'll find her at the foot of the street, just keep on the way yer goin', you can't miss it. Take a slight swing to the left, she lies direct in front of a lamp post so you'll have no trouble readin' her name. Captain Schwartz may not be aboard, but the watch'll have your papers and see that you get stowed away. Have a good voyage, ladies."

Phoebe cleared her throat noisily. "Sir . . . can you tell us? How long it's like to take to get to San Francisco?"

He laughed. "Ah, there's a thing the captain hisself would like to know, I wager! A lot depends on the winds, you know. With any sort of luck at all, I'd say you'd be there in a hundred days." He lifted a hand to wave us on, and our driver clucked at his horses to get them moving.

"A hundred days!" Dodie was staring after the man in something like shock. "But a train can go across the country in less than a week!"

"Only not for a price we can afford," I said grimly. I had sent another telegram to Papa, telling him of the necessity of traveling by ship; I could only hope he received it and wasn't worried frantic about my whereabouts.

There were lamp posts, all right, but they did little to relieve the gloom. We took our "slight swing to the left," the horses slowed to a walk as we dodged traffic, and we strained our eyes to determine which of these ships was our own.

When we found it, an appalled silence settled upon us.

"Is that the one you're booked on, the *Gray Gull?*" the driver asked incredulously. "Don't look big enough to be safe outside the harbor."

I put down my own misgivings. "From the look of it, it's been sailing for some years now without going down. I'm sure it wouldn't be spreading sail for California unless the crew had every expectation that it would get there."

The *Gray Gull* was, indeed, a small and shabby vessel compared to her sister ships on either side. Still, I hadn't expected a modern steamship with incandescent lights, had I? The important thing was to get to Papa in San Francisco, by whatever means possible.

Our luggage was set down beside us on the heavy planks of the wharf, at the foot of a perilous-looking gangplank that had not even the nicety of a handrail, only a few narrow strips of wood across it to keep one's feet from slipping backward.

Our driver took his money, then hesitated. "Do you want me to wait? To be sure . . . I mean, in case it isn't the right ship?"

My words were sharper than I'd intended, perhaps because of my own unadmitted uncertainty. "Of course it's the right ship, the man we paid said the *Gray Gull,* didn't he, out of Newport? There's no need to wait."

Yet as the conveyance clattered away I had an impulse to call him back, to return us to our own village to await word from Papa, no matter how long it took.

"Oh my," Pity said. "Are we supposed to walk up that thing? It . . . it's moving up and down!"

"Very slowly and rhythmically," I pointed out. "If we stay in the center there should be no danger. There surely is someone about to handle our luggage. Ahoy, there! Is anyone on board?"

My question was answered, although not verbally, when a sailor came along the deck above us and lurched rapidly down the gangplank.

"Excuse me," I said. "Is there anyone in charge aboard the *Gray Gull?*"

He was close enough so that I could smell the spirits on his breath, and his eyes appeared to have trouble in coming to focus on me. "Oh, aye, there's a bloody mate some 'eres." He swiveled on his heel and shouted through his hands. "Mr. Doane, sir! There's a lady askin' for yer!"

And then, without waiting to see whether or not anyone came in response to his summons, he made his way on across the street to the nearest bar.

We stood for a moment, reluctant to leave our luggage, equally reluctant to attempt to carry it on board ourselves by the precarious ramp, waiting for Mr. Doane.

When someone finally stirred on deck, there was almost an explosion of furious movement. Two men erupted from the cabin amidships, their voices loud enough to be clearly understood over the racket around us.

"I say you'll fulfill your contract, Mr. Rohann. You signed on for San Francisco, and that's where you'll bloody well leave this ship, sir."

The speaker was a stocky man of middle years, with grizzled hair under an officer's cap. He stalked after the younger man, his voice rising as the other's heels sounded on the wooden decking.

"You and your scummy ship can go to hell," the other retorted. "I'd as soon tie an anchor around my neck and jump into the bay here and now; it would be a more merciful end, Captain. Good evening to you."

The first voice was rough-spoken, uneducated, the second that of a man of some breeding, I thought, although there was little to choose between them either for their dress or the impression they gave of anger and latent violence.

The younger man reached the gangplank, some sort of bag balanced on his shoulder, pausing only when the captain laid a hand upon his arm. "I say ye'll not go, sir, and leave me without a second mate. I've advanced you a sum against your wages, and that you'll repay."

"Maybe I will, but it won't be here and it won't be now." Rohann, if such was his name, shrugged off the restraining hand. "If this miserable little dinghy doesn't sink before that, it'll never last 'round the Horn, I'd bet my boots on that. I may be hard up for my passage home, but I'm not so desperate I'll risk my life on the *Gray Gull,* thank you."

Some of the words the captain flung after him down the gangway I had never heard before, but there was no doubt they were profane as well as impotently furious. Seeming impervious, Rohann strode toward us, the flimsy planking heaving beneath his feet, so that we stepped backward, out of his way.

I was too close to the edge of the dock. My hasty withdrawal brought me up against one of the valises we had set down, so that I was completely overbalanced. I would have gone into the bay but for the quick footwork and strong right arm of the man called Rohann.

At that it might have been less painful than having my arm nearly wrenched out of its socket. I cried out, and felt myself jerked against a solid, muscular chest, and then set on my feet at a safer distance from the edge of the planking.

I stammered some sort of thanks, putting a hand to the strained shoulder, looking up into a pair of pale blue eyes in a face that might have belonged to some ancient Viking, surrounded as it was by a rough red beard and mustache, with more of the tousled red curls showing from beneath a knitted cap.

"You all right?"

"Yes, I think so."

"You want to watch your step, the wharf is a dangerous place. Although," he added, possibly for the benefit of the man at the rail of the ship, "it's safer than the *Gray Gull,* if you're thinking of boarding her." He touched the cap in a perfunctory gesture, and strode briskly away.

◇◇◇◇ 4 ◇◇◇◇

I saw dismay on Phoebe's face, and Dodie made a sort of whimpering sound. I felt rather like whimpering myself. Instead, I stepped once more to the foot of the gangway and spoke with what assurance I could muster. "Captain Schwartz?"

He peered down at me, scowling under the feeble glow from the nearest streetlamp. "Who's that?"

His manner was so intimidating, especially coming on top of the exchange we had just overheard, that I might well have retreated had there been any alternative to boarding his vessel.

"My name is Saunielle Hunter. We've booked passage on the *Gray Gull* for San Francisco."

The scowl deepened. "We don't sail until dawn, day after tomorrow."

Dismay held me speechless until I heard Dodie's indrawn breath behind me. "But surely we can come aboard, sir." I hesitated, because it was not easy to confess our poverty, and then added, "We've very nearly exhausted our resources, Captain. We have no funds to pay for lodgings for two nights." Nor for meals, I remembered. Not if we were to avoid arriving in California completely penniless. Desperation put a bit of starch into my manner. "Could we have someone help us with our luggage, sir?"

For a moment I fought the conviction that he was going to deny us permission to board; I could envision us spending the night in an exhausted heap right here amid the coils of rope and the kegs and crates stacked for loading.

"Very well," he said at last. "I'll send someone to fetch it."

He turned away from the rail, and three pale faces turned toward mine. "Saunielle, do you think it's true, what that man said?" Dodie's tears were near the surface. "That the ship isn't safe? That it hasn't a chance of getting to California?"

"Of course not. Obviously the ship's been in service for years, and it must have gotten to wherever it was going on all the other voyages."

"He was a handsome one, wasn't he?" Phoebe said.

"Who? The captain?"

"No, that Rohann. Not a big man, not nearly so tall as . . ." She stopped, remembering only just in time that the others knew nothing of my relationship with Francis. "Not so tall, but well set up, for all that."

I dismissed Rohann with a sound of exasperation. "He's nothing to us, one way or the other. Poor Aunt Pity is about to drop with weariness. I trust they are prepared for us, I'm done in myself."

The sailor who came for us was little more than a boy. He was trying to grow a beard but needed a few more years to manage it. He eyed us curiously, but said nothing until he'd hauled all our luggage onto the deck. "I'm Tom. Captain said to show you quarters."

"We'd be most obliged if you would," Pity assured him. If the rest of us were worn out, I could imagine what sort of condition she was in. Yet she kept up with the rest of us as we were led across a deck that felt slippery underfoot, and down a ladder into the bowels of the ship.

I fought a wave of nausea that rose when I was enveloped by the fetid air below decks. It smelled of unwashed bodies and human excrement and other things I was afraid to identify.

The boy carried a lantern, not bothering to hoist it high enough to be of much use to anyone but Pity, who was closest, behind him. Dodie stumbled and Phoebe muttered, and I brought up the rear, so deep in misgivings that I was trembling.

Even without the condemnation of the red-bearded Rohann, the *Gray Gull* would have been frightening. She was an old ship, and small to be sailing round the Horn, it seemed to me. To learn that she reeked of decades of occupancy by men without bathing facilities was scarcely promising for a voyage that would take months to complete.

"Are . . . are there other females sailing to California with us?" Pity asked, in a voice that was almost a squeak.

"No'm. We ain't got but space for twelve passengers, and we never had any ladies before, since I been on 'er." The boy paused, throwing open a door so narrow that a man with shoulders of average proportions would have had to turn sideways to pass through the opening.

"How long would that be?" Pity wanted to know, or perhaps she was only reluctant to enter our designated quarters now that we were here.

"Two months. I'll light the lantern for you; it hangs just inside there." He hung his own light on an overhead hook, so low that even I might have hit my head on it.

"You haven't been around the Horn, then." Dodie's voice wavered, and for once I didn't blame her.

"No'm. But I got to git me to California, my brother's there and he's had the good luck to find a fine position in a brewery. Signin' on as a hand was the cheapest way to get there," the boy confessed. He had lighted the lantern and replaced it on its hook, so that it emitted a feeble glow.

None of us spoke to admit our own similar situation. Pity stepped first through the doorway, and then the rest of us, which was actually somewhat of an accomplishment. For the floor space of our cabin was so limited that we could only all stand simultaneously by brushing against one another.

The sailor said, "Evening, ladies," and then he was gone, leaving us with lips that trembled as much from apprehension as from exhaustion.

"Good grief," Pity said, the first to break the silence. "They surely don't mean all four of us to sleep in this cubicle. It's no bigger than an outhouse."

"Sort of smells like one, too," Phoebe contributed. "But there's four bunks, so I expect this is it."

Dodie's eyes swept over the narrow berths, noting as mine did that these consisted of no more than rather lumpy-looking pallets of coarse canvas, without sheets, and a blanket for each one. "Dear heaven. We're to live in this for three months or more?" She looked back at me, and though my panic rivaled hers, I tried to stay calm.

"No doubt we'll be allowed on deck as long as the weather is good. See if that window, or whatever they call it, can be opened, Phoebe. A little fresh air would do wonders to improve the place. Shall we draw straws for the bunks? The three of us, I mean, Aunt Pity shall have a lower, of course."

It was possible to sit in reasonable comfort on the lower bunks, and this added a certain spaciousness to the cabin, although it was difficult to imagine the four of us living this way for an extended period of time without going mad.

The fresh air, even smelling as it did of the wharf area, was a help. By the time the young sailor was back with our valises, Phoebe and Dodie were agreed upon taking the upper bunks, while Pity and I had the lower ones. There was a bit of confusion over where to put our luggage, but the sailor showed us how it could be crammed into the space beneath the lower bunks, in which area was also stowed our rather primitive sanitary facility. This latter had unfortunately not been emptied since the last travelers had used it, but the young man had the grace to offer to do this for us at once.

When this had been accomplished, we were ready to settle in for the night. It didn't take us long to learn that only one person could dress or undress at a time. Pity was given first chance, and got into her nightgown while the rest of us avoided looking at her as best we could.

From her small satchel Phoebe produced a book. "Maybe we

could read a chapter in *Black Beauty*. The light's bad, but if I was to stand up right close to the lantern . . ."

Dodie's gray eyes were large in her thin face as she leaned over the edge of her berth. "I thought we agreed to bring only the minimum of effects, and no books except Aunt Pity's Bible."

Phoebe's fingers gently stroked the cover of the small volume. "I didn't have as much as the rest of you to bring, and this was a Christmas present from Miss Nell. It's the only treasure I've got; I couldn't leave it behind."

I had seen her slip it into the bag and had said nothing, for I knew how she felt. I would have liked to bring what were left of Papa's books, for he had loved them so. But the cost of shipping them would have been excessive, and their very weight have made them difficult for us to manage, so they had been sold to the current village schoolmaster for a fraction of their true value.

"By all means," I said. "Let's hear the first chapter of *Black Beauty*. Only you'll have to try to read from there or no one will be able to get ready for bed."

Phoebe had had to leave school at the age of eleven to go into service, and she had not been an exceptional student while she was there. But at our house she had been caught up, as the rest of us were, in the novels of Miss Alcott and Mr. Dickens. It wasn't long before she came to me to ask if I would tutor her in reading, and she was now a much better reader than Dodie was.

So Phoebe read while the rest of us prepared for sleep. I could very nearly have quoted *Black Beauty* from memory, and my mind wandered. The bunk was very narrow and much less comfortable than my bed at home. It was too warm for the blanket, so I used it as a pillow, although it was somewhat scratchy against my skin.

And when Phoebe had finished her chapter, and we'd all said our good nights and put out the light, I lay awake in the darkness and listened to the gentle slap of water on the hull of the *Gray Gull* and tried not to be afraid.

Inevitably, my thoughts turned to Francis. The official verdict had been that he died by mischance, perhaps when he had been drinking and had fallen into the river. I knew that, like the other village lads, he had learned to swim at an early age, and the verdict seemed unlikely to me. Yet what did it matter? He was gone, and I had only a few treasured moments to remember. To my horror, I found that I had trouble conjuring up his face in my mind's eye. I stared, wide awake for all my weariness, up at the unseen bottom of Dodie's bunk, trying to force the memory to come. He was tall and straight and slim, and his hair and eyes were nearly as dark as my own; I knew those things, and yet his image refused to form.

I scratched at my neck, which was beginning to be irritated by the coarse wool of the blanket. I had thought my world torn apart when Mama died and Papa went away, but it seemed now that my desolation was even more intense. I had at least had the security of Aunt Rachael's household, my own private room with Mama's belongings as keepsakes, and Papa's books. And of course, eventually, Francis.

I squirmed, wondering how the blanket could be causing me to itch even under my gown. And at the same time I heard Phoebe whisper, "Miss Nell?"

"Yes, what is it, Phoebe?"

"Something's biting me."

Biting! I sat upright, and now the itching was a white-hot fury on my neck and arms and across my trunk.

Above me, Dodie wailed. "Saunielle! What is it?" I was out of bed, fumbling for the matches left to us to light the lantern, while I imagined thousands of small, vicious creatures feasting on my flesh.

The light provided no immediate answer, although the bites themselves were beginning to become visible. I stared at the bunk in repugnance. "They must be full of fleas."

"Or bedbugs," Pity said. "I remember the house was infested with them once, during the war. Those Yankee soldiers slept in our beds, and it took us weeks to get rid of the bugs. We boiled everything, and turned out the ticking and put kerosene in little dishes under all the legs of the furniture. It was dreadful."

"Bedbugs!" Dodie's piteous wail made me want to slap her. "Oh, good heavens! What are we going to do?"

And so we began our first night aboard the *Gray Gull*. It would be an exaggeration to say that any of us slept. The very thought of having to live with vermin made me queasy. Indeed, I felt badly enough so that I lay after the others had gotten dressed in the morning.

Only Phoebe regarded me with troubled eyes. "This is a bad time to be sick, miss. There's none of the rest of us know what to do about anything."

I wiped at my mouth with a handkerchief, resisting the urge to scratch. "It's the traveling, and being too tired, no doubt. And what makes you think I know what to do about anything?" If only Francis were with us, I thought in a paroxysm of grief and longing. He would never have let us board this miserable little vessel in the first place.

I began to pull on my clothes, pausing to examine the red blotches that bore witness to my bed partners. "I hope they can do something about these wretched creatures. I wonder if there's any way we can bathe on this misbegotten ship?"

The girl was still watching me in a rather odd fashion, so that I spoke sharply to her. "What's the matter with you?"

"Nothing, miss. Soon as you're ready, shall we go on deck and get a breath of air and maybe find something to eat?"

The last thing I wanted was something to eat; I had a conviction that it would no more than touch bottom than it would turn straight around and come back up. But the fresh air appealed to me.

Fresh air, it turned out, was absolutely the only appealing thing to be had. Breakfast consisted of bowls of watery grits. Lunch was no better, and I wondered what our fare would be at sea if this was the best that could be offered in port.

Pity and Dodie elected to take theirs on deck, where the air was cleaner; Phoebe suggested that we do the same, but I was looking at my bowl of stew with revulsion.

"Aren't you feeling well, Saunielle?" Dodie asked. "You're looking rather white."

"I think it's the motion of the ship," I said, perching on the edge of the bunk. "It seems to be unsettling."

"But we're scarcely moving," Dodie said, and then alarm etched itself into her pale features. "It will be much worse once we're at sea. What if we're all seasick? Oh, I never thought of that!"

"Like as not we'll survive it," Phoebe said, but her gaze was fixed on me in a disquieting way.

When the others had gone, Phoebe remained standing over me, something I couldn't read in her eyes. "Are you overdue your monthly, Miss Saunielle?"

"What?" I jerked my head to look up at her, swallowing hard against the alarm that set my heart to hammering. "What do you mean?"

"I mean I don't like the look of you the past few days. Pale, and sweating, and sick to your stomach."

I moistened my lips and swallowed again. "Anybody'd feel unwell, with all we've had to cope with this past month."

"The rest of us ain't puking into a bucket in the morning," Phoebe pointed out, in a tone so laden with meaning that there was no mistaking it.

For a moment I forgot to breathe. Oh, dear God, no, I thought, it couldn't be *that*.

Her blue eyes with the stubby red lashes were knowing. "You didn't go to your Aunt Sophie's, did you, Miss Nell? You was with him, that Francis Verland, the two nights you was gone."

She was younger than I, hardly more than a child, and yet I felt as if she were much older and wiser and tougher than I for this moment. I felt the sweat, cold and clammy, oozing on my body, irritating the bedbug bites. Yet my mouth was so dry I could scarcely speak.

"Oh, Phoebe. Phoebe . . ."

"Then you could be expecting?" There was no condemnation, only concern in her voice, and she reached out a hand to lay it over mine.

"We were married, Phoebe." Tears welled up, hot, uncontrollable. "We were married secretly, and we were going to go to California together when Papa sent for me, and we didn't want Aunt Rachael to know . . ."

Something relaxed in her manner. "Oh, miss, if you were married that makes it different! Once you reach your Papa he'll see everything's taken care of . . ."

"But I can't prove it, Phoebe. Francis had the marriage certificate, and I don't know what happened to it! I asked Mr. Dunning about it, but he said everything was gone from Francis' room, and they didn't find any papers on his body! I don't know what happened to it!"

Indecision played over her expressive features. "Maybe . . . maybe you ain't . . . aren't . . . *are* you late?"

"I don't know. I haven't given it any thought, we've been so busy and so upset . . ." I tried to remember, counting out on my fingers, undoubtedly growing pale as I did so. "Oh, Phoebe. Twelve days . . . twelve days late."

Our eyes clung, dark brown and pale blue, and though we were so physically dissimilar, we were sisters under the skin.

"Oh, God, what am I going to do?" I said, but Phoebe didn't answer and I knew with a sinking heart that this was one more thing I'd have to deal with by myself.

◇◇◇◇ 5 ◇◇◇◇

To say that I was beset by a dozen new fears would be an understatement. How long could I continue to dress and undress in the tiny compartment with the others before they guessed that I was to have a child? How long, since I'd thrown away the remains of my torn foundation garment and hadn't the means to purchase another, before *anyone* could tell, even when I was fully clothed, about my pregnancy?

I'd been exposed to some of my cousins during their early-married years. I wracked my brain to remember every bit of information any female had ever spoken on the subject in my hearing. Why hadn't I realized sooner that I might be with child? What difference would it have made if I had?

How would Dodie and Pity react? Would they believe that I had married Francis? Or would they think I only lied to cover my own transgressions?

What about Papa? He would surely believe me, but what if we

didn't find him as wealthy as he had led us to hope he would be? What if the burden of a daughter was more than he could bear, let alone a grandchild and the likelihood that everyone would think me a shameless hussy? What if—the frantic questions grew more fearsome—we did not even meet Papa in the strange California city and we were forced to fend for ourselves?

I tried to bring my tumultuous thoughts under control. I was worse than Dodie, who always expected the worst of catastrophes to occur. Of course we would meet Papa, for we had the address where he was staying. No doubt he had long since replied to my letters and telegrams, and he would be there, waiting for us, when we arrived. He would believe me at once and no doubt he would know what was best to do in any event; once I reached him there would be little else to worry about, because he would take care of me as he had done all the time I was growing up.

But the ugly thoughts persisted. When Mama had died not even his love for me, which I never for a moment doubted and did not to this minute, had been strong enough to keep him with me. He had left me with Aunt Rachael, and the promise to send for me, five long years ago.

Of course he had left me with Rachael, since she had told him so many times how unsuitable it was for a lone man to try to care for a young girl. And he had taken rather heavily to drink, in his sorrow and anguish. But he had doubtless gotten over that, as the time passed; certainly there had been nothing in his letters to suggest that he was still drinking too much.

Dear heaven! My head ached from the overabundance of speculations. Aunt Pity asked, when we were finally allowed to return to our quarters, if I was feeling poorly and I lied and said it must be caused by the odor of the sulphur that was to kill the bedbugs.

I lay on my bunk, wondering how on earth I could possibly endure three or four months of confinement in this tiny compartment. Once we were at sea there would be nowhere else to go, except for an occasional walk upon the deck when the weather was fair. My every movement would be observed, my every change in figure. How long had it been before my cousins had begun to show rounded bellies and fuller breasts?

If I were, indeed, carrying Francis' child (and I confess there were moments when I convinced myself that I was *not,* that it was all a mistake, that I was only worn out to the point of senselessness) then long before we reached California it would be apparent to everyone save the most naïve that I was expecting.

The air was so thick and so putrid that I longed for the clean, fresh air of home with a longing that was physically painful. Above me Phoebe scratched and swore that the sulphur couldn't have done its job very well because she'd just discovered a new bite on her arm. Dodie whimpered softly that she was sure the wretched creatures were crawling all over her, under her clothes, and she wished her mother were here.

Pity's voice was tart. "Fat lot of good that would do . . . five people crammed in here where four will scarcely fit. Don't be wailing over your mother, child. It may be she's the lucky one. Went quick, she did, just like her father and her grandfather. My father went that way, too. Active man, he was, always a yelling and a shouting and a smacking someone, if they didn't move fast enough to suit him. And when the day came, he went into one of his rages and just dropped dead, he did. Of the heart, same as Rachael. Nothing for them to worry about now. They're well out of it."

Dodie sobbed quietly, murmuring that it was a cruel way to speak to one who had just lost her mother.

I thought of my own Mama, and the long months during which she had suffered so terribly, when the flesh had wasted away from her bones until at the end she weighed far less than I, a twelve-year-old child. I agreed with Pity that Rachael had been lucky, still vigorous and without pain until the very end. Perhaps there had been pain, those few moments in the garden after Phoebe had seen her fall, but by the time the rest of us reached her there were no lines in her face, nothing to suggest that her last moments had been agony.

Our noon meal came, brought by young Tom. He and Phoebe exchanged a few words over it.

"Nothing but watery soup, it is. Lucky if we've got half a potato apiece in it, and no more of carrot and cabbage. Is this the best we'll get, the entire trip?" Phoebe demanded.

"More than likely. There hasn't been anything much better than that since I've been aboard," Tom admitted. He was watching Phoebe in unconcealed admiration, eyes fixed on her carroty hair. "Don't recall that I ever saw that color hair, before. Quite striking, it is."

Phoebe giggled, and stepped into the corridor with him as he left; we could hear their voices but not the words as they spoke together. Dodie, sitting up on her bunk to eat, stared at the closed door.

"She's flirting with that boy. Shameless, she is."

"Why is she?" I asked. "She's a girl, alone in the world. She can't expect us to keep her forever. She'll want a man and a home of her own one day."

My choice of words was unfortunate. Dodie's eyes filled with tears. "I suppose so. But there's lots of us will never get what we want in this life."

Aunt Pity, seated in the bunk below, sucked noisily on her spoon and then twisted her head to look up at the girl. "That's true enough.

But a girl who smiles instead of going around with a droop to her mouth has a better chance of catching a man. Men don't like tears and complaints. I always figured that was why your father died so young, it was the only way he could get away from Rachael."

Oh, Lord. I glanced up at my cousin, whose mouth had dropped open.

"How can you say such a wicked thing, and Mama not cold in the ground . . ." The tears threatened to become a torrent, and I said quickly, "Aunt Pity doesn't mean to make matters worse, Dodie; you'll have to make allowances for her, she's getting on in years and she's very tired . . ."

"So am I very tired! And I miss my mother, and my home, and I'm afraid . . ."

I put aside the bowl of so-called soup, fearing that I couldn't swallow another mouthful of it. "We're all tired, Dodie. And we miss our mothers and our homes . . ." Why didn't I finish it, admit that we were all afraid, too?

"What are you talking about? Your mother's been dead for five years, and Aunt Pity's mother must have been gone for fifty!"

"Don't matter," Pity said, chewing on some morsel she had found at the bottom of her bowl. "You still miss 'em. I lived in a mansion as a girl, too, you know. Winoweh was every bit as lovely as Hunter's Hill, I assure you, and we had almost as many slaves. My mother was a beautiful woman, much like Saunielle's mama, only she wasn't so dark. Pretty, and dressed fit to kill, with such pretty little white hands . . ." She spread her own old and twisted fingers. "Not like these. She never had to work with hers. Oh, yes, you still miss 'em, even after fifty years."

The wrench of emotion I felt, the overwhelming sorrow for my own mother, brought me out of the bunk. "I'm going on deck for some air," I said, and blindly moved after Phoebe.

The girl was still standing there talking to the sailor; she spoke to me, but I brushed past, not speaking in return. I made my way on deck, literally gasping for the fresh air I was denied below.

I moved to the rail, wondering if everyone on board would know why if I lost my lunch over the side. My eyes stared, unseeing, at the activity below, at the goods being hoisted into the hold, at the scurrying men.

How could I, in such a few short weeks, have been brought from such joy and anticipation, to this?

"Enjoying the air?"

The voice at my elbow brought me around. I knew who the man was; Tom had pointed out the ship's officers to us. Mr. Doane, the first mate. I'd never been this close to him before, and my instinctive reaction was to step back. Since I was already against the rail, however, this was impossible.

He was a man of middle years, with the sagging paunch that comes from unwise eating and drinking. He needed a shave, although not nearly so urgently as he needed a bath.

"It's very close below decks," I said, stepping to one side. He countered this, however, by stepping with me.

"Aye. Little bit of a cabin, and four ladies in it. Very uncomfortable, I daresay." He ran a thumb over lips still greasy from his noon meal . . . or would it be from his breakfast? "Not much privacy on a ship . . . although it's possible to be to one's self if a person is determined enough, eh?" He winked at me.

Revulsion sent me turning in the other direction; again he matched my movement. "Excuse me, sir."

"Ah, you won't run away from me, will you, miss? It's a long voyage, and always the more pleasant if everyone on board is friendly, eh? I'm the only one, outside of the captain himself, who has his own cabin. Was to have shared it with that Rohann fellow, but he's took off . . . too hoity-toity for the likes of us on the *Gray Gull*, eh? But I'm sure you ladies won't be the stand-offish types. After all, it's a long voyage, and if there's anything the first mate can do for you, well . . . nothing wrong with everyone being friendly, is there?"

His leer told me only too clearly what he meant by being "friendly." But there were others all around us, on the docks and on the deck, and two members of the crew on the ship next to us were watching from their superior height. Surely he wouldn't force his attentions on me under these circumstances.

"Excuse me, I must go," I said, and actually had to brush against his outstretched hand to move around him. There was a fine tremor in my legs as I made my way back below decks, a tremor that built until I reached our compartment so that I wondered if I would ever be able to stop shaking.

The mate made no move after me. But why should he? Tomorrow morning we sailed. For the following three or four months, except when we put into various strange ports for provisions and fresh water, I would be trapped on this vessel with the man, having no one to turn to for protection against him but a surly, drunken captain.

No one noticed there was anything wrong with me this time. The others were concerned with Dodie, who was having what promised to be a full case of hysterics in the middle of the cabin.

Phoebe pulled at her ineffectually, trying to get her into one of the lower bunks. "Sit down, Miss Dodie, you'll feel better. It's not likely it'll happen again, and besides, I don't think they'll make you sick, or anything. Not so's to die or anything like that."

Dodie threw off the restraining hand with more force than I'd ob-

served in her since as a child she'd bounced an apple off my head for
some rude remark I'd made. Never a pretty girl, at the moment the
poor thing was a sight, indeed, with her reddened nose and tear-
stained cheeks, her stubby eyelashes sticking together. "I will die!
I'm sick now of this terrible ship and that awful food and I *will* die if
I have to live this way for months and months!"

Dodie's hysteria seemed to have a calming effect on me, for I forgot my legs were shaking. "What's the matter now?"

"There was maggots in her food," Phoebe said apologetically. "I
expect it happens once in a while on board a ship. It wouldn't of
been so bad but she'd bit into one before she noticed it, the light
being so poor in here, and she's been screaming ever since."

For once I didn't blame her. "We'll complain to the captain.
Surely the passengers are entitled to edible food. Stop it, Dodie.
We'll insist that we must have something decent to eat, our money
entitles us to that."

My cousin wiped at her dreary eyes, catching her breath on a hic-
cough. "I don't want to go to California after all, Saunielle. I want
to go home where I can sleep in a clean bed and wash my hair and
eat food without . . . without . . ."

I hardened my voice, because sympathy would have done no good.
"You are at liberty to go wherever you like, of course. But someone
else has undoubtedly moved into the house by this time, so there's no
bed available. The garden and the chickens belong to them, as well.
And I think your share of the purse is somewhere in the neighborhood of eleven dollars and sixty cents, if you think you can accomplish anything with that."

Silence settled over us, until Phoebe asked in a shocked whisper,
"Is that all there is, miss? To get us all the way to California?"

"Our passage is paid, which should also include our meals, something without maggots. It ought to be plenty, for once we get to San
Francisco Papa will meet us and take care of everything."

Dodie began to cry again, this time with a quiet hopelessness that
was almost harder to watch than her hysterics. "Then there's no
choice, is there? We have to endure it, no matter how bad it is."

To say that the afternoon was depressing is not to overstate the
matter. Phoebe tried to rouse us from our black moods by reading
further in *Black Beauty*. I don't know if any of the others listened,
but I didn't. I lay in the narrow bunk, trying to think of something
that would not make me cry, wishing I could give vent to my own
fears without further alarming the rest of them.

Tom brought the evening meal, his mood subdued, his usual chat-
ter stopped. It was Phoebe who noticed why, crying out when he
turned to leave.

"What's happened to you? How did you come to be hurt?"

Hurt? I rolled over and sat up, unenthusiastic about the expected meal but concerned for the only crewman on the *Gray Gull* who had shown us any measure of kindness.

Tom ducked his head as if ashamed for us to see the left side of his face, for it was swollen and badly bruised, and there was a trickle of blood at the corner of his mouth where a tooth had punctured his lip.

"Did you fall?" I asked, thinking of those wicked ladders and the inadequate lighting below decks.

"No." He put a thumb to the lip, testing it. "The captain's in a bad mood because Mr. Rohann pulled out, and it's taking longer to load the cargo than he figured, so he's short-tempered. He gave me a clout that like to split my head because I was late with his supper."

After a moment of appalled silence, Phoebe said, "It's not right that he should do that."

"We're going to complain to him about the food," Dodie said. "There were maggots in mine at noon."

The boy's head bobbed again. "There is, sometimes. But I wouldn't say anything about it, miss. Not tonight, at any rate. I'd stay clear of him, miss."

Again there was a silence, while each of us battled with our own righteous indignation and our own fears.

"Dear God," Dodie said at last, and accepted her own food from Tom, staring at it without interest. "How did we come to this?"

Tom cleared his throat. "There's a bit of grog flowing tonight, last night in port. If you don't mind the advice, it might be wise to stay in your cabin until we're under way in the morning."

There was nothing to say to that. Supper was a slight improvement over our previous meals, being a stew that actually had a bit of meat in it, and though we all looked the bread over carefully, we found no foreign matter in it and we were all able to eat.

Aunt Pity put aside her dish last, patting her lips with her handkerchief in the absence of a napkin. "I remember, when we were at home when I was a girl, how we used to have wine with our meals. Settles one's stomach, my father used to say. The kind I liked best was a ruby red, and it was served in tiny glasses with long stems. Even Rachael didn't object to a glass of wine in the evening, to help one sleep."

She rambled on, about the house she had lived in, and the clothes she had worn, and the flowers and the beaux and the balls. We lay in our bunks and listened to how it had been, all those years ago before the war, when there was plenty of everything and the women had been treated as if they were fragile and priceless.

And gradually she came to the years of the war itself, and how their supplies were requisitioned, first by the Confederate forces, and

then by the Yankees. She told how the women of the South learned
to do the things that had previously been done only by slaves, to
cook and clean and nurse the wounded. She spoke of her father, who
had fallen to a Yankee bullet while trying to defend his home against
McClellan's troops outside of Richmond, and of the brothers and
cousins who had died at Chancellorsville and Fredericksburg, and of
the man she might have wed if he had not fallen at Gettysburg. He
had been Pity's only romance, and I had always thought they had
been young lovers until she spoke now; she had been thirty-two years
old, and he a schoolmaster nearly forty when he died with a bullet in
his throat.

At last her voice grew tired and faded altogether. Our lamp had
burned out and no one came to bring more oil, and no one wanted to
go seeking it. We lay on our lumpy mattresses in the dark, unwilling
to make the effort to undress and prepare for the night. I tried to say
a prayer, but it was so chaotic that not even the good Lord could
have made sense of it, I suspected.

Several times we heard heavy footsteps outside our door, and deep
voices cursing. Once we thought we were being invaded, only to realize moments later that someone the worse for his liquor had simply
stumbled and fallen against the bulkhead.

After a time the ship grew quiet, except for the gentle action of the
water against the side. I dozed, to awaken with my heart in my
mouth when a body fell heavily against our door.

We were all awake, suspending our breathing, waiting for sounds
that did not come. Long minutes passed before we heard anything,
and then it was not what we expected. Someone moaned.

"Someone's hurt," Phoebe hissed, dangling her head over the edge
of her bunk.

"Drunken sots, I hope they all break their necks," Dodie stated.
And then it came again, a drawn-out sound of pain, and a murmured, "Please, please, don't . . ."

Phoebe was out of her bunk in a flash, hitting the floor so solidly
that I knew she hadn't even taken off her shoes. "That sounded like
young Tom . . ."

"Don't open the door!" Dodie said quickly, and I too sat up, in the
fear that it might be a trick.

"But if it's Tom and he's hurt . . ." Phoebe and I collided in the
blackness. "We just can't let him lie there . . ."

I pressed my cheek to the door, listening intently. "Who's there?"

"Please, please . . ."

"It's him, I know it's him. I'm going to open the door," Phoebe
insisted in a low voice, and we fumbled together to find the latch.

The boy was sprawled in the passageway, limp under our groping hands. Phoebe lit a match and held it, strangling on her own cry of protest as we saw him in the briefly flaring light.

Blood flowed freely from his mouth and nose, and his right arm was twisted at such an unnatural angle I could only surmise that it was broken. He lifted his head, eyes glazed and nearly black with pain, then slumped forward helplessly as the match went out.

"We've got to help him," Phoebe said. "He's bad hurt, Miss Saunielle."

Between us, we dragged him into the compartment and onto my bunk. He had passed out and at least didn't make any more distressing sounds. Phoebe located our water container, and I heard her ripping material off her petticoat to use as a washcloth, although how she hoped to accomplish anything in darkness I didn't know.

"It must have been the captain, taking out his anger on the boy," Phoebe said, sounding angry and ready to tackle the entire crew with her fingernails if necessary. "We've got to have light and no doubt he needs a doctor if that arm's broke the way I think it is."

Dodie's voice wafted out of the upper bunk, wavering yet insistent. "Saunielle, we can't do this. We can't stay on this dreadful ship! We'll none of us get to California alive! There must be some other way!"

My tongue moved over lips so dry they felt as if they would crack. "Yes. I agree. It's too awful, we can't be expected to do it."

A startled expectancy greeted my announcement. "What are we going to do, then?" Phoebe demanded.

"We're going to the captain and demand our passage money back."

"But if he's drunk and in a rage he may attack us as he's done with Tom. Do you think there's any chance he'll give us the money?"

"He'll have to," I said, swallowing against the fear that threatened to choke me. "And if he doesn't . . . well, I think that Mr. Rohann was right. We'd be better off dying in Norfolk than staying on this miserable vessel. Dodie, you'll have to come with me, I can't go alone."

Dodie sucked in a horrified breath "Why me? Take Phoebe, she can go . . ."

"Are you willing to get down here and take care of Tom, then? Someone has to see he doesn't drown in his own blood from that broken nose. Are you prepared to do that?"

After a few seconds of silence, Dodie slid down beside me. "All right, I'll go. Let Phoebe do that, you know how the sight of blood affects me."

"We'll have to go quietly. I think the sailors have all passed out in their quarters, but I don't want to rouse any if there's a half-sober one left. Come on. Phoebe, latch the door behind us and don't open it until we get back."

Pity's voice came unexpectedly. "I'll go with you and bring back the first lantern we see. Phoebe can't do much for the boy without a light."

And so the three of us were off together, though Pity found her lantern at the bottom of the first ladder, holding it long enough to show us the way up before she headed back to the cabin.

To my surprise, it was chilly when we gained the deck. The wind raised gooseflesh on my arms, or perhaps that came from my fear of facing the captain. My only experience with a man in his cups had been with Papa, but he had only sunk into a morose silence; he had never been violent. I had no such assurance about Captain Schwartz.

There was a feeble light emanating from his quarters, and when we reached the doorway we found that the man was hunched over his littered table, the brandy bottle empty before him. Talking with him was going to be out of the question, at least for tonight, and we were scheduled to sail at dawn with the tide.

When Dodie made one of her involuntary whimpering sounds, I turned on her fiercely. "Shut up! Do you hear me? Be quiet while I think what we can do."

"I feel as if I'm going to faint."

"You do and I'll give you a bloody nose to match Tom's. We have to get our money back and get off this ship before they weigh anchor, but from the look of him he won't be sobered up by then."

"Maybe we should just take our belongings and get off now."

"Without our money? We paid nearly seventy dollars each for our passage. We can't leave it."

The ship rolled gently, and a precariously balanced dish fell off the table with a crash that shattered the silence and our nerves as well. My fingers dug into Dodie's thin arm, warning her not to cry out. Either the man was used to his crockery smashing or he was too drunk to function, for he only muttered under his breath, not rousing.

"Saunielle, it's no use! We can't talk to him, and it's not likely he'd refund the money anyway! If we get off the ship, at least we're still alive and unhurt, which is more than we'll be if we sail!"

I didn't waste my breath asking what she thought we'd do once we were off the *Gray Gull*. No doubt she'd expect me to come up with something, no matter how impoverished we were. We remained poised in the doorway while my gaze roamed the cabin. It was so sparsely furnished that perhaps I could determine where he kept his monies; if I could, I would simply take what was ours and go with it.

When I said as much to Dodie, it was clear that I'd have no help from her except that possibly she could watch the captain while I searched, though I wasn't sure I could trust her to do even that much.

When Pity spoke from behind us it was too much for Dodie, who spun about with a cry. "Oh! Aunt Pity, talk some sense into her, Saunielle is going to get us all thrown into jail, or worse!"

Pity didn't bother to so much as look at her, but addressed me. "The boy's come around, and he says the captain keeps his cash in a tin box, under his bunk. I'll watch to see he doesn't do anything while you look for it."

She was as cool as if she were at home, searching out pennies from stray corners for the Sunday collection plate. I felt a rush of relief and took her at her word, trying to ignore the man who slumbered heavily and noisily within arm's reach while I knelt beside his bunk.

The compartment was filled with junk, rancid-smelling clothes, rope, a length of chain, and, finally, a tin box. It made a protesting screech when I lifted the lid, so that we all looked at the sleeper, but he was undisturbed.

My fingers trembled as I counted it out . . . $275.

Pity spoke softly. "Phoebe says the boy must go with us, and he's owed two months' wages. Ten dollars."

I added the extra ten, rolling the bills into a packet that would fit down the front of my dress, leaving my hands free to replace the box. My knees were so weak it was all I could do to stand.

And then it was over, and we were out of the cabin, smelling fresh sea air and creosote and fish. Never had air been so sweet.

"Get our belongings," I said hoarsely. "They've left the gangway down, let's get out of here before they discover us."

And like thieves in the night, we crept off the ship, Phoebe and I supporting young Tom between us, in the hour before dawn. I did not know what we were going to do, nor how we would now reach California, but like Mr. Rohann before us, I felt that we had done the right thing in fleeing the *Gray Gull.*

❖❖❖❖ 6 ❖❖❖❖

A few hours later we were on our way, having accomplished a great deal. My initial reluctance to include Tom in our party, not because I didn't sympathize with him but because of our pitifully inadequate funds, was quickly overcome. For once his arm had been strapped to his chest (his shoulder was dislocated, not broken, the doctor said), Tom proved invaluable.

He found us a bath house, not inexpensive at twenty-five cents apiece, but well worth it to us to rid ourselves of both dirt and insect life. He procured bread and cheese upon which we breakfasted with considerable relish; even I felt no more nausea once I'd left the *Gray Gull,* and even allowed myself to hope that perhaps Phoebe's diagnosis might prove wrong.

Clean and fed, though still weary, we then held a council at which Tom was far more useful than any of the others. I had decided there was no recourse but for me to sell Mama's pearl necklace, for a telephone call to our home village (my first experience in speaking on this marvelous instrument) made it clear that no word had come from my father since our departure. Inquiry along the docks in Norfolk had failed to turn up any ship bound for California upon which we could possibly afford passage, and although there would be such within a matter of weeks we felt we could not wait for them. No, selling the pearls was the only sensible thing to do, for they would surely raise sufficient funds to put us all aboard a train heading west.

My attempt to find a buyer was an upsetting one, for I was offered far less than I knew the pearls to be worth. Again Tom took over, saying that it was too obvious that I was in need; one had only to look at me to imagine that I would settle for any paltry sum. He was convinced that he could do better, and he did. While still falling short of the actual value, the amount he got would at least suffice for our railway tickets, including one for Tom, if we traveled second class. And of course, Tom assured us, his brother who worked at the brewery would reimburse us for Tom's fare once we reached San Francisco.

We might have boarded the train in Norfolk, but since it did not go directly to Richmond, Tom suggested that we find a ride with one of the farmers who brought their wagons into the city with produce, and who would therefore be returning with empty carts, a less expensive way to travel. It was he who knew where to find the market and made the arrangements for us.

To our astonishment, the farmer who agreed to take us was a man from our own county. We did not know him personally, but his name was familiar, and he knew us by name as well. He had heard of Rachael's death and expressed his condolences in an awkward fashion.

We were loaded into his wagon, which was not too uncomfortable with a bit of hay to sit upon, and set off on the jolting journey. The only thing noteworthy about the encounter was a question he addressed to me when he set us down where our routes diverged.

"Did he catch up with ye, that feller was looking for ye?"

Startled, I hesitated in the act of lowering my valise to the ground from the wagon bed. "What fellow was that, sir?"

"Why, the one came into the village right after ye left. Happened to be there mysel', selling off my vegetables, like. Thin little man dressed in black, asking for Miss Saunielle Hunter. Man at the market told him you was off to California, and he seemed right agitated, he did."

I felt a bit of a chill. "Did he say what his business was?"

"Not in my hearing, he didn't, but he was still talking when I left. I knowed about your aunt passing on, and I took it maybe he was a tax collector or a bill collector, one. Them people don't even let a body die in peace any more, they don't." He shook his head, handing down Tom's small bundle of clothes. "Ah well, I expect you done the best you could with the bills, like all the rest of us. And I wouldn't be worrying if the tax collector never caught up with me, if I was you."

He clucked to his horses and slapped their rumps with the reins, and he was off, leaving us standing at the roadside.

"What was that all about?" Dodie wanted to know, her forehead furrowed as she looked after the old man.

"I'm not sure. Should we have paid some sort of taxes, after Aunt Rachael died?" My grip tightened on the purse that held the proceeds from the sale of Mama's necklace, as if the man might even now step out of the bushes and confiscate it.

"I don't know. Maybe taxes on the house. But they weren't due yet, I don't think, so let the new owner take care of them. What are we going to do now? I didn't realize he'd put us down right out in the country like this."

Tom had no doubt slept less well than the rest of us in the back of the wagon, for the jolting must surely have pained his injured shoulder. He was rather pale, and his face was bruised and his nose tilted slightly to one side, but he was fairly cheerful for all that. He had accepted his pack with his good hand and slung it off into the dusty grass.

"No sense going any further with him, since he's not going the right direction. There's plenty of bread and cheese left, and we can drink from the creek yonder, so I say let's rest a bit and hope someone else comes along to offer us a lift." He dropped beside his pack and began to lay out the lunch, with Phoebe's willing assistance.

"I declare, I hope the next one has a softer wagon bed," Pity observed, massaging her ancient bones. "If the rest of this trip is like the first of it, I'll never last to California."

I looked at her in some concern, for it had indeed been very tiring, and she was an old woman. Yet she ate her share of bread and cheese with good appetite, which was reassuring.

Twice travelers came along, and Tom walked out to talk with them, both times coming back to join us as the wagons rumbled on.

"No sense of taking up with anyone who isn't going more than a mile or two," he said. "We got to get us all the way to Richmond, and on the main road that ought to be possible to do. In the meantime, we'll rest up some more."

Dodie's head was bent as she examined one shoe, the sole of which was coming loose. "I don't understand why we want to go to Richmond, anyway. Isn't it out of our way, to go north instead of west?"

"Straight west is mountains," Tom pointed out. "The railroads go through them, but only in a few passes. We'll have to go even further north out of Richmond before we can cut across to the west."

Phoebe regarded him with open admiration. "How do you know so much about the railroads? Have you traveled on the trains?"

"No, but Mr. Rohann talked about 'em. You remember Mr. Rohann, the second mate that left the ship the night you came aboard? He's been everywhere, all around the world, I reckon. He comes from a good family, plenty of money, sounded like, out in San Francisco. He didn't exactly say he was the black sheep of the family, so to speak, but it could be that he is. Said he'd had a quarrel with his family, anyway, and hadn't seen any of 'em for two years, nearly. He's been in London most lately, and before that he was in China. He told us all about the people there, they have yellow skins and slanty eyes. It's the truth, I saw one myself once. Anyway, he's been on lots of trains." He bit off a chunk of crusty bread and chewed for a minute. "He shipped on the *Gray Gull* because he was broke, but it didn't seem to bother him much. Only when he found out what kind of ship it was, and what sort of captain, he said he'd find a better way to get home, and he'd only signed on when he was drunk, anyway."

"And he told you how to get to California on the train?" Phoebe prompted.

"That's right. He said as how he was going to go, and I remember what he said. It might even be that we'd catch up to him somewhere along the way. I wouldn't mind that. He was nice to me, Mr. Rohann was."

I couldn't deny that the rest was welcome, but the sun was settling toward the mountains, and I began to worry that we might have to spend the night in the open, a prospect anything but pleasant. Summer was over and the nights could grow chill; we hadn't even a blanket between us, and we'd devoured all but a few crumbs of bread.

I dozed there in the shade of a hickory tree, falling into an uneasy dream of Papa and Francis, who finally merged into one person. Phoebe woke me with an urgent hand on my shoulder.

"Wake up, miss, we've got a ride! Tom says the man will take us all the way to Richmond!"

Pity's wish for a softer wagon was not realized, but at least it was not any worse. We had enough room to stretch out and sleep, so that by dusk, when we stopped for the night, I was feeling almost my old self.

Had we been alone, we would certainly have felt the need to find lodgings. With Tom shepherding us, however, our accommodations were less grand but also less costly. We slept in a barn, surrounded by the familiar odors of cows and chickens, and as Tom had bought bread from the farmer's wife, as well as fresh milk warm from the cow and jam for the bread, we went to sleep comfortably fed.

By the time we reached Richmond, I trusted Tom enough to hand over the money and let him make the arrangements for us all. And the following morning, after a good night's sleep in an inn (where we had our last chance to bathe for some time) we boarded the train for California.

◇◇◇◇◇◇

There were no bedbugs, but there were other disadvantages to train travel, including smoke and hot cinders, and hard seats. Once again we might have done worse than to have Tom with us, for it was he who procured food to eat on our journey.

"There'll be people at the main stops, selling things," he told us, "but they'll charge more than I paid for this. I got a couple of pillows, too, to make sleeping a bit easier."

Tom was, we discovered, twenty years old. I had taken him for about my own age and was glad I hadn't let him know how young I thought him to be. He had little or no formal schooling, although he could read and write; almost at once Phoebe undertook to improve those skills, and they were huddled over *Black Beauty* for hours of every day, which was more than the rest of us had to pass the time.

The first part of our journey was through the lovely Blue Ridge Mountains, where the trees were already beginning to turn scarlet and orange and gold. We chugged slowly along, Aunt Pity tatting lace antimacassars that never came out quite right any more, Dodie listening to the readers behind her or watching the other passengers, and I . . . I watched out the open windows, occasionally brushing off a cinder before it should burn through my clothes, and let my mind wander where it would.

Inevitably, I thought of Francis. Inevitably, too, I thought of the child I was carrying although as yet it had little reality for me, and I continued to hope that there might not be a child, at all, that at any time Phoebe would be proved wrong. I thought about Papa, and prayed that he would have received my letters and be there to welcome us. My spirits rose, because now I knew it would be only days, not months, before we were together again.

Our coach was filled with travelers, all of them as uncomfortable as ourselves, and most of them little more prosperous. Everyone carried baskets of food; it was a rare time when one could look around without seeing someone eating fried chicken or bread or fruit.

Nights were the difficult time, because while we had all heard of the elegant Pullman cars with sleeping accommodations, our train had no such compartments. We had to arrange ourselves and our baggage . . . and the blessed pillows Tom had acquired . . . in whatever comfort we might manage. Around us people snored and coughed, swore and shifted position, and for almost the entire trip there was a group who played cards at the end of the compartment, their voices an accompaniment to the clack of the wheels on the rails.

Twice we had to change trains, each time losing a few familiar faces and gaining new ones that were somehow just the same. Since we had so few belongings this was not a hardship, particularly; in fact, I welcomed the chance to alight and stretch my legs and work some circulation back into them. During these intervals Tom was quick to see what could be had at a moderate price to keep us fed for the next lap.

The final stretch of our journey, from Omaha to San Francisco, would be made in one long jump. As we waited to board for the last lap, Phoebe and Tom went together to bargain for food and another set of pillows, although we had been assured that this coach would be more comfortably furnished.

The novelty of traveling had vanished, even in so short a time, for I felt dirty and bruised and exhausted. Underneath my excitement at the thought of seeing Papa lay that small but insistent worry: what if he should not be there? What if I had to cope with a coming baby without him to help me?

"Come on, Tom's got our seats picked out!" Phoebe's voice cut into my thoughts, and I reached once more for my satchel and my pillow. "It's ever so much grander than that little thing we rode out of Richmond. There's plush padded seats, and separate conveniences for ladies and gentlemen, with a mirror in the ladies'. I looked, just to see. I heard a man say that on the flatlands this train will go nearly a hundred miles an hour! Just think of that!"

I followed the others without comment, giving little credit to her statement. A hundred miles an hour, what rot. How people did exaggerate. Even I, who felt as if I'd been traveling for weeks. Well, at least we were not on the *Gray Gull,* at the mercies of Captain Schwartz and his mate.

"Guess what?" Phoebe turned back to assist me in climbing the steps into our chosen car. "Tom says that Mr. Rohann is here in

Omaha, he's talked to someone who's met him! Wouldn't it be interesting if he were riding on the same train?"

"I thought he was signed on the *Gray Gull* because he couldn't afford train fare," I observed, not caring one way or the other.

Phoebe giggled. "Maybe he sold his mother's necklace, too. Or something."

"More likely 'or something.' He didn't look the type to be carrying his mother's jewels." I followed her along the aisle, jostling and being jostled by all the other people who were also trying to convey their luggage to their seats.

Tom had chosen a spot nearest the ladies' convenience, which was thoughtful of him, because by the time the train got under way the aisles were as full as the seats, with valises and parcels and even a crate of chickens to climb over or around. The seats were much more comfortable, there being some padding under the dark red velvet covers, and we could open or close the windows as we chose.

What this meant was that we could have them closed, and feel stifled by the much-used air within the coach, or open them and have the soot and cinders flying in on us. As the weather, at least in the daytime, was still warm, we mostly traveled with them open, keeping a careful watch that a coal didn't land in someone's hair or lap without being noticed.

As on the previous coaches, a card game quickly developed at one end of the car. This time Tom sauntered over to talk with them, and after a time came back with a grin on his face.

"He's on the train, somewhere. Mr. Rohann. I'm going to go take a look, and say hello."

I closed my eyes, settling against the pillow, surrendering to the motion of the train. Only a few more days and our traveling would be over; wherever Papa was living, there would be water to bathe in and wash our clothes, and real beds . . . I drifted off, dreaming of clean sheets and blissful quiet . . .

The train may not have been going a hundred miles an hour, but it was certainly much faster than the ones we had ridden through the mountains and the eastern plains. Since the scenery here was of little interest to any of us, this was to the good, but the motion tended to make me queasy again.

Eating helped somewhat, when Tom came back. He had found the red-bearded Mr. Rohann, whose first name was Sebastian, two cars ahead. "Told me I did the only sensible thing, jumping ship. And he says I won't have any trouble getting work in California, once my shoulder heals. There's plenty of work for everyone, he says."

"How does he know if he hasn't been there for two years?" Dodie asked.

Tom was not put down by this. "Oh, there's letters and news-papers, miss. I got us a few pears; does anybody want one?"

The fruit was juicy and sweet, and reminded me of home. Home . . . would there be a home waiting for me, with Papa? Or was his hope of wealth enough to provide a home only another of his pipe dreams, as Rachael had called them?

We slept well enough that first night, but I woke in the morning struggling against nausea. The coach swayed from side to side in a rhythm that must be every bit as bad as that of a ship at sea. Most of the windows had been closed against the night chill, and the air was thick with stale cigar smoke and the odors of travelers too long in their clothes.

I gulped against the sudden spasm in my mid-section, and scrambled over Phoebe's inert figure into the aisle. She roused enough to look after me, but the others slept on.

Fortunately no one was in the ladies' convenience to bar my en-trance or see me vomit. I clung, weak and shaking, to the brass bar secured to the wall, until I thought I could walk back to my seat.

There was a small rectangle of mirror on the wall, and I stared into it at the countenance of a stranger. A wild-eyed girl, with no semblance of prettiness, her dark hair in need of combing, stared back at me. My skin was white and in the early morning light seemed almost to have a greenish tinge. I was wearing a black dress, having thought it most suitable both for mourning and travel, but I hadn't reckoned on the dust; I looked like a dressmaker's dummy that had stood in the attic for years.

The door opened a crack and Phoebe stuck her head into the aper-ture. "Miss Saunielle? You all right?"

"As all right as I can be, I suppose. Would you . . . would you fetch me a dipper of water from the barrel?"

She hesitated. "There's no mistake, is there, miss?"

"I'm afraid not. Do you think anyone else has noticed, Phoebe?"

"I don't think so, miss. Miss Dodie is not thinking of anything but herself, and Miss Pity . . . well, she doesn't notice as much as she used to. I'll get the water, miss."

I sipped at it carefully, then wet a handkerchief with the rest of it to sponge my face and neck. It wasn't much, but the best I could do at the moment.

We returned to our seats, where the others continued to sleep. I felt somewhat better, although the motion of the train kept me un-easy.

I managed to eat and retain my share of breakfast when the time came, and as the coach awoke the activity distracted me a bit from my own indisposition.

Late the second day, when we had crossed Nebraska and were

hurtling through the southern part of Wyoming, where the scenery was all red rock and occasional sparse sagebrush, Sebastian Rohann came to our coach.

He stood grinning at Tom, his oddly light blue eyes skimming us and dismissing us as of no consequence. "I hear there's a poker game back here. You a poker player, Tom?"

"No, sir. Never learned how, and I haven't got much money."

"Neither did I have, but what I had I parlayed into a train ticket and a change of clothes. Come along, I'll teach you a few things."

Alarmed, Phoebe sat up straighter, although she said nothing. Perhaps the man sensed our disapproval, for his grin widened. "No harm to be done, miss. I won't let him play, just watch at first. Passes the time, and there's too much of that."

Tom agreed with alacrity, handing back to Phoebe the book he had been reading aloud. "It's a thing a man ought to learn," he said.

Rohann nodded politely to us, then led the way down the aisle. Again his eyes had taken little note of us.

I found myself resenting it, although after seeing myself in the mirror I knew we deserved no more. We were tired and dirty and needed our hair combed and dressed, yet I could remember a time when I had been thought pretty and desirable. I swallowed the lump in my throat, turning toward the window to hide the tears I couldn't control.

"Horrid sort of country, isn't it?" Pity said from the opposite seat. "I can't imagine why anyone ever left Virginia to cross this place. Imagine driving an ox team through this!"

The day was hot, adding to our discomfort when perspiration soaked through our clothes, leaving wet stains under arms and across shoulders. When night fell, however, the temperature dropped sharply, so that we welcomed our shawls. The poker game at the end of the car went on for hours, and even from our distant vantage point it was obvious that Sebastian Rohann was winning. Tom watched intently, and came back to report at suppertime, when we shared out the last of the chicken and biscuits.

"That little fellow, Mr. Sipes, he's won about two dollars. But Mr. Rohann's ahead nearly twenty."

"Does he cheat?" I asked, to be rebuked by a pained expression.

"He don't have to cheat, Miss Saunielle. He's just a good poker player."

"He must be," I said dryly, "if he won his train fare and pocket money in only a few days' time."

"He didn't leave Norfolk until after we did; he was playing poker there, too. That reminds me, miss, he said something about that same man. At least I think it was the same man."

"What man is that?"

"The one that was asking after you, remember, the old farmer mentioned him? A little man in a dark suit. A tax collector, or whatever. He must have followed you to the city. Anyways, he was asking after you around the docks. The *Gray Gull* had already sailed by the time he got there, and didn't anybody know but what you were on it. Mr. Rohann said he seemed perturbed, like."

I shifted uneasily in my seat. "Did Mr. Rohann talk to him?"

"No. He just was there in the saloon when the man was talking to some sailors. He didn't know your name then, but from the description he figured it was you. Anyways, I don't reckon a tax collector would follow you to California." He stripped the meat off a chicken leg and threw the bone out the window. "I wouldn't want to get into that game with no more'n ten dollars to my name, but I'm learning a bit." He went on about the card game, explaining to Phoebe how the game was played.

My mind had halted back there on the small dark-suited man who might be a tax collector. I hadn't deliberately run from a creditor, although I well might have if it meant handing over any of our resources to one. I hoped to heaven Tom was right about his giving up the pursuit once he thought we had sailed for the Pacific Coast.

Occasionally the engine had to stop for water. When that happened, most of us got out and walked around, easing muscles cramped from so many hours in a sitting position. If we were lucky there might be a small town or at least a ranch house where we could obtain a little extra water for washing the exposed portions of our bodies. Mostly, however, there was only a tank filled by a windmill, and nothing to see but bare earth or dry grasses stretching to the horizon.

Pity worried me. She seemed to have aged ten years since we'd left home, and her mind wandered at times. She talked a lot about her girlhood, and the years she'd spent in other people's homes, rearing other people's children, the lot of an unmarried lady with no marital or financial prospects. There was nothing wrong with that, and it helped to pass the time. But once in a while she would be disoriented, wanting to know where we were going, and why.

No doubt she felt, as I did, that the train seat had become a painful growth attached to her own anatomy.

On our last night on the train, our routine was changed, and not for the better.

We had all begun to settle down a bit earlier than usual, I think, except for the men in the poker game at the far end of the car where the lights still burned a little after ten o'clock. The rest of us had blown out the lanterns, adjusted our windows and our pillows, and were trying to find reasonably comfortable positions. Across the aisle a fat man was snoring loudly, and an irate seatmate punched him in the ribs with an elbow and delivered a sharp admonition.

Phoebe and Tom, in the seat behind me, were murmuring softly. If I'd had a bit more energy I might have worried about them, too, although their opportunities for getting into trouble had not been great while we remained on a crowded train. And with my example to follow, I hoped she would not do anything foolish.

Pity was asleep with her mouth open, her tatting still in her lap, and I reached over to take it gently out of her hands and tuck it into her reticule. Dodie slept, too, her face almost a mirror-image of my own weariness and worry, her clothes as rumpled and soiled. No wonder Tom's Mr. Rohann wasn't taken by our looks.

I loosened my collar, and in so doing touched the chain there, from which hung the ring Francis had been wearing when he died. I pulled it out and enclosed it in my fingers until it warmed there, giving in to the sorrow it evoked but feeling some comfort, too. Francis had loved me, and perhaps sometime, somewhere, there would be another who would find me pleasant and attractive.

I closed my eyes, and at once it seemed that the speed of the train had slackened. Another watering stop coming up, but from what Tom had reported (he circulated among the other passengers and brought back all sorts of information) there would be nothing but the water tower. I debated, very briefly, getting off to stretch my legs, and then decided against it. It was cold out there after dark.

The brakes made a protesting sound, so that my fellow travelers stirred uneasily and muttered in their sleep, but no one got up to get off. One of the poker players made a coarse remark and the others laughed in a subdued fashion.

And then the laughter died abruptly, unnaturally, and a muffled oath was also cut off.

I opened my eyes and saw them, three men wearing jeans and flannel shirts and bandanas tied around their faces. They had appeared through the doorway at the back of the car, just beyond the card players, and I knew even before my gaze dropped to their weapons that we were being robbed.

◇◇◇◇ 7 ◇◇◇◇

Paralysis held us all as motionless as if we were having photographs taken. Sebastian Rohann stood just beneath one of the lanterns, his red curly hair and beard a spot of color against the blackness of the open doorway. I heard Tom's quick intake of breath behind me, only a second behind my own.

"Just everybody stay put. Don't do nothing foolish and nobody will get hurt," one of the masked men said.

For a moment it seemed that no one breathed. Those who had been asleep awakened, except for the fat man who continued to snore. Pity jerked upright, swiveling around to see what the rest of us were looking at.

"All we want is your valuables. Money, watches, jewelry. Don't hold nothing back or you'll be sorry. Put everything in the hat when Harry holds it out to you."

Two of the men stayed where they were, at the door. The third began to move along the aisle, the hat extended to people too astounded and too frightened to resist. There were a few verbal protests, quickly silenced when Harry reached out to hurry slow fingers with a brutal nudge from the weapon he carried.

I watched his approach with a sick sense of shock and outrage. We had so little, and to have it taken from us this way would mean that we would arrive in San Francisco penniless, and no way of knowing what would be required to reach Papa. On both sides of the aisle travelers were dropping their valuables into the outstretched hat, a ring, a watch, the contents of a purse. My own small purse lay on top of my valise, and there was nothing I could do to hide it.

Down the length of the car my eyes met those of Sebastian Rohann, who still stood motionless, and I felt a stronger flicker of fear. He did not have the attitude of a man who has given in, a man resigned to the inevitable. He was not a big man, but he had heavy shoulders and biceps, well muscled from doing manual labor, I suspected, and he was poised as if he expected to use them.

I had the fleeting hope that he would do nothing that would get him shot, and then Harry was opposite our seats, the hard muzzle of the revolver bringing to an end the snoring of our neighbor. The man jerked awake, eyes rolling as he gasped for breath.

"Ha . . . wha . . . what's going on?"

"Hand over your money. And that ring, and the watch. Come on, hurry up, we ain't got all night."

The man, dazed, failed to respond, and Harry jerked at the chain across the fat man's waistcoat so that it snapped and the watch at the end of it went into the hat. The other passenger in the double seat hastily added his own contribution with a hand that was visibly trembling.

And now the bandit was here, looking at us, and I had been able to do nothing to save our precious few dollars. Dodie gave a frightened yip when the hat was passed in front of her, shaking her head.

"Come on, don't waste time, lady. Give me your purse."

"There's . . . there's nothing in it, I have nothing . . ." She demonstrated, turning it inside out, her eyes glazed it terror.

The man made a sound of disgust, reaching out with his left hand to rip the brooch from the neck of her dress with a slight tearing sound. Pity regarded him with dignity and more control, opening her own reticule to display her tatting and two copper pennies, which she dropped disdainfully into the hat. I wondered what she'd done with her twelve dollars and hoped the man wasn't going to search anyone.

"Just like the damn Yankees," Pity said clearly, with more bravery than good sense.

Harry was in too much of a hurry to bother with her, however, and moved on to me. "Come on, open up that satchel. Let's have it."

There was nothing I could do but comply; a glance at the man's face was enough to convince me he wouldn't hesitate to shoot anyone who failed to cooperate. However, I didn't move with sufficient haste, and he hit my hand a glancing blow with the barrel of his weapon, so that I cried out in pain.

"Let's have this, too," he said, and through the blur of tears I saw his hand come out again. The chain cut deeply into my neck, resisting his effort to jerk away the Jaubert ring; if Phoebe had not leaned quickly forward and loosed the clasp I might have had a severe injury. As it was, my right hand was briefly crippled and the other came away touched with blood where the chain had broken my skin.

The man moved on, the length of the car, his hat overflowing by this time with small treasures. He turned back to his companions, only then realizing that he had bypassed Sebastian Rohann.

"You, too," was the order. I watched the tensing of muscle, and then Rohann brought the roll of poker winnings out of his pocket, a far thicker roll than the mere twenty dollars Tom had reported earlier. There was a grunt of satisfaction from the man called Harry, and then he was out of the door while the remaining gunmen looked us over.

"Stay in your seats. It'll be a few more minutes before we're finished, and you can go on your way. Anybody sticks his head through that door gets a bullet through it, so don't try anything."

They were gone; we heard their feet clattering on the steps, and then nothing, not even our own breathing, for a matter of seconds.

Sebastian Rohann was the first to break the silence. "Has anybody got a gun?"

There were murmurs from several directions, but none of the speakers made any move to get up. "I got a .45, but I ain't aiming to get my head blown off," one of them said.

Rohann was already moving down the aisle, a hand outstretched. "Give it to me, then. I'm not letting anybody take every cent I've got.

If anybody wants to come with me, I'll welcome the help, but if you don't I'm going out there anyway."

"You'll get killed, mister. I couldn't see much of their faces but I saw their eyes, and them guys was crazy mean. They're gonna shoot if you go after 'em."

"Not unless they see me coming." Rohann was so light on his feet he reminded me of a cat. He looked over the .45 and hefted it as if it felt natural in his hand. "Put out the rest of the lights. Every blessed thing, including any smokes anybody's got going. Keep them out, and there won't any of us be silhouetted against a light. And everybody get your heads down below the level of the windows."

He moved with the assurance of a man used to command. Tom was out of his seat and moving too.

"I don't know how much use I can be with only one arm, but I'll come if you need me, Mr. Rohann," he offered.

Rohann flashed him a grin. "One arm and two good eyes, that's more than some people have. Come on," he said.

Just before the last of the lights was put out, two young men in western garb much like that of the bandits stood up, having produced similar weapons. They looked like brothers.

"We'll go with you, mister. They got away with six hundred dollars of our money, and the old man ain't going to take kindly to us coming home without a year's profit," one of them said grimly.

Three armed men and a crippled boy. It didn't seem an adequate contingent to send, I thought as silence settled over the darkened coach. For there must be more than the three men who had appeared in our car. Someone had held a gun on the engineer, certainly, or the train wouldn't still be immobilized. And I knew there was a baggage and mail coach which could be expected to offer more than they'd taken off the passengers.

Phoebe's hand sought me in the dark, and I grasped it with my uninjured one, squeezing for a moment, then reiterating Rohann's orders. "Get down below the level of the windows, he said."

"What for?" Dodie asked, and someone across the aisle saved me the trouble of replying.

"If there's any shooting you're a lot less likely to get a bullet in you, girlie."

We crouched on the dusty floor, limbs cramping, elbows gouging ribs and posteriors. I suspect the rest of them, as I did, prayed, although I couldn't have said afterward whether I'd prayed for the men brave enough to leave the train or for the return of the funds we needed so badly.

It seemed hours that we knelt there between the seats. The air grew thick and too warm and malodorous, and Dodie was shaking so that her fear was infectious. Pity kept mumbling something about the "damn Yankees" and I wondered if she thought she was being besieged by McClellan again.

I suppose we were all expecting gunfire, but when it came there was a general reaction that sent us groveling under the seats, or trying to. A man yelled, as if he'd been hit, and then there were half a dozen more shots, followed by silence except for a muttered curse from inside the train.

I knew I had to move or be permanently crippled. The darkness was not so intense now that my eyes had adjusted to it, and I very cautiously brought up my head to peer out a window.

Several others were doing the same thing. "By George," observed the fat man who'd lost his watch, "I think they've stopped them! I think they've got our money back!"

And so it proved, when our impromptu vigilantes returned a short time later. Between the group from our coach and a heroic guard on a payroll shipment, the bandits were rounded up, trussed like fowl for the market, and stowed into a corner of the baggage car. As soon as our water had been replenished, we were once more on our way.

Rohann and the others were grinning, joking, inordinately pleased with themselves. They passed among us, sorting out our belongings, determining who had had what amount of money taken. Rohann passed over Pity's two pennies, and my small collection of bills, again showing no more interest than he did in the fat man across the aisle.

It was some time before we slept again, and even the poker players left off their game and put out the lights, except for one burning to light the way to the conveniences.

Tomorrow, I thought. Tomorrow night we will be in San Francisco, and Papa will be there, and everything will be all right. Hugging the hope to me with the fervency of prayer, I fell asleep.

◇◇◇◇ 8 ◇◇◇◇

San Francisco! How many times I had imagined it, as described by my father in his letters. A city built on hills, with a sparkling blue bay on one side and the Pacific Ocean on the other, with its magnificent public buildings and city parks!

Even the grandeur of the mountains through which we passed, so much higher and more rugged than our Appalachians, and still carrying last winter's snows, could not draw my attention from the expectancy I felt at reaching San Francisco.

The mountains behind us, we crossed the strange and frightening desert land of Nevada, and climbed once more as we worked our way through a Sierra mountain pass, and then we were down the western slopes, rushing toward the sea.

The California valleys were lush with vegetation, even at this time of year when harvesting was in full swing, although Tom (who gained knowledge a jump ahead of the rest of us and was only too happy to share it) said that no rain fell here during the summer and all water must be brought from the mountains for irrigation purposes.

We approached the city from the south, since we had to skirt the seventy-mile length of San Francisco Bay and return up the far side of it. Fatigue was forgotten in our excitement, and long before we reached the depot we had our belongings in hand, ready to depart.

The weather was everything we had been promised: blue sky and bright sunshine, yet without the heat of the interior valleys. The very air seemed to set our pulses tingling as if we'd drunk champagne.

Dodie pressed her face against the window, showing the most animation I had ever seen from her. "Do you think Uncle Edward will meet us, Saunielle? Your last telegram told him we were arriving, didn't it?"

"I told him the day. But of course he may not have received the telegram; apparently he didn't get the earlier ones. No doubt when he moved into . . . into the house he intended to buy, he neglected to make arrangements for his mail to be forwarded to the new address. I hope he's taken care of it by now, so that it won't be difficult to find him. But I'd be most amazed if he met us."

The engine chuffed to a halt and there was a frantic press of movement, as if after days of riding we could not wait to get off the train. I saw that Pity was literally carried away from us by the surging passengers, and I called to her to wait on the platform, hoping that her reticule and valise wouldn't be torn from her grasp in the crush.

I suppose, despite my attempts to be realistic, I was secretly cherishing the hope that Papa would, after all, have received that final message. For my eyes swept over the waiting crowd and the carriages drawn up to meet the newcomers, searching for a tall and gently smiling man with dark hair and friendly blue eyes. Papa had always had a flair for clothes, and I pictured him much as he had been when he left home, elegant in a good dark suit, with a high white collar and possibly a rather daring vest and a silk tie.

Of course it had been five years since I'd seen him, and at the age of fifty-two no doubt there would be a touch of gray at his temples, although there had certainly been none when he left Virginia. His letters had assured me that he had stopped drinking . . . at least, that he drank no more than any gentleman does in a sociable evening with his fellows . . . and I hoped to find him fit and happy as he had been in the old days, before Mama's death.

There were well-dressed gentlemen aplenty, but none who looked familiar. We had been separated in our descent from the train, and we quickly regrouped, taking inventory to make sure we hadn't left anything behind.

"What do we do now?" Pity asked with an air of practicality. "I declare, I didn't think I'd need to sit again for a week, but I'm already a bit out of wind. How are we to find Edward?"

"I have the address where he was when he last wrote to me," I said, consulting the crumpled enveloped in my small purse. "Perhaps we should just take a hired carriage there. What do you think, Tom?"

Tom, looking well recovered from his bout with Captain Schwartz except for the fact that his right arm was immobilized, turned from an earnest and low-voiced conversation with Phoebe. "That sounds sensible to me. Let's see if I can find out how far it is to the lodging place, and what it will cost. Oh, there comes Mr. Rohann, I'll want to speak to him . . . Good-by, sir, and thanks for everything. I wouldn't have liked landing here without a cent on me, and I sure would have if you hadn't had the courage to take off after those bandits."

Rohann, in contrast to our own insecure state, seemed confident and at ease, including us all in his smile. "They had over two hundred dollars of my hard-earned money. I wasn't about to lose it, since those poor fellows on the train didn't have that much for me to win from them to replace it. I had no choice but to go after it."

I stifled the sense of disapproval his words aroused in me, yet he must have read something of my attitude in my face.

"Don't approve of a man playing poker for his bread and butter, Miss . . . Hunter, is it?" The idea was not in the least disconcerting to him, for the grin widened. "Well, it's a damned sight better than sailing round the Horn on a leaky old tub and maybe settling for a watery grave. People who can't afford to lose shouldn't gamble, and it's not my fault if they don't use good judgment about that, is it? I spent two nights in Norfolk easing the pockets of a few incautious souls, so that Captain Schwartz had his piddling wages returned and couldn't send the constable after me, and I wasn't about to have to walk to California." That was as much justifying as he intended to do, for he turned his attention to Tom. "Going off to find your brother in the brewery, are you?"

"Yes, sir. Of course I can't very well take a job until this arm works again, but I reckon Jack will have a place where I can sleep until then."

"Well, I wish you luck. If the brewery doesn't pan out, look me up and I may be able to turn something your way. I'm heading for the family home on Taylor Street, right on the cable-car line, so it's easy to get to. Ask the motorman, he's sure to know it, the Rohann place." The oddly pale blue eyes swept across us, the poor drab females who, but for his intervention, would have arrived here penniless. "And I wish you luck, too, ladies, in your job hunting. When I left there was a considerable demand for maids and waitresses, so I don't doubt you'll get on all right."

I failed to be charmed by his parting smile, staring after him in something close to outrage. Humiliation warmed my face. "Why, that wretched man thinks we're no more than poor white trash!"

"Oh, miss, he's never seen you dressed up and with your hair done," Phoebe cried. "He'd be stunned at what a beauty you are, it's only all this traveling and soot blowing in on us, and none of us with a proper bath since God knows when."

Aunt Pity fixed an eye on my mid-section and pursed her lips. "I shouldn't wonder if he took any female that wasn't wearing a decent corset not to be a lady, after all."

Logic told me that a pregnancy no further advanced than my own could not be obvious, but I was unable to control pressing a hand to my stomach, which still seemed perfectly flat. "Am I bulging so much as all that? But my dress fastens all right . . . the corset came apart in my hands, it wasn't fixable, really it wasn't . . . and I've been afraid to spend the money for a new one . . ."

"You look perfectly all right to me." Dodie, too, stared after our recent benefactor with resentment. "Anyone who gambles for a living has his nerve looking down on *us*. We come of good stock, as good as any in Virginia, and I wouldn't doubt if some of his ancestors were among the damned Yankees who came swarming down and ruined everything for us."

I was staring down at myself, trying to assess my own waistline. "Is it obvious to everyone that I don't have a foundation garment?"

"I've noticed you haven't been wearing one since we left home," Pity said. "Oh, I suppose it's not something every stranger would remark, but that man had his arm around you back there in Norfolk, to keep you from falling into the water, and any man can tell the difference between stays and flesh under his hand."

That made me flush more deeply than before, at the thought that Sebastian Rohann had felt my flesh, no matter how briefly nor through how many layers of petticoat and chemise and dress fabric. I pounced upon Tom in my haste to turn the subject. "I thought you were going to determine how we are to get to this address."

Tom, who had been taking this all in with his mouth slightly agape, closed it and took the paper from my hand. "Ah yes, ma'am.

Market Street, opposite the Palace Hotel. That oughtn't to be hard to find. I'll be right back."

He darted off into the crowd, and to my relief no one returned to the matter of my corsetless state, although I was uncomfortably conscious of it. "It looks as if everyone's being met but us, doesn't it?"

"I never saw so many people in all my life," Dodie declared. The excitement of our arrival had brought a becoming touch of color to her usually pale face. "Oh, Saunielle, isn't it going to be exciting, living in the city?"

"I hope so. After years of doing nothing but sewing and entertaining ourselves reading *Little Women* during the evenings, I'll be ready for some diversion," I said. And then I thought of choir practice and walking home from church with Francis and the brief hours we had had together, and of the coming child who would so drastically affect my future, and I didn't want to pursue *that* topic, either.

Phoebe was staring off after Tom, although he had vanished somewhere among all these people who seemed so clean and well-dressed compared to us. "I suppose once he's put us in a carriage and we're off to find Mr. Hunter, we'll never see Tom again."

"I certainly hope we'll see him again, since he owes us for his railroad fare," I reminded her. "That's a considerable sum, and one we may have a good deal of use for."

Her freckled face brightened. "I'd forgotten that. You're right, of course, he'll have to be in touch, won't he?"

Tom returned in a short time, and gestured toward one of the waiting carriages for hire. "It's not far, he said. I've left the slip with the driver, he'll see you there safely. I've . . ." he glanced at Phoebe, then back at me. "I've wrote down Jack's address, it's a boardinghouse, and that's where I'll be. As soon as you know where you'll be staying, send me a note there, and I'll be in touch. I'll be getting your money to you as soon as may be, Miss Saunielle. I'd give you the ten dollars I got now, but I'm sort of afraid to until I know where the next is coming from, you know?"

We and our luggage were loaded into the carriage; we all waved good-by to Tom, and then we were rolling up Fourth Street to Market, on the next lap of our journey. On what, I prayed, would be the very last step before falling into Papa's arms.

The rooming house was a respectable-looking one, certainly not the sort in which a derelict would live. I wasn't conscious that I had worried about that, that Papa would be down and out, as Aunt Rachael would have said. The neat sign on the front porch of the narrow, three-storied house stated that the proprietor was a Mrs. Annie Morton, and that the rates were five dollars a week and up for board and lodging. I did a bit of rapid mental arithmetic, conscious of the few bills remaining in my purse, and hoped to heaven I wouldn't have to pay for lodgings for any period of time, if at all.

The driver took it for granted that this was our destination, and handed down first his passengers and then the luggage. Now that I had had my personal shortcomings so painfully pointed out, I was most conscious of the shabbiness of the luggage, as well, in contrast to the fresh tan paint and potted flowers along the porch rail. I paid the carriage man, unable to control the tremor in my hand as I both feared and anticipated what I would find in this place.

We got ourselves and our belongings up the high steps to the main floor and I twisted the iron knob that rang a bell within the house. There were freshly washed and ironed lace curtains in the window that precluded our seeing in until a stout matron with an apron over her shirtwaist and skirt came to the door.

"Yes?"

"I'm . . . I'm looking for my father, Edward Hunter. He gave this as an address some few months ago." My heart was hammering, the prayer a constant accompaniment to it, *Please, God, let him be here.*

"Edward Hunter? Oh, yes, we did have Mr. Hunter here. And you're his daughter?" She looked me over, critically, I thought.

"We've just come all the way from Virginia, on the train." I brushed at one shoulder and was mortified to see the small puff of dust emanate from my clothing. "Is Mr. Hunter here now?"

"Why, no, he ain't. You didn't hear from him, before you left Virginia?"

A cold chill had begun to creep in both directions from the pit of my stomach. "I have his last letter here, from . . . nearly three months ago. Do you know where he's gone? Did he leave a forwarding address?"

She shook her head. "No, that he did not. Stayed until his rent was up, and then he left. Very nice gentleman, Mr. Hunter was. I was sorry to see him go. Well mannered, paid his rent when it was due, never one for drinking and causing trouble. But I don't recollect that he said where he was going. Never talked about his personal affairs, he didn't. Very refined gentleman he was."

Dismay brought a painful ache to my throat. "You have no idea at all where he went? Perhaps he talked to some of the other roomers? He might have told someone else what he intended to do?"

"Well, he might have. If he did, I don't know about it." Her eyes flickered over the rest of our party. "Are you all together? All his family?"

"Yes. This is my aunt, Miss Pity Calhoon, and my cousin Dorothea Calhoon, and Phoebe is our . . . our maid." I thought that sounded better than "hired girl." "Mrs. Morton . . . you are Mrs. Morton? . . . could we come inside? If my father isn't here, I'd like very much to talk to the others who might know something about him. And in any event, we'll have to have lodgings for the night, or until we locate him." A portion of my mind noted that this was undoubtedly one of the better-class rooming houses in the city, and that we would do well to locate a cheaper one if we had to spend more than a day or two finding Papa. Another part, more purely physical, begged that we were exhausted and we had no idea how to locate a less expensive house, and that we might risk one night here, at least.

"Four of you? Two to a bed?" We nodded. At this point, we might well have settled for four to a bed, if we could have a meal and a bath thrown in. Shrewdly, she assessed our financial situation. "Seventy-five cents apiece for the rooms, payable in advance. It's cheaper if you stay a week."

"I don't know yet about that . . . if we can find Papa . . . but we'll stay for the night, at least. We'll be needing supper and breakfast, I'd say, and as soon after that as I can make a decision, we'll let you know about more than that. Will that be satisfactory?"

"Supper's twenty-five cents. I set a good table, your pa agreed to that. Breakfast is fifteen cents."

Determined to think positively, I smiled and nodded. By tomorrow, at the latest, we would find Papa and would then not have to worry about every penny. "Would that include baths, Mrs. Morton? We're so looking forward to bathing."

"No extra charge for bathing, long as you don't do more than one a week. If you do, it's ten cents for the extra hot water," she said, and stepped backward so that we could enter her hallway.

It was a plain house inside, but spotlessly clean. She led us up a stairway to the second floor and toward the rear of the house, which ran very deep on the lot; I would discover that this was a characteristic of many San Francisco houses.

Our two rooms were across the hall from one another. Dodie and Pity took one, Phoebe and I the other. Each contained a heavy, ornate dresser, a matching bed, two chairs, a writing table, and a commode; Mrs. Morton opened the latter to display the customary white china set, this one decorated with tiny pink rose buds.

"There's a bathroom on each floor, I'll show you. Now's a good time to use it, if you've a mind for a bath, before the men comes home from work. Supper's at six-thirty sharp."

She waited while I counted out her money, putting it into her apron pocket with an air of having concluded a profitable transaction, and then showed us the bathroom.

We decided that we would use that facility in the order of our ages, starting with Aunt Pity. She was almost reeling with weariness, and I stayed to help her run water into the enormous claw-footed enamel tub and to undo her buttons. I had deliberately not looked at her when she undressed on board ship, but it was impossible to avoid seeing her now, and I was concerned that she was so old and so fragile, the blue veins showing everywhere through pale skin, the bones seeming about to poke through at any moment.

"Will you need any more help? Shall I stay with you?" I asked, helping her into the tub.

She sank into the warm water with a sigh of pleasure. "No, run along, child. I'll soak a few minutes, and then you might help me with my hair, when I'm out. Oh, how good it will be to be clean again!"

That was a sentiment echoed by all of us. A bath, washing my hair, and getting into fresh clothes was one of the most pleasant experiences of my life.

I stood in the large, sunny room, brushing my hair until it dried, grateful that it had some natural curl so that I didn't have to do it up on curling rags or draw it back in one of those skinned-rabbit hair styles.

How far I had come in so short a time, I thought. If only Francis could have been here with me! I would have no fears about finding Papa if Francis were here, if I were sharing this room with him instead of with Phoebe.

This was a new world, as unknown as if I'd gone to the moon. The city was far different from our little country village in Virginia. It was easy to see from the people who had been at the depot and on the streets that this was a more affluent society than we were used to, and there would be many new and exciting and, possibly, frightening things to adjust to. None of them would be frightening if Francis were here . . . or when I found Papa, of course. He would laugh and rumple my hair as he had done when I was a child, and say that he would take care of everything, that from now on I would have nothing to worry about.

Deliberately, I led myself away from memories of Francis, for they brought tears to my eyes and I did not want to have to explain them. What if . . . I turned about the room, tracing the pattern of cabbage roses on the wallpaper, fingering the fine lace of the curtains, peering out onto the opposing windows of the next house . . . what if Papa had bought such a house as this? We would keep house for him, Dodie and I, and Aunt Pity could sit and crochet her lopsided antimacassars and doilies, and Phoebe . . . Phoebe would be welcome with us as long as she liked, of course, but I had a suspicion young Tom might eventually have something to say about that.

That made me think of Francis again, so that my eyes were slightly reddened when Phoebe returned from her own ablutions. She was scrubbed bright pink, and she'd dressed in a blue and white gingham dress that had been her Sunday best.

"I feel ten pounds lighter," she confessed. "What are we going to do about our dirty clothes? These are such a mess I'd throw them out if I had anything to replace them with."

"We're all in that shape, I'm afraid. But when we find Papa we can take care of that. I hope supper is as good as our landlady says it will be; I'm so hungry for a hot meal!"

"It can't help but be superior to what we got on the *Gray Gull*," Phoebe offered, and I had to agree with that.

As a matter of fact, supper was excellent. Mrs. Morton did her own cooking, with the help of a sturdy young girl, and she served us a leg of lamb and potatoes whipped and dripping with butter, and freshly baked bread, and green beans cooked with bits of bacon in them, and a salad of fresh vegetables such as Aunt Rachael had made for us at home. It seemed months since we'd tasted anything so good, and after we had all eaten our fill, she brought in dried apple pie, spicy with cinnamon and warm from the oven, with a crust as tender as any I'd ever eaten. No wonder Papa had praised her cooking.

Only after the food had been tucked in and the table cleared away did Mrs. Morton put my question to the other lodgers.

"This young lady here is Mr. Edward Hunter's daughter, and she's come all the way from Virginia to find him. She wants to know if anyone knows where he went?"

There were curious glances aplenty, then, from the mostly male boarders. One by one, however, they shook their heads.

"Don't know as he said where he was going."

"I didn't even know he was leaving, until after he'd gone."

"Wasn't a man for visiting with us working-type blokes, much. Always had his nose in a book. Not that he wasn't polite, and all that, but he didn't know nothing about making beer and I didn't know nothing about books, so there wasn't all that much to talk about, I reckon."

"Seems like I heard he was coming into some money. Don't know who he told that to, likely Johansen, but I overheard it. Right pleased he was, about getting some money."

My heart leapt, because that, at least, was verified. "He must have gotten it, do you think? Or he wouldn't have left?" I asked eagerly.

The faces were of good, decent men. They would have liked to help me.

"Could be. Could well be, miss. If anybody knows anything, it'd be Johansen, but he ain't here tonight. Works over to the foundry as night watchman, so he's ate and gone already. Be here at breakfast, though, shouldn't wonder. He and Mr. Hunter used to talk, some, because Johansen reads books once in a while. You just ask Johansen in the morning."

I had to be content with that. Indeed, I was encouraged to think that Johansen would undoubtedly be able to tell us exactly where to go, and I went to sleep reasonably content, or the closest to it I'd been since Francis and Aunt Rachael died.

◇◇◇◇ 9 ◇◇◇◇

We were up early, refreshed and ravenous. There was no sun today, only swirling mist that obscured everything beyond our own front porch, but it couldn't dampen my spirits. Today Mr. Johansen would tell me where Papa was, and I couldn't wait to get down to the breakfast table for this information.

Mr. Johansen was a burly man in working clothes, obviously tired from his night's work, and he had been told about me in advance. He smiled, putting out a hand to shake mine.

"I'm happy to meet you, Miss Hunter. Your father spoke of you, said you were a right pretty girl, and he wasn't exaggerating."

I smiled back, perhaps the first genuinely happy smile in a month or more. "And I'm happy to meet any friend of Papa's, Mr. Johansen."

"Well, I don't know that I could claim to be a friend of his, exactly, although he was an educated man and I do like to read a book once in a while. He loaned me several of his, and told me when he got his new library together I could come over and borrow some of them. Said his family used to have a marvelous library, back in Virginia, before the war, and he was going to have one again now that he could afford it."

My smile deepened. "Yes. He's always loved books. He did get the money, then, that he wrote me about."

"Well, I assume he did. He wasn't a man to talk too much about his private affairs, so I don't even know where it was coming from . . . some sort of investment, I guess. But he wasn't going to leave until he had it, so I reckon he came into it, all right."

"Do you have his address? I want to contact him as soon as I can."

His smile faded. "Well, I don't rightly know where he is, miss. He said he'd be in touch when he got his house in order . . . he was going to buy a house, had it all picked out, I think, although he didn't say anything about where it was . . . but he never did. I ran

into him down on Market Street about a week after he left here, with
a lady, he was, and he was as friendly as ever, and said he'd be
calling me. I kept thinking he would, any time, but so far he hasn't."

I ought to be getting used to shocks, I thought, but I wasn't. Why
on earth would Papa have told this man he'd be in touch, and then
failed to do so? That wasn't like him, any more than it was like him
to promise me something he would not subsequently deliver.

I think it was at that moment that the premonition of disaster first
touched me. For that was the crux of the entire matter: Papa was a
man who kept his word, who didn't make idle promises. And he had
promised to send for me, had promised me a home, and then he had
not replied to either my letters or my telegrams. To find that he had
made a promise to this man, however casual the friendship might
have been, and then had not kept it, was a matter of grave concern.

My mind fastened on the one small bit of information that was totally unexpected. "You said he was with a lady?"

"Yes, that he was. In a good-looking carriage, they were, and they
pulled up long enough to speak a minute. Very handsome woman,
she was, had red hair and was very stylishly dressed."

I started to lick my lips and then stopped. "Did he introduce you
to her?"

"Yes, he did. I wonder if I can remember who she was. Come to
think of it, I ran across her name again, in the paper, just a few days
ago. Maybe if there's a newspaper around I can find it again, soon as
I've had something to eat."

And so my hope was resurrected, though still tinged with that
undefined dread that something might have happened to my father.
I had to eat, and contain myself, until Mr. Johansen had been fed.

Breakfast was well worth fifteen cents, I had to agree. There were
fried eggs and strips of lean bacon and little hot cakes dripping butter and honey, and hot, fragrant coffee. This time, however, I did
less than justice to it, for my stomach was acting up again. Not the
morning sickness of pregnancy, I believed, but uncertainty and apprehension were responsible for it.

Someone brought forth a San Francisco *Chronicle,* dated two days
previously, and as soon as he'd reached his final cup of coffee and
the dishes were cleared away, Mr. Johansen spread it on the table
and began to look through the classified ads.

"Seems like it was back here somewhere, just a minute now . . ."
He read down the page, keeping his place with a forefinger, and at
last exclaimed in satisfaction. "Here it is. Right here." He pushed the
paper toward me, turning it at an angle I could read. "Mrs. Belle
Fox. That's it. Belle Fox."

I read the words in the tiny box. *Mrs. Belle Fox announces that
she will receive selected guests into her home at reasonable rates.*

Privacy assured, as well as a good address for the discriminating gentleman. Only those with impeccable references need apply.

My eyes blurred before I had read the address. Surely if this woman had been in a carriage with Papa, she would know where he was to be found!

"If she's a friend of his . . ." I swallowed.

"They seemed to be on friendly terms," Mr. Johansen said, taking out his pocketknife to remove the ad from the paper, being careful not to cut deeply enough to damage the tablecloth. "In fact, I'd say they were out for an outing, having a good time, you know. Smiling and pleasant, they both were. So more than likely there's your answer, this Mrs. Fox will know where he is."

He handed me the clipping, and I accepted it gratefully. "I'd like to go there at once, if someone can tell me how to get there. Will I have to hire a carriage?"

"Be a lot less expensive to go on the cable cars. You can get one right out there on the corner, here on Market Street. I'll have to ask Mrs. Morton which car you want to get to Fell Street, where her house is, but I think there's one goes out along Hayes to Golden Gate Park. I expect the motorman can tell you where to get off if you give him the house number, and then it's only a walk of a block or two to Fell Street. It's a good neighborhood, no reason why a young lady alone should worry about going out there alone. Or will one of the others be going with you?"

I considered. I'd appreciate the company and the moral support, but unless Papa were one of her "selected guests" there would be little to be gained by having the others along. "How expensive is the cabel-car fare?"

"A nickel. Each way, that is."

That settled it. I couldn't afford to waste an extra dime on a companion. Mrs. Morton was called into conference, and she wrote down for me the car that I must take.

And so I set out, wondering if I would ever accustom myself to this nervousness in the stomach, and then hoping devoutly that there would be no need to get used to it. Quite likely when Papa had come into the proceeds of his investment, whatever that had been, he had simply moved into a fancier rooming house until his plans were fully matured. Oh, how I prayed that this might be so!

Several cable cars came along before one arrived bearing the proper number, and I had a chance to inspect them. They were brightly painted in red and gray with yellow trim, and I couldn't tell which end was intended to be the front and which the back. Each of them rang a jolly-sounding bell, in case one wasn't paying attention, making it impossible not to know when one was arriving.

I paid my five-cent fare when a man came through the car collecting it, and concentrated on enjoying the ride and trying to determine how the thing was powered. No doubt Tom could have told me, had he been there, I thought with amusement, and resolved to ask him the next time we met. If he rode on one of them he was certain to learn what made it run. I guessed that he'd have to ask, for there was certainly nothing obvious in sight, no motor of any sort.

Market Street ran in a southwesterly direction, with the streets on my left intersecting it at perpendicular angles, the streets on the right coming in on sharper angles from the north. There were many people about, and the fog was lifting by the time we turned off onto Larkin Street; my spirits lifted with the mists, and by the time we had reached the stop where the motorman said I should get off, I was almost my normal self again.

The man gave me quite specific directions as to how I should reach my destination, and the smile that went with them was enough to boost my spirits another notch. Phoebe was right; being cleaned up and reasonably dressed, even if only in an ordinary dark skirt and my best white shirtwaist, and having washed my hair, made me far more presentable. If I ever saw Mr. Rohann again, which wasn't likely, I might be thought something other than a hired girl.

I climbed off the colorful cable car on Hayes Street, and walked briskly south as directed until I came to Fell, which turned out to be an attractive residential avenue facing a sort of park; this latter was a scant block wide and perhaps eight or nine blocks long, very narrow but with a pleasant band of greenery between the two rows of houses facing it.

The houses themselves were substantial and unostentatiously prosperous, being much of a style and painted in a variety of colors quite different from what I was used to. All were three stories plus an attic, very narrow at the front but extending deep into the lots, and the front doors were reached by climbing seven or eight steep steps. There was a good deal of colored glass in the windows and the double doors, and a considerable amount of the wooden scrollwork known as gingerbread, so that I was reminded of the picturesque illustrations in one of my old fairy tale books.

The number I sought was a comparatively severe dark brown in color and a bit less ornate than its neighbors, but it was richly endowed with some striking colored-glass windows, and the lace curtains in the triple-windowed bays on all three floors were rich and expensive-looking. It did not, in truth, look at all like a rooming house, and I checked again the newspaper advertisement to be sure I had the right place, for there was no sign, however discreet, to suggest that it was anything but an elegant private house.

I climbed the steps with an accelerating heartbeat and a small prayer. The bell was similar to the one at Mrs. Morton's house, being an iron handle to be twisted to produce a strident sound that must have been audible even on the third floor. I turned it and waited.

There was no sound of footsteps to announce activity within. One half of the double door was suddenly opened, and a woman stood there who must surely be the one Mr. Johansen had described.

I would have guessed her age at about fifty. She was taller than I, a robust woman with a full figure, a bosom of magnificent proportions swelling upward from her tightly corseted waist. She wore brown, but there was nothing drab about it, the fabric being an extremely rich and heavy brocaded mohair brilliantine; it seemed somewhat dressy for a lady at this time of day unless she was going out, was my first thought. It was adorned by an elaborately hand-painted locket on a gold chain, a locket that was mesmerizing as it rose and fell on a sea of brown.

Lifting my gaze from her bosom to her face, I decided at once that her hair, while professionally styled, was of too vivid an auburn to be real; it had to have had assistance, although that too was professional for it was carefully done. The touch of rouge on each cheek was less skillfully applied, for I recognized it for what it was.

One rather large hand rested on the other half of the door, fingers laden with four rings, one of them a wedding band.

"Yes?" she said in a throaty voice, the word taking a number of seconds to climb out of her well-developed chest.

"Mrs. Belle Fox?"

"Yes." She inclined her head, then looked more sharply at me, evaluating my costume so that I was glad I hadn't turned up here in yesterday's travel-stained clothes. "Were you looking for living accommodations? I do have a few rooms left, but they're rather expensive." Her tone suggested that they were quite beyond my means, although she was being gracious about saying so.

I sucked air into cramped lungs before I remembered the instructions I'd had on behaving like a lady. "I've come . . . I've come to ask you about Mr. Edward Hunter."

The smile congealed on her wide mouth and for a matter of seconds the locket stopped rising and falling on her breast. "Mr. Edward Hunter?"

"Yes. You are the Mrs. Belle Fox he introduced to Mr. Johansen, aren't you?"

Her eyes were dark and, at the moment, hard, as they looked down into mine. "What do you want with Mr. Hunter? Who are you?"

"I'm his daughter, and I've come all the way from Virginia . . ."

The natural color slid away out of her face, drained as if a cork had been drawn out of a bottle, allowing it to empty. This left only the twin spots of pink high on her cheekbones. And then an astonishing thing happened.

Her mouth opened and closed several times, as if she were attempting to speak, but no sound emerged. She sucked for oxygen, even as I had done, only it seemed that she couldn't get it, which made her gasp the more. And to my alarm her knees buckled and she slid into an ungraceful faint at my feet.

◇◇◇◇ 10 ◇◇◇◇

"Mrs. Fox! Mrs. Fox, please . . ." I knelt beside the prostrate woman, feeling that I ought to loosen her clothing but unable to see how to accomplish this. When I put out a hand to touch her outflung wrist, I was stopped by a low growl.

A dog stood just beyond her, not a large dog but one with formidable teeth all the same, one of the ugliest bulls I had ever encountered. I quickly withdrew my hand, since he seemed to object to my touching his mistress, but I couldn't simply leave her lying here in a heap in the hallway.

The woman showed no sign of rousing even when her pet sniffed at her temple. I called out into the spacious entryway, but there was no response, so I reached for the bell and twisted it, not once but half a dozen times, in an urgent appeal for help. Dear Lord, what if I'd unwittingly caused the woman to have a stroke or something! What if she, my only clue to the whereabouts of my father, should never be able to relay to me what she knew about him? I twisted the bell again, and this time finally heard footsteps, and then an irate female voice.

"I'm coming, I'm coming! You needn't pull the house down! What's . . . oh!"

She came through a doorway at the rear of the hall, a thin young woman some four or five years my senior. I had only the most superficial impression of her at the moment, as being blond and overdressed in something a curious shade of pink, for I was concerned with Mrs. Fox. I could tell now that she was breathing, but it was with an effort beyond the normal.

The newcomer shot a glance at me, then knelt beside the stricken woman, pushing away the bulldog. "Get out of the way, Alfred. What's happened? Aunt Belle? Aunt Belle?"

"She . . . she fainted," I said inadequately.

The young woman pursed her lips. "I can see that. She *will* wear

that thing laced so tight she can't breathe. Here, take her other arm
and help me get her inside, and I'll try to loosen her stays."

This was accomplished with considerable effort, for Mrs. Fox was
much heavier than either of us, and we were hampered by Alfred's
nipping at my ankles until my companion fetched him a swift kick
that sent him back into a corner.

"Confounded dog! There, if I can get another hook or two undone
it should let a little air into her. Aunt Belle, can you hear me? Aunt
Belle?"

Mrs. Fox moaned slightly, which seemed to satisfy her niece.

"There, she's coming around. What happened? Did she just keel
over?"

"I . . . I was talking to her, and I asked about Edward Hunter,
and she . . ." I stopped, for the same peculiar expression was coming over *her* face, now. She wasn't so tightly laced, and she didn't
faint, but there was no contradicting the fact that she went pale.

I looked at her more closely, this girl who was not exactly pretty
because she was so thin and her nose so sharp, this girl wearing what
was surely, now that I looked at it, an evening dress, at only ten
o'clock in the morning. She had colored her lips, although it wasn't
noticeable until she became so pale.

She ran her tongue over her lips to moisten them. "Edward
Hunter? Were you asking about him?"

"Yes. He's my father, and I was told . . ." I stopped, for her dismay was apparent.

"Your father. Oh, God." She sounded sick, and indeed she looked
it as well.

"I don't understand. What is it? Is he here, is my father here?"

She glanced down at the inert form of her aunt, now breathing
loudly enough to have caused alarm had it not been such an improvement over her condition minutes earlier. "What did she say to
you?"

"Not much of anything. She said . . . I think her exact words were
'What do you want with Mr. Hunter? Who are you?' And then she
sort of gasped for breath and fainted."

"I'll just bet she did. His daughter. Oh, God."

At our feet, Belle Fox made a gurgling sound, and flailed out with
her arms. "Oh, oh, my . . . Estelle . . . Estelle, is that you?"

"I loosened your stays, Aunt Belle. Are you feeling better? Well
enough to get up? Here, if the young lady will help me, maybe we
can get you into the front parlor, and I'll get your smelling salts."

There was nothing I could do but as she suggested; my own emo-
tions were sufficiently tumultuous to shorten my breath, as did the
effort of getting the woman to her feet and easing her through the
nearest doorway and onto a sofa. By the time the smelling salts were

brought, I wouldn't have minded a whiff of them myself, for certainly something was very wrong here.

Mrs. Fox inhaled deeply, then flopped against a cushion, staring up at me. "You said . . . you were . . ." Abruptly, her eyes rolled and she sank again into a semi-conscious condition, muttering something under her breath that I couldn't understand.

"Perhaps a doctor . . ." I said tentatively, but this time the younger woman only made a wry face.

"If she'd stop insisting she's got a twenty-inch waist when any fool can see it's thirty inches, she wouldn't have such trouble. She's got the salts in her hand, she can hold them under her own nose." And then she turned her attention fully to me. "It's you I want to know about. You're Miss Hunter?"

"That's right." With an apprehensive backward glance at Mrs. Fox, I followed the niece into the entry hall. "What is it? Has something happened to him?"

The girl called Estelle hesitated. "She didn't tell you anything?"

"No. Nothing. Please, if you know where my father is, tell me!"

She swallowed, and then firmed her shoulders and looked me straight in the face.

"I'm sorry, Miss Hunter. To be the one to have to tell you, I mean. Mr. Hunter is dead. Your father is dead."

The words took me like a blow to the face. I think I may even have staggered back, as if the blow were a physical one.

She moved forward, a compassionate hand outstretched, to guide me toward a chair. "Here, sit down, or you'll be fainting too, although you don't look as if you're corseted to death. It'll be a shock, I know . . . it's always a shock to lose somebody we love . . . but that's the way of life. There, sit a minute; put your head between your knees if you feel dizzy, until it goes away."

Until it went away . . . the initial shock had been great, but the wave that followed it was worse. It went deep, and tore with a brutality that made me wish I could escape, like Mrs. Fox, into unconsciousness. Only I did not; I was crushed beyond bearing, yet it must be borne, and I leaned forward in a paroxysm of grief so overpowering that as yet I did not think of myself and my problems, only of Papa.

"Estelle!" The voice from the parlor had regained some of its vigor, and I was left alone, tears beginning to stream down my face, as Estelle went to minister to her aunt. I heard the low murmur of their voices without being able to make out the words, until Mrs. Fox's voice rose in a sort of shriek and there was a sound of something heavy falling onto the floor.

"You fool! You stupid fool!"

I didn't care about them. I only cared that I had arrived too late, that I would never see Papa again. Gradually, as the muffled voices behind me took on a low-toned intensity, the realization came to me that not only would I not see him, he would not help me to care for the others or see me through the ordeal of bearing the expected child. And even at a time like this I must think of the fact that my purse held enough money to see us through no more than a few weeks at most at Mrs. Morton's house, or a month at a cheaper place. And then we would have nothing.

I drew in a breath and tried to pull myself together. When I opened my eyes, I was staring into the face of the little bulldog, who recognized that fact by a deep-throated growl. Ignoring him, I got to my feet and made my way back to the door of the parlor, leaning against the door jamb with one hand while the other unconsciously massaged my throat.

"Mrs. Fox . . ." They both turned to face me, and for a moment there was a curious lack of expression on either face. Mrs. Fox had sat up and was still utilizing the smelling salts; she'd been pried nearly all the way out of her restricting foundation garments and presented a most undignified appearance. "Please . . . please tell me. About Papa. How he died."

"Oh, my dear. Oh, my dear . . . Saunielle, isn't that your name? Oh, dear. Please, come sit down. Estelle, help me back into my clothes, I'm a disgrace . . . forgive me, my dear, but it was such a shock, finding you on my doorstep. I never dreamed you were coming to California! Dear Edward told me about you, of course, but I understood that you were securely settled with your aunt in Virginia, and I never dreamed you'd do anything so rash as to come all the way out here . . . I didn't have an address for you, and I couldn't remember the name of the village you lived in, or I'd have written to you . . ."

I allowed myself to be maneuvered onto the sofa beside her while her niece helped get her back into her clothes. *Dear Edward,* she had said. Why did that send such a sense of unease through me? *Dear Edward?*

"But Papa wrote to me, to say . . ." I broke off, suddenly reluctant to confide in this woman who spoke so intimately of *dear Edward.* How close would their relationship have been, if he had not mentioned that he planned to send for me very shortly? "Tell me what happened. Was he involved in an accident?"

There was a moment's hesitation while the eyes of the two women met. Mrs. Fox spoke first. "What did you tell her, Estelle?"

"Not much of anything, I didn't have time. Only that he died."

"When?" I demanded, thinking of all those letters and telegrams . . . where had they ended up? Mrs. Morton hadn't mentioned having them.

"Two months ago, the fourth of August," Estelle said promptly.

I closed my eyes, leaning back into the brocaded surface, fighting for self-control. Within a few days of the time I'd received his happy and expectant letter, he had been dead. All the time I was dreaming of our reunion, dreaming of coming with Francis to see Papa, he had been dead and forever lost to me.

With a supreme effort, I formed the words: "How did it happen?"

"It was his heart," Belle Fox said. "Poor man, he went just like that! One minute he was talking and the next he'd folded right over and he was gone. It was a great shock to me personally, you understand, but I did think of you, too, for I knew he had a daughter he'd left behind as a little girl. But he hadn't time to say anything, no final messages or anything like that. And I had no idea you'd be coming West, nor any way to know how to reach you. I suppose you'll be wanting to go back to your aunt in Virginia now, won't you?"

"My aunt died," I said dully. "Of her heart. I have nothing to go back to."

"Oh my." One of the plump, ringed hands, closed over mine in a brief squeeze. "Oh dear. You poor thing."

"Was he . . . was he living here? Was he . . . one of your guests, at the time he died?" I asked.

Again I was aware of a small silence, and then Estelle said rather harshly, "You're going to tell her, aren't you?"

"Tell me what?" I was still braced for bad news, although what could be worse than this was unimaginable, but I was in no way prepared for what was to be revealed.

Belle Fox had withdrawn her hand, and now she twisted at the wedding band on her third finger. "I don't suppose he wrote to you about me?"

I shook my head. "No. No, he didn't." He had only written that he would be able to afford to make a home for us, the two of us.

The rich brown fabric swelled with her inhalation. "I see. Well, it was all rather sudden, and we were both so busy, I suppose there was no time. The truth of the matter is, my dear, that only a short time before he . . . before his death, Edward and I were married."

For a moment the word was meaningless to me. Married? Papa? And to this woman who painted her face and dyed her hair?

The contrast between Belle Fox and my own dear Mama was so great that I couldn't credit what she'd said. Papa had delighted in my mother, who was slim and pretty and gay, who came from a good family in her native France and was accepted into the best of society in Virginia, what there was left of it after the war. After loving Angélique Jaubert, could he then have loved a woman like Belle Fox?

"But . . . the ad in the paper said your name was Belle *Fox* . . ."

She twisted her mouth expressively, patting a coil of auburn hair to be sure that her pins had not let it fall. "Yes. Well, of course for the mere three days that we were married I was Mrs. *Hunter*. Only so few people knew about it, and I was already established *here*. To tell you the truth, I hardly felt that I'd been *married,* the time was so short, and I'd been Mrs. Fox for . . . for many years. So it seemed more natural, you know, to revert to being Mrs. Fox, so much less confusing for everyone. You do understand, don't you?"

"Yes," I said, though in truth I didn't understand anything. Was *this* what Papa had meant when he said he was going to come into money, that he would be able to make a home for me? This woman's house, this woman's money?

No, no. I rejected it even as I thought of it. Papa would never have married for such a reason, I was convinced of that. If he had married her, it was because he cared for her.

"Do you have his belongings?" Did I imagine the almost electrical silence? "He must have left papers, letters, things like that. A will, perhaps?"

Belle Fox made her reply quite decisive. "Nothing at all that I'm aware of, aside from a few unpaid bills. Very small ones, nothing to be alarmed at, and I've taken care of them, of course. If there had been letters, no doubt I'd have known where to write to you, but we found nothing of that sort at all."

The small flicker of hope, so tiny it could hardly be called a flame, vanished. "There was no will, then."

"No. A man in his prime doesn't feel the need of wills, I suspect. And of course there wasn't much to dispose of . . . no money or property, that is to say."

Dully, I stared at the elaborate French wallpaper in a tasteful pattern of white and blue and gold. No money or property. There was no home to return to, and no home here, not even a small legacy to tide us over until we could all find employment. Mr. Rohann had been more right than we knew in his estimate of us as maids and waitresses, though who would knowingly hire one in my condition?

Resolutions to the contrary aside, I began to cry. Not loudly or noisily, but silently, the tears welling up in such quantities that it was no wonder Mrs. Fox began to look alarmed.

"Estelle, I shouldn't wonder if poor Miss Hunter . . . or may I call you Saunielle, since you are my stepdaughter, aren't you? . . . could do with a cup of tea. She's quite undone, I think."

Estelle looked down on me dispassionately. "A glass of brandy would be more to the point, I'd think, for someone in a state of shock."

"Brandy, yes, yes, brandy. Bring her some brandy. Bring me some as well, this has been an ordeal for both of us."

I was not unfamiliar with the smell of brandy, since it had been

Papa's drink when he was not socializing with a crowd, but this was the first time I'd ever drunk it myself. I took a bit too much, and coughed and then regained control as the heat of it began to spread through me with far greater rapidity than that from any mustard plaster I'd ever had applied. I even began to perspire.

"Easy does it, takes a bit of getting used to," my self-described stepmother said. She demonstrated. "A sip at a time, that'll do it. It'll make you feel better."

As a matter of fact, it did. Physically, at least. But there was still the problem of what to do with my small ménage, who were waiting hopefully for me at Mrs. Morton's rooming house over on Market Street.

"I don't know what I'm going to do," I said, the courage to put the problem into words perhaps shored up by the brandy. I took another sip of it. "I haven't any money . . . at least, very little. I had to sell Mama's pearls in order to raise the money for the train fare."

"Your aunt didn't leave anything?"

"Only enough to cover the bills." I thought about the man who had followed me to Norfolk. "Maybe not quite even enough for that. I had thought Papa would . . ." I bit my lip; the brandy was not enough to overcome the basic emotional upheaval.

"Of course you did. But you're a young girl, healthy, and very pretty. Edward said you were pretty, but you never know about a father's evaluation of his daughter's looks, do you? There must be various things you can do to enable you to get on."

"Back home my cousin and I took in sewing. I'm fairly expert at dressmaking." This was the time to have added that I was also pregnant, but I couldn't quite bring myself to make the necessary explanations to these people who were, after all, strangers. I took another sip of the brandy.

"Well, there you are, then. Any community as fashion-conscious as this one will certainly support an expert seamstress and dressmaker. As a matter of fact, I'm in need of some sewing myself, aren't I, Estelle? I'll tell you what, why don't you move in here until you're able to find a position, and in the meantime you can sew up some things for me. How would that be?"

Gratitude brought new tears to my eyes. "I would appreciate that very much, ma'am."

"Good. Good. That's settled. Estelle, I think the little room at the east on the third floor, don't you? Since it hasn't any view it won't bring as good a rental as the others, anyway."

Estelle was still standing, her thin, almost feral-looking face enigmatic; I had, for a moment, the strongest impression that she was going to voice strenuous objections to the plan. And then she shrugged and agreed. "Why not?"

I drained my glass and the resulting warmth gave me the additional bravery I needed. "There's only one thing."

"Oh? What's that?" Belle Fox had drained her glass, too, and was refilling it from a handsome decanter.

"I didn't come to San Francisco alone."

They watched me, alert and wary.

"You brought someone with you?"

"My cousin, Dorothea. She's twenty. And Aunt Pity . . . she was really the aunt of Aunt Rachael's husband, he died many years ago, and she had nowhere else to go, so she lived with us. And Phoebe, Phoebe was our . . . our maid."

There was no doubt, even to my rather brandy-numbed mind, that four people were a bit more than they'd bargained for. Yet what else could I have done but to tell them? I couldn't abandon the others, there was no way I could do that.

"A cousin, an aunt, and a maid." Estelle shot a look at her aunt. "Any of them cook?"

"Yes, we all cook, although probably Phoebe's the best at it." Perhaps a hired kitchen girl had merit, after all. "She's cooked under Aunt Rachael's supervision for several years."

"And the cousin, Dorothea, sews?"

I decided this was not the time to state too explicitly the quality of Dodie's needlework. "That's right."

"And how about the aunt? She's an elderly lady?"

"Yes. She isn't capable of earning her keep, I'm afraid, at least not fully. Her eyesight isn't good enough to enable her to sew much any more. But she doesn't eat much and she isn't any trouble . . ."

"I see. Well, four of you." Mrs. Fox was digesting this along with her second glass of brandy, which disappeared so quickly that it was clear she was more practiced in taking it than I.

"Two to sew, and one who can cook," Estelle summarized. "Well, what do you think, Aunt Belle? Since it's only temporary . . ."

"Yes. Yes, quite right. We could put them all to good use for a time, couldn't we? Why not? Well, that will mean reorganizing a bit, to find space for everyone, but I think we can manage. When would you like to move in, dear?"

"This afternoon?"

"Why not?" she said again. She patted her ample bosom with one ringed hand. "I declare, this has quite tired me out. Estelle, you can see Saunielle out, and then we'll decide what to do about rooms. And we'll be expecting you back in time to settle in before dinner, which is at six-thirty. How will that be?"

Gratitude and relief brought new tears to my eyes. "I'm most grateful, ma'am."

"Well, well, since I *am* your stepmama, what else could we do? I wonder, would you be rested enough from your travel to look at some materials I have? Maybe tomorrow you could cut out that blue serge for me."

"Yes, of course." At the moment, delivered from my most urgent financial difficulties, I would have promised to make a robe for an elephant tomorrow, if that would have pleased her. "I'll start any time you like."

The fat little bulldog had waddled into the room, and climbed up to scratch at his mistress' knee; she scooped him up onto her lap and stroked his ugly head. I was glad of that, for he looked as if he'd welcome the opportunity to have another go at my ankles, and in my present impoverished state I could hardly spare the stockings.

Estelle went with me to the front door. "While you're making up the suit for Aunt Belle, do you think your cousin would run up a few things for me?"

Recklessly, I promised on Dodie's behalf. "I'm sure she would."

She nodded, a small smile curling her thin mouth. She was more attractive when she smiled. "Good. We'll see you back here in a few hours, then."

I went down the front steps with mingled feelings. To say that it was a terrible shock to learn that Papa was gone was to put it truthfully. Yet for a short time my fears for those of us still living had taken precedence over my sorrow, for our needs were immediate and our resources so limited.

I walked back to the corner opposite the one where I'd left the cable car, feeling the slightest bit tipsy. Or perhaps it was only the result of everything that had happened to me, and the emotional letting-go when I'd been offered refuge, however temporary it might turn out to be.

Another nickel was required for the return trip, and it would cost us twenty cents to come back here, the four of us. I wondered if I would dare invest in some new undergarments, and a pair of shoes for Dodie, for she'd repaired the sole on one of hers so amateurishly that it was a wonder walking on it didn't cripple her.

I rode along on the car, moving just as mysteriously as its counterpart which I had ridden earlier, making plans in my mind. Why hadn't I confessed to Mrs. Fox that I was carrying a child and that I couldn't expect to go out and find a position in a public place? Would it be feasible to advertise (discreetly, of course) and seek out customers such as we had had at home, who would let me come and work in their homes even though I was pregnant? Or who would trust me to make up garments for them in Mrs. Fox's establishment?

Beyond the point at which the baby would be born, I refused to think. The child itself was as yet unreal to me, although I knew that had Francis been with me I would have been overjoyed to be having his infant.

I almost missed my stop on Market Street, getting out of my seat only just in time. I had eaten little breakfast, because I was so nervous, and now I was suddenly ravenous. I hoped the noon meal hadn't been served before I got there.

It occurred to me then that I had neglected to ask where Papa was buried. I could not see him, but I could visit his grave and perhaps put a few flowers on it, as he and I had often done at Mama's before he went away. Perhaps that would ease my grief somewhat, to know that we were as close to each other as it was possible to get.

I went into Mrs. Morton's rooming house and gathered my resources to relate it all to them as the faces turned questioningly in my direction.

◊◊◊◊ 11 ◊◊◊◊

"What's the house like?" Dodie asked, torn between nervousness and excitement.

"I didn't notice all that much, to be truthful. Very elegant, I think. The sofa was covered in some sort of blue brocade, and the wallpaper in the front parlor was white and blue and gold. There was a crystal chandelier . . . I think there were gaslights, but I'm not sure. I suppose it's more like Hunter's Hill than anything we've ever seen."

"What's she like, this Mrs. Fox?" Aunt Pity wanted to know.

I hesitated. "Well, she's . . . she's about fifty, I'd say. And she has auburn hair . . . and I think she uses a bit of rouge. She was wearing some valuable-looking rings, and her dress was of very fine material . . . very much like that stuff we made up for Miss Harbinger, remember, Dodie, the brocaded mohair brilliantine? Only this was brown instead of blue."

Dodie nodded, impressed. "If I remember, she paid fifty cents a yard for that. Lovely stuff, it was. I don't mind sewing so much if it's on nice goods. And this niece, Estelle . . . what's she like, Saunielle? She's my age?"

"Or a year or two older. It's hard to judge. She has a . . . an *experienced* air about her, which makes her seem older, perhaps."

"What do you mean, experienced?" Pity demanded.

"Only . . . less sheltered than we were, I mean. I suspect that she wasn't brought up to be quite a lady, although I'm not sure why I say that. A lady might well have offered brandy under those circumstances, and I did feel better after I'd drunk it. Maybe it was her dress; it was pink, and rather low cut for anything but an evening dress."

They asked a lot of questions, most of which I couldn't answer, as we readied ourselves for the move. For fifteen cents each, Mrs. Morton had provided an excellent luncheon of homemade bean soup with ham, and fresh bread with plenty of butter, so that we left her house in better condition than when we'd arrived.

"Hadn't we better leave a message here for Tom?" I said, as we were ready to walk out the front door. "Give him the address where we'll be."

Phoebe hastily scribbled it down to give to Mrs. Morton, but added, "I have the address where he is, Saunielle. He was here right after you left. His brother was able to get a cot for him brought into his own room, and he's been promised a job at the brewery as soon as he can use his arm." Her freckled face was flushed and excited. "We took a cable-car ride, to the Ferry Landing at the end of Market Street. We're going to take a ferry ride one of these Sundays, he says, although he may be getting a bicycle instead of spending five cents on the cable car every time he wants to get somewhere."

We said good-by to Mrs. Morton, and I asked her to thank Mr. Johansen again for me, for putting me onto the way of finding Mrs. Fox, and then we all trooped out to catch the next cable car going out to Hayes Street.

While we waited for the proper car, Phoebe explained how they were powered; as I had anticipated, Tom had been quick to determine this.

"There's a sort of cable thing in a slot in the ground, between tracks, you see. It's all hooked up to some big gears and pulleys in the car barn, and the car is pulled along with it until he looses it and uses the brakes to stop, and then when he wants to go again he 'takes rope,' they call it, until the next stop. It even works on those high hills, Tom says, and that's why a man named Mr. Hallidie invented the first one in the first place. So many horses slipped and fell in horrible accidents on the hills, because they're so steep and slippery, and the grip man told Tom they hardly ever have an accident with a cable car on the hills."

"Hardly ever" wasn't totally reassuring, but since our immediate journey involved no hills to speak of, I decided to worry about that later. I was more concerned that we should be assimilated into Mrs. Fox's household without friction, and that we be able to earn our keep there until some other arrangements could be made.

We were not the most prepossessing group I'd ever seen. Although we'd all changed into our best clothes and redone our hair, we were definitely shabby. It hadn't been particularly notable at home, where our small country village boasted few people of real wealth any more; but here in San Francisco everyone seemed to dress very smartly. I could only hope that our benefactress would not find us too ill turned out to be seen by her "quality" guests.

There were none of these in evidence when we arrived at the Fell Street house. Mrs. Fox herself let us in, smiling a welcome as she acknowledged my introductions.

"Such a sad way to meet, isn't it? But that's the way of things. I was married to my first husband, Mr. Fox, for only two years, and I've been a widow fifteen. We never know what lies ahead of us. Come inside and put your things down here in the hallway; I thought you'd like a cup of tea before we get you settled in. Estelle and I have attempted to make suitable arrangements for you all." She led the way into the front parlor, where I had been before.

This time I was a bit more observant, noting the excellent quality of the furnishings and the tastefulness of the decorating as a whole. We were all seated, on the sofa and on chairs drawn up in front of a low, marble-topped table, and then Mrs. Fox went to bring in the tea.

Pity stared after her with interest. "You know, I think she dyes her hair."

"Perhaps she does, but I'd speak of it only in private and in a very low voice, considering our circumstances," I suggested.

"Very nice goods in her dress," Dodie said quietly. "In fact, the entire place is most elegant. Look at that lamp, it's exquisite."

Pity examined it at close hand. "It's oil, not gas. I'm surprised they don't have those newfangled electric lights. But it's all very nice. Could use antimacassars on this lovely furniture, should get some on before anyone damages them with hair oil. I'll offer to make her some."

I might have commented on that if Phoebe hadn't suddenly let out a yelp. "Good grief, is that a dog? It's the ugliest creature I've ever seen!"

Alfred stood in the doorway, his little fangs showing, although he was not growling. None of us moved or said anything more until his mistress returned with the tea tray.

"Get out of the way, Alfred. He's a dear, such good company, but he will get underfoot. There we go, tea for everyone." The tea service was magnificent, consisting of a heavy silver tray with an ornate pattern around its edges, with matching teapot, sugar bowl, creamer, and a pot to hold the spoons.

The beverage was served in delicate, thin china cups which even Aunt Pity regarded with unalloyed approval, and while it had not quite the restorative powers of brandy, the tea was warming and welcome.

"I have four guests at the present time, all gentlemen," Mrs. Fox informed us as we sipped. "Mr. Simons, Mr. Quayle, Mr. Goodwin, and Mr. Dillingham. All very nice. Mr. Goodwin's retired, Mr. Quayle is a clergyman and semi-retired, and the others go out to business. Mr. Simons is in dry goods, Mr. Dillingham's in crackers."

"No ladies?" Dodie asked politely. She was trying to sit so that the shoe with the loose sole would not be apparent.

"No ladies. I prefer gentlemen, actually. They're far less trouble. Eat what's put before them, don't object to poor Alfred . . ." Here she dropped an affectionate hand to the head of the bulldog. "Less trouble, all around."

We drank our tea, and then she led us grandly up the stairs to be distributed among the various bedrooms. Twice when she had made some pronouncement, Aunt Pity responded with "How's that?" until at last Mrs. Fox looked at me and murmured, "Hard of hearing, is she?"

Actually, I didn't think she was; I thought it more likely that she'd simply been too engrossed in her surroundings and hadn't been paying attention, so I only murmured in return, not wanting her to think Pity unmannerly.

The stairs took several turnings, broad and substantial but with a beautifully carved balustrade in some rich dark wood with a high polish. The stairs were carpeted, as was the second-floor hall, which stretched so far back that I was amazed at the size of the house. No wonder, if she were suffering financial reverses, she had decided to rent out rooms. There were dozens of them.

"You'll note we've put up a card on the door of each room that is occupied. That's to simplify finding one's own room. Mr. Quayle, he's the clergyman, had a little difficulty in remembering whether his room was the third on the left, or the fourth on the left, and as there are so many doors and they're all alike, Estelle made the cards. She has a neat style, don't you think?"

I could sympathize with Mr. Quayle's dilemma. The doors were of the same highly varnished wood as the balustrade, set at regular intervals in the expanse of French wallpaper; up here, it was in a pattern of white and rose with faint touches of pale green, and I thought how Mama would have loved it. She'd had something rather similar in her own bedroom at home, long ago.

Mrs. Fox moved ahead of us like a ship in full sail. "You'll want to be oriented, in regard to the rest of us. We're putting you on the top floor, since the second floor is nearly filled except for our very best front rooms, and as those will bring the highest rental, of course I'll want to rent them." She patted the perspiration off her upper lip with a lacy handkerchief, proof that climbing the stairs had taken some exertion. "I'm hoping that renting out rooms in my home will not be necessary indefinitely, but financial reverses can happen to the best of us, and my investments haven't quite worked out the way I expected. There," she gestured along the second-floor hallway, which ran straight through from the front of the house to the back, "is Mr. Dillingham's room, on the left, then Mr. Quayle, and Mr. Goodwin. Beyond there, on the left, is the back stairs that come out near the kitchen. The bathroom is on the right, opposite the stairs. I'm next to the bathroom, and coming back this way we have Mr. Simons. I'll show you this room, which would be ideal for a lady."

She pushed open the door and stood back to let us troop in ahead of her for a look.

I missed the reactions of the others, because I stood entranced on the threshold of what might have been my own dream room.

Ideal for a lady, indeed. Whoever had decorated this house had used a lavish hand with imported wallpapers and fine furnishings. The color scheme was pink and white, and the canopied mahogany bed was right out of Hunter's Hill, as Aunt Rachael had so often described it.

The rug was a pale cream color with a design worked in pink and deeper rose, the most exquisite I had ever seen. There were a large wardrobe, a dresser with a mirror that could be tilted to suit one's convenience, a small roll-top writing desk with a chair, and a chaise heaped with inviting cushions, ready for one to curl up with a good book.

Phoebe's eyes were large. "It's beautiful! I'm surprised you don't want to sleep in it yourself, ma'am!"

Mrs. Fox laughed, pleased. "It's a room for a brunette, not a redhead, I'm afraid. And of course since it's the finest bedroom of all, it's worth far more to me as a rental. My own room is quite to my liking."

She showed us the other empty rooms at the front of the second floor, a man's bedroom and adjoining study. The others exclaimed appropriately over the furnishings there, but I was still back in the pink bedroom, wondering what it would be like to live in such a fairyland of perfection.

And then we went on to the third floor. I hoped that so much climbing wouldn't prove too much for Pity, but she wasn't panting any more than the rest of us when we reached the upper level.

Our first stop was the sewing room, at the very front of the house, overlooking the street. This would have been a choice room (aside from the climb to reach it) except that it was so small; it took up the space that corresponded to the landing on the floor below.

At that, it was larger than our sewing room at home. And against one wall, between tall windows, was a sewing machine.

Dodie and I had speculated on the luxury of owning one of these devices, which could sew tremendously long seams in only minutes simply by working a treadle with one's foot. We'd never actually seen one, only pictures, and Dodie now crossed to poke tentatively at the treadle, jumping when it moved.

"Is it as fast as they say?"

Mrs. Fox shrugged. "I couldn't say. I don't know how to operate it. I bought some fabrics, as you can see, with the idea of hiring a seamstress to run them up. There's a folder of instructions with it; I'm sure it's simple to use."

We admired her yard goods, and she told me what she had in mind to do with them, and then we went on to our sleeping quarters.

My room was a large, pleasant one next to the sewing room, also overlooking the street and the parklike strip of greenery between Fell and Oak Street. There was no mahogany bed with a ruffled canopy, but the iron bed was new, as was the mattress, and the green-and-white sprigged paper and complementary furnishings were certainly attractive and comfortable. Dodie had the room adjoining mine to the back, Pity the one beyond that, and Phoebe was across the hall from Dodie. I was sure it was by far the grandest room Phoebe had ever occupied; for all its simplicity, she was quite taken with it. Estelle, we were told, had the room the farthest back on the right, with the bath beyond.

Opposite Estelle's room, right next to the back stairs, was a room which was used for storage. "I have some rather valuable things in there, so I keep it locked," Belle Fox said. "Of course I don't think any of my lodgers would touch anything, but in forty-two years I've learned prudence, if nothing else."

Phoebe and I locked glances behind the woman's back. Forty-two years? I'd have guessed her at least ten years older than that. Phoebe made an exaggerated grimace of disbelief, and I was forced to smile.

There was an empty room next to the storage room, and then Phoebe's quarters. Pity embarrassed us by immediately trying out the bed, bouncing like a child, and pronounced it satisfactory. She also commented on the chamber pot so that Dodie blushed, but Belle Fox seemed not to notice.

We were warned again that supper was at six-thirty sharp and then left to ourselves. Only Estelle slept on our floor, and she was apparently not in her room for the door stood open; for half an hour we visited with one another, examining one another's quarters. We also tested the taps in the bathroom and admired the plumbing. There was a device for heating water, which must be lit some half hour previous to one's bathing. None of us wanted to attempt this, as we were totally unfamiliar with the use of gas, until we'd seen someone else demonstrate its safety.

There was heated water on the first floor, we had been told, but since the climb was so high through the pipes, it was very wasteful to attempt to pump it to the upper floors, so we must either light the heater or use cold water. After our several nights on the *Gray Gull,* and nearly a week on trains, the luxury of water of any temperature seemed so great that no one bemoaned the lack of heat.

Phoebe, testing out my bed much as Pity had done her own, pronounced herself awed by the entire place. "If you had to get yourself a stepmother, Miss Saunielle, it's nice you got a rich one."

"She's not rich; she's reduced to taking in lodgers," I pointed out.

"Lodgers-smodgers. Anybody who has a house like this is *rich,*" Phoebe pronounced. "I can't see sleeping way in the back of the house in a rather ordinary room, though, not when she's got the gorgeous room at the front. Ummmm, lovely!"

"She told you why, it's a room that will rent for a good price. And we haven't seen *her* room; it's quite likely every bit as luxurious. Besides, it's next to the bathroom. Possibly she has to get up at night. Many older people do."

Phoebe giggled. "I dare you to refer to her as an older person to her face. Forty-two! She's fifty-two if she's a day!"

"Well, certainly fifty," I agreed. "That pink room is beautiful, isn't it? I shall close my eyes tonight and imagine that I'm sleeping in it."

"Funny," Phoebe said, getting off the bed and walking across the room to examine herself in the mirror over the dresser. "About that room. I wonder why she had it decorated that way? I mean, it's obviously for a lady . . . for a *beautiful* lady . . . but she said she wanted to take in only gentlemen lodgers because they're so much less trouble."

"She probably didn't decorate with the idea of taking in lodgers; she said she'd only recently suffered financial reverses."

"I shouldn't wonder, if she did this house as recently as it looks like. Everything's spanking new, you know. Every blessed thing. And it must have cost a fortune. It'd run anybody into the poorhouse."

Phoebe struck a pose in the mirror, pushing at her carroty hair as if it were styled in the latest fashion. "Do you think I look all right, to go down to dinner? Or should I change into my black sateen?"

"I hope we all look all right the way we are; we haven't much of anything to change into. There looked to be an awful lot of material in there; I wonder if there's any possibility she'd let us use the leftovers to replenish our wardrobes?"

"Ask her," Phoebe suggested. "Tell her we're in rags. I don't suppose she'll want me to eat with the family, the way I did in Virginia, will she? I know that didn't even set right with your Aunt Rachael, at first. A hired girl setting down to the table with the family. But when there's only the kitchen for eating, and one table, and it's so hard to keep the food hot . . . I know you're the one persuaded her, miss. I always appreciated that, I did."

"Never mind about that. No doubt Mrs. Fox will tell you what she expects. Run along, I want to work with my hair a bit before supper, Phoebe. And I think we'd best allow a quarter of an hour to get downstairs and catch our breath before we go into the dining room."

"All right." Phoebe made a final face at herself in the mirror. "I hope the food's as good as everything else in this place. It might even fatten Miss Dodie up."

I was smiling when she left the room, but when she had gone I took my own turn before the mirror, unsmiling. I turned sideways and pressed my skirt against my abdomen, wondering how long it would be before everyone in the world could tell.

It was hard to find anything to think about that didn't make me want to cry, and I was determined not to do that. Not now, not when I had to go downstairs and meet those strangers, face Mrs. Fox and Estelle. Of course they knew some of my reasons for sorrow, but I've yet to meet anyone who isn't disconcerted by grief, and I didn't want to be sufficiently depressing so they would be reluctant to have me around. Not until I'd worked out . . . something.

I should go to Mrs. Fox and tell her just how difficult my circumstances were, I thought. She had a right to know. And perhaps, in her superior age, she would have some idea what I ought to do.

Do? I thought bitterly, examining the face of the girl in the mirror. What could one do, when a child was on the way and there was no marriage paper, not even a wedding ring to indicate there had been a husband . . .

A wedding ring. I clutched at my throat, pulling open the neck of my dress, searching for the chain and the ring . . .

It was gone. The Jaubert ring was no longer around my neck. What . . . And then I remembered. The man on the train had tried to jerk it off my neck . . . I could still see the marks the chain had left on my flesh. Phoebe, seated behind me, had loosed the clasp, and the chain and ring had gone into that upturned hat.

Sebastian Rohann had brought back our money and other valuables, but he hadn't returned the Jaubert ring. Had he retrieved it, or was it lost forever, the last thing I had of Mama's?

There was nothing I could do about it now, but the next time we saw Tom I would ask him to find out for me if Rohann had the ring and had simply not realized who it belonged to.

I would feel badly if I didn't get it back. But I had a more urgent problem, one that I must face up to as quickly as possible.

Tonight, after supper, I must approach Mrs. Fox and tell her that I was expecting a child.

◇◇◇◇ **12** ◇◇◇◇

I knew at once that in this house "supper" must be known as "dinner." Any meal, however simple, served in that charming dining room, under one of the most magnificent chandeliers I had ever seen, must be known by a grander name than "supper."

The table was enormous, like the legendary one at Hunter's Hill. It was not covered with a cloth but was set with individual linen mats. On each of these was arranged, in formal fashion, a place setting of fine, thin china in a pattern of pale blue forget-me-nots and gold-tracing. I wanted to turn it over to be sure, but I knew without doing so that it was Haviland china, from Limoges in France, for Mama had had some exactly like it, china that was sold when Papa lost his job as the village schoolmaster.

The silver pattern was not familiar, simply because we had never had any silver. The Yankees had confiscated the Hunter and Calhoon silver and silverplate when McClellan swept through our part of Virginia before the end of the war. This was heavy, ornate, and gleamed with the reflected light.

Phoebe confessed later that she was glad she wasn't to sit with the rest of us, once she'd seen that table. "I'd have knocked over one of those crystal glasses, or broke a cup, or something. There's just ordinary china in the kitchen, the sort you dare to touch."

She was pressed into service with Estelle, who then joined us at table. The gentlemen lodgers were there, and we were introduced to them. My initial impression was a vague one, since I was concerned with the necessity for care in handling the china and the crystal, and more concerned yet with the ordeal that lay ahead when I could get Mrs. Fox off to myself.

Mr. Dillingham (crackers) was massively obese. Mr. Simons (dry goods) was tall and thin and humorless. Mr. Quayle, the clergyman, was a small, dried-up man with little to say unless directly addressed, and then he was vague and said, "How's that?" to everything before he answered it.

The lodger who sat at my left was Mr. Goodwin (brewery, retired). He was the youngest of the foursome, being perhaps fifty. He was a prosperous-appearing man, with a gold watch and chain across an expansive stomach that suggested he might have imbibed his own product with some regularity over the years. A lingering odor on his breath confirmed this surmise.

He was genial, however, and pleasant, offering me the bread and butter, holding the platter while I helped myself to roast beef, and in other ways trying to make me feel at home. He asked me questions about Virginia, and hoped I would like San Francisco, which he assured me was the only place in the country worth living, and I could take his word for it.

The meal was adequate, but I thought Phoebe could have done better, considering what the cook had had to work with. I gathered from the conversation that Estelle had done the honors, and that she'd welcome the excuse to abandon the duty to anyone else willing to take it on.

Thinking of what I must soon say to my stepmother (I had to force myself to think of her in that light) as I did, the food was of secondary importance. Aunt Pity and Mr. Dillingham carried on an animated if tedious conversation regarding the possibility that some Calhoons he had known in North Carolina were related to her own family in Virginia.

Mrs. Fox, at the head of the table, regal in a deep blue dinner gown cut low to reveal more of her frontal structure, smiled and nodded and kept Phoebe running back and forth to refill water glasses and serving dishes. Alfred, the bulldog, sat on a stool with an embroidered cover and accepted tidbits from his mistress at frequent intervals.

It was a relief to me when the meal was over, although I dreaded what might come next. But it was too soon for a private conference; once the meal was cleared away, the gentlemen must have their cigars and their port or their brandy. Each man supplied his own of those things, and they were kept in a locked cabinet and opened only for the half hour following the evening meal.

The rest of us, with the exception of Phoebe, who was washing up, retired to the back parlor. This room matched its counterpart in decor, for if the need arose, sliding doors could be opened to throw the two rooms together. However, by itself it seemed slightly less formal. There was a gramophone which played the new flat records, and we must have music.

We had known a family in Virginia who had the older-style graphophone with the cylindrical records, though we had never seen one like this. The others were content to sit and listen to it, but after a few minutes I was unable to do this. I kept going over my planned speech in my mind: *I will say, Mrs. Fox, there is something you must know. I'm going to have a baby.* No, no, that wouldn't do. Her reaction would be that of any well-brought-up female, and I might totally alienate her before she heard my extenuating circumstances. I must say something like, *I fell in love with this young man, but we knew my aunt wouldn't give us permission to marry. So we married secretly, planning to announce it when it was time for us to come West to meet Papa. Only Francis ran away with some money from the bank where he worked, or they thought he had, and then he was found dead in the river, and they said maybe another young man had taken the money. At any rate, I was married, but Francis had the papers and I can't prove it. And now I'm going to have a baby . . .*

I squirmed in my chair, wondering if she would believe me. Would *I* believe anyone who told me such a tale?

Mrs. Fox misinterpreted my squirming. "There's a lavatory on this floor, all the way to the back, off the kitchen."

Only too glad of an excuse to leave, I slipped out the room, leaving Dodie entranced by a Strauss waltz. I would talk to Phoebe while she did the dishes, and perhaps she would help build up my courage.

She was up to her elbows in soap suds and turned to meet me with a sober face. "Have you told her yet?"

"No. How did you know I was planning to talk to her?"

"What else can you do, miss? I heard what she said, we're only here temporary like. She thinks once you've sewed up all her goods you'll go looking for work somewhere else. You've got to tell her why you can't, at least not for long. And what happens after the baby comes? You can't go out to work, then. If she's a charitable woman she'll give you a home, you and the baby."

I put both hands to the back of my neck, rubbing at an aching spot. "How am I going to tell her, Phoebe? So she'll believe me, that Francis I *were* married."

"Just tell the truth, I guess. It won't matter in the long run, whether you're believed or not. The babe will still come along in due time. I reckon it's a fearsome job, all right, to tackle that woman. But the sooner you do it, the better for all concerned, Miss Saunielle. I'm sure of that." Her tone was earnest and brought me dangerously close to tears.

Our relationship had undergone a subtle change in the past few weeks, I thought. Not that we hadn't always been friendly, but Phoebe had been a servant in our home, and impoverished though we were Aunt Rachael insisted we maintain our proper places as the young ladies in the family.

But since Rachael's death, on our travels and after Phoebe had guessed that I was pregnant, this hired girl and I had become closer than Dodie and I had ever been. It was almost as if Phoebe were the sister I had never had.

"I know. I'm going to tell her tonight, Phoebe. But not until the others have gone upstairs. I don't want them to know, not yet. And I'm frankly terrified as to what she'll say. What if she throws me out of the house?"

"She won't. She married your papa, didn't she? She's your stepmother, and she's doing the decent thing by taking us all in because of you. Even if she does expect to get something for it. She didn't say anything about paying any of us wages, did she?"

"No. Phoebe, I know that you could find work elsewhere, as a maid in someone else's home. There are hundreds of houses in San Francisco that look as if they belong to very wealthy people. Anyone living in a house the size of this one must have servants. They'd pay you a wage as well as provide meals and lodgings. You don't have to stay here because of us, you know."

She wiped suds off her arms and reached for a towel. "There's no hurry about that. You might need me yet, and I've not forgot your generosity in bringing me along, Miss Nell. You paid my fare as if I was a member of the family, with money from the sale of your mama's pearls, and I know how you hated to part with them. I think Mrs. Fox is going to take care of you, all right. But if she shouldn't . . . well, if you've got trouble, I'll share it, the same as you've shared mine, miss."

At that I had to clasp her hand and squeeze it, for Phoebe's offer of help was of far more value than anything Pity or Dodie could give.

"Those gentleman must be finished with the sherry by this time. There's just their glasses to wash, and I'll be finished. It's frightening, handling those lovely, delicate things. Do you think she'd have me drawn and quartered if I broke one?"

"More than likely," I admitted. "Come on, I'll help you with the rest of them."

So we finished clearing the dining room, redolent as it was of the scent of expensive cigars. With the vast kitchen tidied up, we were free to rejoin the others listening to records, but it was the last thing I wanted. "Did you have a chance to eat, Phoebe?"

"Oh yes, I ate between running back and forth. I also got a peek or two at the rest of the house. Come along, Miss Saunielle, I want to show you!"

As if we were indeed sisters, she reached for my hand and led me down the corridor toward the front of the house. Opposite the dining room she threw open a door and stood back in triumph. "Look at that! I think it must be nearly a match for the library your family had at Hunter's Hill, before the war! If the missus has no objection to our browsing, we won't have to go to sleep to *Black Beauty* any more. Not that I don't love that book, I do, but all these nights and days of nothing else to read, I'm ready for a change."

I stood there, looking around the big room with its high ceiling and paneled walls and ruby-colored carpet. There were easy chairs, and a cabinet that looked as if it might have been intended for the brandy bottle and glasses, and good reading lamps at strategic places. But most of all there were books.

Hundreds of books, from floor to ceiling, most of them behind glass doors to protect them from dust and damp, but some on open shelves that suggested they were favorites and would be often read.

My eyes filled with tears. "How Papa would have loved this room. Look, there's even one of those ladders on the little wheels and the track at the top, to move around and get at the books on the top shelves! Oh, Phoebe, what a magnificent room!"

She gave me a little shove closer to the nearest bank of shelves. "See there. The Encyclopaedia Britannica, thirty volumes. Do you suppose anyone's ever read the entire thing?"

I ran a respectful finger over the green silk bindings. "Papa always wanted a set, but they cost nearly fifty dollars and he never could afford it. Look, there's a Webster's International Dictionary. And a Ladies Medical Guide. And The New Physician."

Phoebe moved ahead of me, displaying her recently acquired reading skill. "Look, here are Miss Alcott's novels, all the ones we had at home and more besides! We never had *Eight Cousins,* did we?"

For a few minutes we forgot that in a short time I would have to face Mrs. Fox with my appalling revelation. We immersed ourselves in the titles and the leather and silk bindings and the familiar author's names . . . a complete set of the Horatio Alger books, twelve volumes of T. S. Arthur, Charlotte Brontë's *Jane Eyre,* Anne Brontë's *Tenant of Wildfell Hall,* and Emily Brontë's *Wuthering Heights.* We found James Fenimore Cooper's novels, and a sixteen-volume set on the Battles of the Civil War, which was obviously written by some Yankee, Phoebe said. There were the Elsie Dinsmore books, which Mama had read to me as a little girl, and the works of George Eliot and and Ralph Waldo Emerson and Richard Harding Davis, and Charles Dickens, and on and on until we were nearly dizzy trying to comprehend the riches of this marvelous room.

It was there that Mrs. Fox found us, engrossed in an illustrated *The Hoosier School Boy.* We spun around sharply, guiltily, when she spoke. "Ah, there you are. I wondered where you'd gotten off to. Your aunt and your cousin have gone up to bed, pleading weariness after all this moving about. I thought perhaps you'd gone up, too."

"No. I . . . we . . . we saw the library and . . . I hope we aren't intruding here . . ."

She waved a careless hand. "Help yourself. It's dusty in here, no doubt; since none of us read much I don't think Estelle has been tidying up this room. Luckily most of the books are behind glass, so it doesn't particularly matter."

"Nobody reads?" I echoed, incredulous. "With a selection of books like this available?"

"My eyes aren't what they used to be," she replied, but I knew from the way that she didn't even glance at the books, that they meant nothing to her.

Phoebe bobbed her head in what she thought was a proper attitude for a cook-maid. "I'll be going up myself, ma'am. Will you be wanting me to do the breakfast in the morning, then?"

"We serve at eight. Estelle will work with you tomorrow, until you're familiar with the kitchen," Mrs. Fox confirmed. "And I like to have tea brought to my room at seven-thirty. Very *hot* tea."

"Very good, ma'am. Good night, then. Good night, Miss Saunielle." She gave me a very meaningful look, and I'd no doubt she would have administered a pinch as well, if she could have done so undetected.

I knew perfectly well what the look was for. I cleared my throat. "Mrs. Fox . . . ma'am . . . I would like very much to speak to you privately, if I might."

"Certainly, my dear. Only let's go into the parlor, shall we? I have a fire in there, and it's much cosier. It's rather depressing in here, with all those books climbing the walls."

I was pondering why anyone who found books depressing should have spent hundreds, perhaps thousands, of dollars filling the library. And it hadn't been a random buying of anything that would look well on the shelves, either; the selection was too perfect, too varied and all-encompassing, to have been done other than by someone to whom the books meant a great deal.

I followed her across the hall, dismayed to see that all the gentlemen were there. But even as we entered, they stood and began to file out, making their good nights.

Mr. Goodwin was the last to leave. He beamed at us, nodding approvingly at me. "Very nice to have a fresh young face in the house. Especially when it's such a pretty face, eh? I see you've been inspecting the library. Quite a collection, isn't it? I used to read a bit, but the eyes won't do it any more. Tried it the other day, something called *The Labor Movement in America,* by Professor R. T. Ely. But I had to give it up, the strain was too much." His smile widened. "Maybe one day when you haven't too much else to do you'd spend an hour reading aloud to an old man, eh? I'd enjoy that no end."

I murmured something unintelligible, trusting that if I ever was at loose ends I could find something better to do than read anything so dull sounding as *The Labor Movement in America* to anyone.

He seemed to find my response favorable, however, and told us both good night. A moment later we were alone in the parlor, with the fire burning cheerily on the hearth, and I almost wished the old men hadn't gone.

Belle Fox settled herself in a chair, letting the ugly little dog climb into her lap, and motioned me to the sofa. Somewhere in the house a clock chimed ten. The fire crackled and sent out a pleasant fragrance.

"Now, we can have a cosy little talk," the woman said, stroking her pet's head. "What did you have on your mind, my dear?"

I opened my mouth to speak and suddenly found it impossible, for my throat had closed up as if around a hard, painful knot.

There was only one lamp lit, so perhaps the lack of light made it seem that she was gazing at me with malevolence. Why would she do that? Certainly when she spoke her voice was ordinary enough, and not unkind.

"I hope your room is satisfactory?"

With a supreme effort, I broke through the lump. "Yes, it's very nice, and I'm most grateful, ma'am."

"Then what is it you want to say to me?"

"I . . . I have something I must explain, and it's . . . rather difficult . . ."

"Difficulties may usually be handled if we take them one step at a time. I realize that you and your family have run through your funds, but you and your cousin are handy at sewing so it shouldn't be much of a problem. There are plenty of goods up there to go around, to make each of you a dress or two and some underwear, a nightgown, whatever you need."

"Thank you. It's true we do need clothing, but that isn't what I wanted to talk to you about."

She leaned forward, lifting her hand from the dog to pat my arm. "Saunielle, my dear, you needn't be afraid to confide in me as if I were your own mother. I never had a daughter, and Estelle is only the child of my first husband's brother, but I do think I might have made a good mother, had I had the chance. Speak up, don't hesitate!"

And then it all came out, in a jumbled flood, exactly the way I had warned myself *not* to do it. My pregnancy, Francis (I even mentioned that he'd been accused of taking money from the bank, although the bank president had later told me he believed they were mistaken in that regard) and I wound up exhausted from the ordeal and shaking uncontrollably.

Her expression had not changed greatly as she listened. If she condemned me, if she did not believe it, none of this was evident from her face. When I had finished and sat trying to control the trembling of the hands in my lap, she stood up and moved to unlock a cabinet.

"I think we'd both benefit from a bit of brandy," she said. "Has a good deal of medicinal properties, brandy does." She poured two glasses and brought one back to me, taking her place in the chair to toss hers off rather quickly. "Drink up, you need the warmth on your innards, from the look of you."

She waited until I had taken several sips before she said anything else. Then, "How far along are you?"

"About . . . no, exactly . . . two months, lacking three days."

"And you're sure you *are* carrying this young man's child?"

I told her the reasons why I was so convinced.

She nodded, her face settling into a mold of shrewdness. "I see. Yes, you're quite right to have come to me at once. It takes a mature woman to find the solution to such a problem. And a problem it is, mark you, I don't minimize it. I am quite certain that you are telling the truth about being married to this Francis, both because of what your father told me about you and what I observe for myself. It is most unfortunate that the marriage papers could not have been found, but that's beside the point at this stage of things. What is to the point is that no one, outside of me and your family, is going to believe a word of it. They're going to say that you were simply a foolish girl who allowed herself to be seduced and is now unable to come up with a more plausible-sounding story to explain why she is two months with child."

Even the brandy wasn't enough to make me feel much better. I continued to sip at it, determined not to give way to tears.

"What am I going to do?" I asked, not really expecting an answer. For it was, after all, my problem. There was no reason for her to allow me to bring disgrace upon her household if she were not inclined to do so.

"That seems obvious. If you weren't so distraught you'd have thought of it yourself. You'll have to be married, and as soon as possible."

"Married!" I gaped at her. "But . . . I don't . . . I have only been in this city since yesterday, I don't know a soul, and it's most unlikely any man is going to want to marry me . . ."

Her lips tightened with determination and confidence. "Oh, not if he knows you're carrying another man's child, no. Who else knows your condition?"

"Only Phoebe. She guessed. In fact, she realized it before I did."

"And she'll keep her mouth shut, I'm sure, especially if you warn her to do so. No, the thing is to keep absolutely quiet about it, and I'll find you a husband. A quick, quiet ceremony; you haven't met anyone yet who's likely to remember exactly when you came here and in what apparent condition. That's the only answer, a wedding. There are lots of premature babies born, even into the best of families, I assure you. You run on up to bed and don't worry about it, my dear. I promise you, I will take care of everything. I will find you a husband with as little delay as possible. You can trust me."

She stood up, spilling the little bulldog onto the floor, indicating the interview was at an end.

I stood too, feeling somewhat giddy from the brandy. The solution might well be logical, and obvious, and everything else she had said.

But it filled me with no more joy and relief than did the infant that was the cause of my predicament.

I wanted a husband no more than I wanted a baby.

◇◇◇◇ 13 ◇◇◇◇

Had it not been for the brandy I probably would not have slept at all that night. For once I was safely closed in my room the tears soaked my face and my handkerchief and even my dress front, flowing as copiously as a spring freshet.

Tears for Francis, for Papa and finally for myself.

I didn't hear Phoebe's light tapping at the door. I only knew she was there when I felt the bed give beneath her weight and then felt her arm across my shoulders.

"Ah, miss, miss, don't take on so! You'll make yourself sick."

Of course this did nothing to stop me, but after a time the sobs subsided and I sat up, mopping at my face with the clean handkerchief she offered.

"Was she absolutely horrid about it, then?"

I shook my head and blew my nose. "No. Actually, she was very practical and she didn't say a word to reproach me. She said she would take care of everything. But oh, Phoebe, she says the only thing to do is find me a husband!"

Phoebe nodded a little, to my dismay. "She's right. It's the only sensible thing to do, unless you're prepared to do away with the little thing."

Startled, I sat up straighter. "Do away with it! What do you mean?"

"Well, I don't know how they do it, but I understand there's ways to get rid of a child if you don't want it. I think maybe it's dangerous, though. If you're going to have it, you'd best have a husband. That would solve some other problems, too. Like how you're going to care for yourself and a child."

"There's a lot more to marriage than being taken care of." I felt strangely resentful that Phoebe should so quickly agree with what seemed to me an atrocious idea. "Whoever he was, I'd have to live with him the rest of my life."

"You planned to live with Francis, didn't you?"

"That was different. I was in love with Francis! And he loved me. And it was his own baby. He would have been so happy if he'd known about the baby, if we could have been together." That set off another episode of tears, which Phoebe patiently waited through.

"Well, if you could be in love with Francis, and enjoy going to bed with him, then there's another man somewhere you can love, too. There's hundreds of men and women in the world, and we can't all be intended for just one other person out of them all, or it stands to reason most of us would never find the proper one, don't you see? No doubt it will all be a bit strange, but if Mrs. Fox says she'll find you a husband I'm sure she'll do it. Here, I'll help you out of your dress and into bed. A good night's rest will make it all seem brighter, I'm sure."

And so I allowed her to undress me, and pull the blankets up to my chin, and between weariness and the brandy, I at last fell asleep.

The following day was a gloomy one. Not only because of my own inner turmoil and fear, but because of the fog that rolled in through the fabled Golden Gate, that narrow mouth to San Francisco Bay. Fog, thick enough to stifle one just looking into it; I couldn't see the miniature park in front of the house, only the steps of the house itself.

We felt as if we were shut away from the world. Mr. Simons and Mr. Dillingham, who normally went out to business, elected to remain indoors today, feeling it was too risky on the streets. Mr. Goodwin greeted me with obvious pleasure at breakfast, suggesting that this might be a good day to spend an hour or two in the library if I'd care to read aloud to him?

I quickly informed him that I had duties to perform, much to his disappointment, and as soon as the meal was completed I retired to the sewing room with Mrs. Fox to do the preliminary work on the first of her garments.

There was one bad thing about sewing. I could do it in my sleep. It required no conscious thought on my part, which meant that as I cut and pinned and fitted the garment to her voluminous curves, I was able to keep right on thinking about myself. Myself and the husband Belle Fox had promised to find.

Dodie took over the sewing machine, finding to her delight that it was easily operated and that she could accomplish a great deal in a short period of time. Since she was not talkative, she did nothing to take my mind off myself for more than a few seconds at a time. We agreed that she should do the long straight seams on the machine and I would do the more delicate handwork.

I am afraid that the work I did that day was not of my best, but Belle Fox didn't appear to know the difference, expressing herself as well satisfied when she joined us late in the afternoon for a fitting.

As she turned to go, Mrs. Fox paused in the doorway. "Oh, Saunielle, that little matter we were discussing last night. If you'll come down a few minutes early for dinner I'd like to take it further with you; I have, I think, an admirable solution to the problem."

With that she swept away in her expensive green watered-silk frock.

Dodie looked around from the sewing machine. "What's she talking about, Saunielle? What problem?"

I had stopped stitching, my respiratory system nearly paralyzed. A solution could mean only one thing.

"Saunielle? What is she going to talk to you about?"

"Ah . . . I told her we were all in need of clothes," I improvised, so as not to be entirely untruthful. "She thought we might use some of the goods she has on hand to run up underclothes and a dress or two for each of us."

"Oh, I hope so! My black got so much wear and tear while we were traveling that I'm afraid it will fall apart before it's washed another time or two. And the sole is nearly off one shoe . . . do you think our making up these things for her would be worth a pair of shoes, too?"

"I'll see," I said, and forced myself to pick up the needle and begin to work again.

Phoebe looked in on us late in the afternoon, by which time I was on the verge of nervous prostration and welcomed any sort of diversion.

"I brought you both some tea. She's having some, in her room, so I thought if I was climbing all the way to the second floor with it I might as well come the rest of the way up here. There's cookies with it, if you're hungry."

Dodie fell upon the cookies with a cry of delight. I wasn't hungry (how could I be until I knew what . . . or who? . . . Mrs. Fox had in mind?) but the tea was hot and sweet and I drank it greedily.

"Thank you, Phoebe. It was very good of you."

Phoebe nibbled at one of the cookies herself. "I'm doing the dinner by myself tonight. It'll be a better one than that Estelle cooked, too. She don't like cooking, and a person don't like it can't do it well, I guess. Have you been cooped up here all day or have you had a chance to explore a bit?"

"No exploring. We even had lunch up here."

"Then you haven't seen the music room?"

I swung around to face her more directly. "Music room? No, is there one?"

"It's the door roughly across from the back parlor, just in front of the library. There's a grand piano that looks as if it must have cost a mint, and it's a beautiful room. But they got it all shut up and gathering dust, just like the library. I asked Estelle who played the piano and she said nobody, the gramophone was good enough for her and plenty of exercise winding it up between records. I thought you'd want to see it, though."

I drained my cup and put it down. "I think I'll go see it now. My back's beginning to hurt from sitting so long. If you took tea to Mrs. Fox's room, did you get a good look at it?"

"Oh yes. It's all very elegant, thick rugs and lots of velvet cushions and a chaise. But it doesn't have the style of the pink room, not by a sight, it doesn't. Can't imagine anyone decorating a house to suit herself and not taking that pink room, I can't. Well, I'd best pick up the tea things from her and get back to the kitchen. If I hear the piano, I'll know you found it."

We parted, she to go down the back stairs, I down the front ones. There seemed to be no one around except Mr. Quayle, the clergyman, reading a newspaper in the front parlor.

I passed by the open doorway without calling attention to myself As Phoebe had said, the door was closed, but it opened readily at my touch.

And once more I stood entranced. Perhaps it seems strange that I should be so taken with these beautiful rooms, but I had been raised on the stories of the fine houses both my parents had lived in as young people. Both Pity and Rachael had lived largely in their memories of the days before the War Between the States, when gracious living was taken for granted, and when it was gone they had missed it sorely and bitterly.

Many times Mama had described to me the music room in her family home in Limoges in France. Until she died, we had had our own piano, for Papa had not been able to deny her that even if he had to sacrifice mightily to pay for it, and some of my happiest memories were of sitting beside Mama on the bench and singing with her as she played. As soon as I was big enough to comfortably reach the keyboard, long before my fingers could span an octave, I was taking lessons so that I might play myself. And when I moved to Aunt Rachael's house, the piano went with me, that she might earn a little money by giving lessons on it.

As Phoebe had said, the room was lovely. The carpeting here was a deep rich blue, almost a shade of peacock, with a pattern in cream and pale rose and a lighter blue. The draperies were of a matching blue velvet, caught back with gold cords so that the light could come in through the lace panels underneath.

I suppose there were other furnishings, but all I saw that first day was the piano itself.

I knew at once that it was much finer than the one Mama had had. I brushed the dust from it as I raised the lid and then uncovered the keys. I wouldn't have been surprised to find it badly out of tune, since it was obviously not in current use, but perhaps it had not been here long. Its notes were clear and sweet and true.

There was sheet music as well as books of familiar pieces, and I was drawn to sit down and try my hand at "The Merry Widow Waltz."

For the first time all day I forgot the approaching ordeal of another discussion with Mrs. Fox. I played for perhaps half an hour, and then, in an interval of silence, I heard voices and knew that it must be nearly dinnertime. Had I missed the appointed talk?

But no. There was no sign of either Estelle or Mrs. Fox, although the beastly little Alfred was sitting in a rocking chair in the back parlor, warning off anyone who came too near by displaying his canines. Pity and Dodie were there, however, so I joined them.

Mr. Quayle had left his newspaper and Dodie was glancing over it. "Oh, Saunielle, there you are. I heard you playing, it was lovely. Look, I've been skimming the classified ads in the *Chronicle*. Someone is advertising for a seamstress. Do you think it would be worth my while to apply? Of course I'm not nearly so good as you are, but it says they have a sewing machine, and I'd be expected to live in."

"By all means, inquire into it," I encouraged her. God only knew how long I'd be able to do anything to see to her keep.

"There's ever so much more in this paper than in our little weekly at home. There's an ad for ladies shoes, all summer styles, at a dollar thirty-five to a dollar and a half per pair."

"I have that much in cash. I'll let you take it and you can get some shoes."

I sat down beside Dodie, careful to stay well away from Alfred, and Dodie opened the paper so that it lay partially across my knees.

"There are a number of positions open for females, Saunielle. Besides the seamstress one they want young ladies to learn to operate the typewriting machines. And someone to teach guitar and vocal lessons. Perhaps you could teach piano; you're every bit as accomplished as Mama was."

My own gaze fell upon a curiously appropriate insertion in the list of advertisements, and I felt my stomach knotting up again. *German midwife. Ladies attended at their residence on shortest notice and at reasonable rates.*

Would I have a residence, when the time came? Or would I be out on the street somewhere, one of those lost women . . . I caught myself up short. My stepmother had said she would find a solution to my problem, and only a short time ago had additionally indicated that she had indeed found it. My only fear was that it would turn out to be worse for me than bearing an apparently illegitimate child.

"Oh, look." Dodie's voice cut through my thoughts. "Portraits taken; deceased persons and children a specialty."

Shocked out of my reverie, I exclaimed, "Why on earth are you reading *that?*"

"I don't have a picture of Mama, except that very old one when she was a bride. It doesn't even look like her. I should very much have liked to have one taken."

"After she had *died?* Dodie, you can't mean that!"

"It would be better than no picture at all, wouldn't it? Don't you wish you had a photograph of your papa?"

"Not one taken after he was dead," I said firmly, pushing the paper aside and standing up. Alfred growled menacingly and I spoke sharply to him.

"Be quiet, you nasty beast. If you nip at me again I'll hit you with something."

"My goodness, Saunielle, you're in a strange mood. Is something wrong?" my cousin demanded.

"Nothing at all. I simply don't like being intimidated by that wretched creature. Excuse me."

"Where are you going?" Dodie called after me, but I pretended I didn't hear.

I could bear it no longer. It lacked only twenty minutes of being dinnertime, and I didn't think I could get through the meal without knowing what Mrs. Fox had come up with to assist me. If she had not come down stairs, then I would seek her out in her room.

Alfred jumped out of his chair and waddled after me, panting with the effort, so that I might have felt sorry for him if I hadn't disliked him so much.

The kitchen was full of tempting odors, but it would take more than food to hold my attention now. Phoebe offered me a taste of a dressing she was trying out, but I shook my head.

"It's good, I think. I never had so many things to do with. The pantry and the icebox are both full. Fancy, miss, they have an ice man who comes twice a week and puts this big block of ice into that thing!"

"That's nice. Has Mrs. Fox come downstairs yet?"

"No, miss."

"Then I'm going upstairs to talk to her. She said . . . she said she'd . . . found a solution to my . . . problem."

"Found you a husband, you mean?" Phoebe looked quickly around, as if we might be overheard. "Already, Miss Saunielle? Who is it?"

"I don't know! That's what's driving me mad, I haven't had a chance to speak with her! She said before dinner . . . I'm going upstairs."

I took a few steps toward the door that opened on the back stairs, but when I did so Alfred moved in front of me and barred my way, displaying his fangs in a decidedly unfriendly manner.

"What on earth's the matter with him? Get out of my way!" I commanded, but the animal did not move. Indeed, he curled back his disgusting lip and snarled.

"He did the same to me, at first, when I wanted to use the back stairs," Phoebe said. "And then Mrs. Fox came along and told him it was all right."

"You mean he won't let me go upstairs unless she says I may? Good grief, how absurd!"

Phoebe nodded. "Maybe I can coax him away with a sliver of the roast. Here, Alfred. See what I've got for you."

The dog hesitated, torn between his duty as he saw it and the savory morsel. Greed won out; when he trotted over to take the meat and lick at Phoebe's fingers, I ran quickly up the stairs.

I paused, out of breath, on the second-floor landing, to orient myself. Mrs. Fox's room was directly across the hall from the head of the stairs, and as soon as my breathing slowed I lifted a hand to knock.

I did not knock, however, for there were voices within: Belle Fox and Estelle were in conversation, and it was immediately apparent that they were at odds about something. The last thing I wanted was to walk into the midst of a family quarrel.

"You're a fool," Estelle said, loudly enough to be heard clearly through the panels of the door. "It's dangerous, you must see that it's absolutely mad to go on this way!"

The reply, while spoken in a lower and more controlled voice, was equally audible. "This is my house, if you'll care to remember that. What goes on in it is up to me. I don't need a snip of a girl to tell me how to handle my affairs."

"All right. Don't listen to me. Go on, play the fool, and see what it gets you, Belle! Because you're playing with fire, and I'll wager everything I have that you're going to get burned! I only hope I don't get burned, too!"

The conversation was sufficiently intriguing to make me want to know what they were talking about. However, if either of them opened that door and caught me standing here it would put me in rather a bad light. I considered retreating and coming up again, more noisily.

And then I didn't have time to do that, for I had left the door ajar at the foot of the stairs and the sound of smashing crockery came clearly to my ears. Since there was a momentary lull in the dialogue in Belle Fox's room, it was evident that they heard it too, for the door was suddenly pulled open.

"For heaven's sake, go downstairs and see what that wretched girl has broken! Oh, Saunielle, you're here. Do you know what's broken?"

"No, ma'am. I suspect poor Phoebe's dropped something. She's very nervous of handling such nice things. I hope it wasn't anything very valuable."

"Needless to say, so do I. Go on, Estelle, see what it is. Come in, my dear, we have a few minutes before dinner, do we not? No doubt you're anxious to know what I've managed to do."

I was ushered into her room, scarcely aware of my surroundings except for an impression of too much furniture, too heavy and ornate, crowded into the spacious room. Belle had changed her gown for dinner, the fourth I had seen her wear in the twenty-four hours we'd been in the house, and I wondered why she needed to have so many new costumes made, since she already had such an ample array.

"Sit down, sit down. That chair will do. Alfred usually sits there, so there may be a few hairs, but he doesn't shed the way most dogs do. Yes, that's it." She was smiling, as if pleased with herself. "Now, you'll be wanting to know your future. Well, put your worries at rest, my dear. I told you a mature woman could solve your problem, and I have done so. A husband you need, and a husband you shall have."

Dread held me in a painfully uncomfortable position, even though the chair was deep and soft. I could not speak, I could only wait.

"Married you shall be, and as quickly as anyone could like. We have agreed upon next Saturday afternoon. The gentleman himself would have found tomorrow satisfactory, but I told him that of course you must have time to make some preparations. A bride can't go to her husband in ragged underwear, after all." Her smile broadened with satisfaction. "I shall, of course, be only too happy to assist you there. I will turn over to you such goods as you think necessary to make a reasonably adequate trousseau. No great number of things, of course," she added hastily, "for he is quite comfortably well off and will no doubt provide you with anything you want, once you are safely married."

Her dark eyes sparkled and she leaned forward to pat my hand, and then for a moment held me, her own hand heavy with rings that cut into my flesh.

"Ah, you see, I've kept my promise! Your worries will be over, just like that! I shouldn't be surprised but what he might be persuaded to provide as well for your aunt, and your cousin might even fit into some niche or other once you're established into your own household."

The pain in my chest was so severe that I spared a moment's thought for the possibility that the heart ailment that had taken Rachael and Papa might be hereditary and that I was on the verge of an attack; however, not even imminent death was quite so frightening as the prospect of marrying whatever man had been persuaded into this alliance.

I wanted to shout at her, to demand of her that she end my suspense immediately. I could not utter a sound.

"Yes, yes. A very suitable match. He will not know you are expecting a child, of course, and since he's not a particularly observant person it may be some time before it is necessary to tell him. And I'm convinced that he will easily be persuaded as to a premature birth. Since he has no female relatives living it's most unlikely anyone will ever question it. And your own future will be quite secure, quite secure. You will lack for nothing, neither you nor the child."

"Who?" The word was a whisper, so faint I scarcely heard it myself.

She was nodding and smiling, rocking a little in her chair. "Why, you've already met him, my dear, so it won't be as if he were a stranger. It's Alastair Goodwin, of course."

◇◇◇◇ 14 ◇◇◇◇

Mr. Goodwin? The paunchy man, nearly as old as Papa, who smelled of beer and cigars and whose idea of a pleasant evening was to have me read to him on the subject of *The Labor Movement in America?*

Before I had been apprehensive. Now I was terrified. She could not be serious. A seventeen-year-old girl and a man old enough to be her father?

My chest heaved with the effort to control my breathing, which threatened to cease altogether unless I consciously commanded it to continue.

"Ma'am . . . oh, ma'am, you can't mean old Mr. Goodwin!"

The good humor faded from her face. *"Old* Mr. Goodwin? He's only fifty, I believe. It's not at all unusual for a mature gentlemen to marry a very young lady . . . and it certainly has a good many advantages for the lady herself, in that he's far more comfortably fixed than a younger man would be. That *is* one of your primary concerns, is it not? That you and your child should have a home and be taken care of?"

Her dark eyes, so animated only moments ago, had gone cold. Perhaps I should have given way before them, but I could not. Revulsion fanned my agitation.

"But that's nearly as old as Papa was! And there must be more to life than having a roof over one's head . . . there must be friendship and respect and love . . ."

"Love will come with time," she assured me smoothly, her lips curving once more into what seemed to me a parody of a smile. "As for friendship and respect . . . I hope you realize that I would not have arranged for you to marry anyone who was not a perfectly decent and respectable man. The second most important consideration, or perhaps it is first, is that of your good name, is it not? Any woman who has ever attempted to rear a child without a father will tell you how difficult that is, if not completely impossible. Suicide often seems a more pleasant alternative."

"But he's . . . he's *fat* . . . and I'd be expected . . ." I couldn't put it into words, but I didn't have to. Her smile deepened, as if she had genuine liking and compassion for me, although that was hard to credit if she expected me to marry this man.

"My dear child, you had only a few nights with your Francis, and you think romance is all! Truly, in the dark there is little to choose between men, and at any rate you will soon accustom yourself to the marital duties."

I scrambled to my feet, knocking over the straight chair on which I had been seated, my voice rising in spite of my determination to retain control of it. "Is that what you did with my papa? *Accustomed yourself to the marital duties?* Is that how you felt about him, that in the dark there is little to choose between one man and another?" I knew I was becoming hysterical, that I must not earn this woman's ill will, yet my voice continued to climb. "I don't believe Papa married you! I don't believe he would have done such a thing!"

For a moment it appeared that I had overstepped what my self-proclaimed stepmother would allow, for she rose, too. She was taller and heavier than I, and when her hand moved I had not time to dodge it and took the open-palmed slap full strength across the cheek.

"You are hysterical," she said then, quite calm. "I think you forget yourself, Saunielle."

Even now I could not stop my tongue. I started to cry, not because of the blow, although it had been painful, but in sheer misery and willful repudiation. "You say you married Papa, but I've only your word for it! I haven't seen *your* marriage papers, either!"

She surveyed me in a detached fashion for a moment. "So you

haven't. Well, if that will make you feel any better, I'll show them to you. What I said was not meant as any disrespect for your father, my dear. I admired him and I liked him. To say that we enjoyed a grand passion at our ages would be absurd. But we married because of our mutual loneliness and need, which is a perfectly respectable reason to marry. I have no reason to think that if dear Edward had lived we would have been anything but companionably satisfied." She walked to her dresser and began to rummage in a remarkedly untidy drawer. "Well, I don't seem to be able to locate the marriage papers at the moment, but they're here somewhere. I'll find them when I have time for a more leisurely search."

She came back to face me, standing sobbing quietly as I now was. "Under the circumstances, I choose to forgive you for your anger and your rash words. As your stepmother, I have undertaken to provide for you to the best of my ability. Within a matter of weeks it will be apparent to everyone that you are carrying a child. Since you have seen fit not to confide in your own family that you were married to this Francis, it seems unlikely to me that even they will accept your explanations as true at this late date, although they may pretend to. You will have to admit the entire story sounds rather farfetched."

I made no reply, mopping ineffectually at my face with a handkerchief so sodden that it was of no use whatever.

"You are, of course, at liberty to order your own life in any way that you choose. If you care to bear a child, and undertake its support and to rear it in shame and disgrace, that is entirely your affair. I will certainly take no steps to force you into this proposed marriage, although I personally, from a mature point of view, believe it to be the only course that is not completely foolhardy. Quite possibly you are not at this moment capable of making a rational judgment, and I suggest that before rejecting dear Alastair out of hand . . . and he is a very kind and generous man, I assure you . . . you give it some thought."

She withdrew from somewhere on her person a handkerchief which she pressed into my hand. "I do not think you are in any condition to exhibit yourself at the table, so perhaps it would be best if Phoebe brought your dinner to your room. I hope that you will bathe your face and eyes and get a good night's sleep . . . and do some serious thinking! In the morning you can tell me what you have decided, so that I may convey to Alastair your final decision."

I do not know how I found my way back to my own room. I do remember that I had exhausted myself in a fit of tears by the time Phoebe appeared with a tray, her face grave and concerned.

I took one look at the enticingly prepared tray and pushed it aside. "Take it away. I'm not hungry."

"But you need to eat, miss. For the baby's sake, if not your own," she added cunningly, thinking that would provide the proper impetus.

I looked down at my still-flat stomach. "I hate it. I don't want it, I don't ever want a child!"

"Oh, miss! Oh, you know that isn't so! The poor little baby didn't do anything to cause this predicament!"

This was quite true, but I was in no mood to be logical. "If it weren't growing there I wouldn't have to do anything I didn't want to do. I'd be free to find a position to support myself. She couldn't force me into a disastrous marriage if it weren't for the baby!"

"Oh, Miss Saunielle! Is that what she's trying to do? But she's only your stepmother, and you're nearly of an age to do what you like. Surely she can't force you to marry someone if you don't want to!"

At that the tears I had thought exhausted flowed anew. "It's monstrous, Phoebe! It's cruel and wicked and wrong to expect me to marry Alastair Goodwin, and he *is* old, even if she said he wasn't!"

Her jaw dropped. "Mr. Goodwin? Is that who she wants you to marry?"

"You see! Even you think it's monstrous, because it is! Phoebe, what am I going to do?"

She moistened her lips, thinking furiously, but no more successfully than I. "I don't know, miss, but it might not be so bad. I mean, he's a kind gentleman, I think. And he has enough money to set you up in your own home, I'm sure. He'd take care of you."

"Take care of me! Is that what you think is the most important thing? A roof over my head and food in my mouth?"

"Well, it's important enough to think about very carefully, miss. On the other hand, I don't see how she can actually make you marry him if you don't want to."

I knew that, of course. Mrs. Fox herself had said it, very neatly tossing it into my lap. It was up to me. Yet she had made it clear that if I did *not* follow her advice and marry Alastair Goodwin, she would wash her hands of me. I would be on my own.

I flung myself face down on the pillow with a cry of anguish. "I can't do it, Phoebe! I can't! Oh, if only Papa were here, he'd never suggest such a terrible thing. I know he wouldn't! Or if only Francis had not died!"

"Were you really in love with Francis, miss?"

It was asked so calmly that it took a few moments to penetrate my rebellious mind. When it did, I sat up and stared at her. "What do you mean by that? Of course I was in love with him!"

"You scarcely had time to get to know him, did you, miss? Only a few evenings at choir practice, and maybe walking home from

church. The only time you had alone with him was when your aunt
went off to Petersburg for a few days, wasn't it?"

"What's that got to do with it? Falling in love doesn't take months,
you know."

"No," Phoebe agreed. Her mouth softened, and I knew she was
thinking of Tom, although she was too considerate to mention her
own happiness in the face of my despair. "But it takes a little time,
miss, to get to really know a person. Talking to them and learning
how they think and feel about things, that's just as important as
touching. Touching can be so exciting it makes you think you're in
love when you aren't, not really."

"When did you become such an expert? Oh, Phoebe, I'm sorry, I
don't mean to be horrid to you, it's only that I don't want to marry
an old man and I'm frightened of what will happen to me if I don't!"

"I know that, miss. I don't mind if you're a bit sharp, I would be
myself, I guess, in your shoes. Only they did say that Mr. Francis
Verland stole money from the bank, and if he was really that sort of
person it doesn't seem likely he'd be one you'd fall in love with, not
if you knew him all the way through."

"That was a mistake, Phoebe. They only thought he took the
money because it was gone and he'd disappeared, too. Only then
they found out the other clerk was gone, as well, that Lionel Erquart,
and Francis . . . Francis was in the river."

"There was talk in the village they might both have been in on it,
and had a falling out," Phoebe said, "and that would explain how he
came to be in the river."

This at least served the purpose of taking my mind off myself momentarily. "I can't believe that, Phoebe."

"No, miss, I know it's hard to accept. But the truth of the matter is
nobody knows for sure, since one was dead and the other left for
parts unknown, but a lot of people who knew Mr. Verland a lot
longer and probably better than you did think that might have been
the way of it."

"Phoebe, do people think Francis was . . . was killed? Deliberately, because he had a disagreement with Mr. Erquart, and they
quarreled?"

"It's only guessing, miss. But certainly a number of people think
so."

"But you never said anything like that to me!"

"No, miss. Wasn't much point, with him dead and you already carrying enough burdens for two. But now . . . well, now maybe it
would help you to face up to things, if you didn't think that Mr.
Verland was so perfect. Because," and she screwed up her small
freckled face in her urgency to make me understand, "if you thought
you loved him, and he wasn't worthy of your loving at all, miss, then

maybe the other way around could work out, too. I mean, you think of Mr. Goodwin as old, but there's lots of older men make good husbands, and if he's kind and pleasant it's possible you could come to love him, miss. Isn't it?"

I stared at her, numb and mute in my emotional torment, and I could not reply. But I was convinced within my heart that loving Alastair Goodwin was forever beyond my capabilities.

◇◇◇◇◇

There was nothing for it but to face the gentleman at the breakfast table. I thought of pleading illness and not going down, but Phoebe persuaded me of the lack of wisdom in such a course. For might not all the others wonder what caused this illness and at some future time speculate on the prematurity, or lack of it, when my child was born?

I had spent a wretched night and my eyes showed it, for all that I bathed them in cold water and accepted some of Belle Fox's face powder to try to cover the worst of the ravages.

I could not have been an entirely pretty sight when I finally descended the stairs, but Alastair Goodwin was there to greet me with a smile at the foot of the stairs. Though my every impulse was to turn and flee, I kept going until I reached him, wondering if he were already under the impression that I had agreed to marry him.

"Good morning, my dear Saunielle. You don't mind if I call you that, do you?"

I murmured something noncommittal, managing not to flinch when he lifted his hand and put it over mine on the banister as I reached the last step.

"I only wanted to tell you that . . . that I do hope you will consider becoming my wife. I was most taken with you the moment I saw you, you know. Very pretty girl, and very sweet. I know you're very young, but my mother was sixteen years younger than my father, and they were very happy together. I'm sure we can be, too, you know."

Estelle, coming in from the front porch with a newspaper in her hand, eyed us sharply. "Good morning," she said, pleasantly enough, but I saw that her gaze roved over my figure and I knew that Belle Fox had told her about me. It was impossible to restrain the color that flooded my face and throat.

"Good morning," my intended bridegroom said, and the smile he bestowed on both of us was so sunny and genial I might have warmed to him had he been engaged to anyone else.

However, sitting beside him at the vast table, forcing myself to make some pretense of eating, I imagined countless mornings such as this, with this man as my husband across the table, my abdomen swelling perceptibly, as I listened to him discuss the dreary small events that made up his days. I had spent a good part of the night imagining what it would be like to share a bed with him, and regardless of Belle Fox's "mature opinions" I knew that so far as *I* was concerned there was a great deal to choose between men, in the dark or otherwise.

Happily oblivious of my inner turmoil (was it that or the pregnancy that made me feel queasy again?), Mr. Goodwin chattered on about the stock market and the price of beer and the possibility that I might do him the honor of reading aloud from a volume he had discovered in the library on the history of Napoleon.

Mrs. Fox paid me no special attention; she might even have forgotten our session yesterday evening. But I was acutely aware of her presence, her dark eyes as they occasionally swept around the assembled company, and knew that she missed nothing about my appearance or demeanor.

The ordeal of breakfast was finally over and I had managed not to lose any of it as yet when we all stood and moved out of the room and on our various ways. Pity created a diversion by announcing rather loudly that there were rats on the third floor.

There was a moment of embarrassed silence, and then our hostess said with a touch of frost, "I think that is most unlikely, Miss Calhoon."

"I heard them," Pity said with the asperity of one whose word is questioned. "Scritch-scratching around. Rats."

I had been over almost all of the house by this time and had found it to be clean and tight and well kept, and I, too, thought it most unlikely, although any house of course might entertain an occasional mouse. "A house makes various sounds at night, Aunt Pity. Perhaps it was only the timbers creaking as the temperature changed."

The old lady made a sound of disgust. "I've been living in big houses for seventy years, and I know the sound of the timbers creaking. This was rats. And it wasn't at night, it was in the daytime. I'd put out some traps, if I were you, ma'am."

With that she swept away. I didn't know what Pity was doing to occupy herself while Dodie and I had been sewing. If only she hadn't been so old and her mind so apt to wander, I would have been pleased to have consulted her rather than Mrs. Fox in my troubles. But Pity could no longer be of help to anyone, not even herself.

I believe the others were in more of a hurry than usual to quit the dining room, fearing perhaps that Pity's observation would call for some comment on their own part and not wanting to make one. Only Mr. Goodwin lingered at my side.

"Mrs. Fox told me that you need a short time to consider, my dear. Naturally you may have all the time you wish to make up your mind regarding such an important step" (he could not know the irony of this) "but I urge you not to delay, for both our sakes. An innocent young girl needs a protector in a big city like this. And I'm fully prepared to make a generous financial settlement as soon as you say the word. Of course, as my wife, you would want for nothing, and I would make you a generous personal allowance. You have only to let me know, or if you are too shy for that, relay the information through Mrs. Fox. Fine woman, Mrs. Fox."

He was off to peruse the newspaper, leaving me gazing after him in a decidedly unsettled state of mind.

A generous financial settlement? *And* a generous personal allowance? Did he mean them both for me? Or—an insidious idea crept into my mind—was he referring to a financial settlement with Mrs. Fox?

Surely that wasn't what he'd meant at all. The notion was so gross as to be untenable, that my stepmother in her avowed concern for me would sell me, at a profit to herself, to an older man.

Yet something in the man's voice, his tone . . . dear heaven, what was I to think? More important, what was I to *do?*

I made my way toward the kitchen, to where Phoebe was once more immersed in suds, and the ugly little bulldog squatted at the foot of the back stairs, his bulging eyes keeping us both under surveillance.

Phoebe looked quickly at me to ascertain my frame of mind. "You're looking a little better this morning, miss."

"I'm not feeling any better. In fact I'm feeling upset and angry. Phoebe, I think there's a possibility that Mrs. Fox told Mr. Goodwin she'd arrange for me to marry him for a price."

"A price? But you haven't any money."

"I don't mean that I would be expected to pay *him,* I mean that he expects to make some sort of financial settlement upon *her,* if I agree to marry him."

She forgot about the dishes. "Whatever makes you think that?"

"Something he just said to me. Phoebe, talk to Estelle, see if you can find out if she's made any such agreement!"

"I'll try, miss, but we don't talk all that much. She's too snooty for the likes of me, and all she's interested in is clothes and men and getting her hands on some money and some jewels one day. She only speaks to tell me where the scrub brushes are, that sort of thing."

"There's a mercenary streak in her," I admitted. "And I'm wondering if the same streak runs through her aunt."

"She's not overgenerous, Miss Saunielle, except in matters pertaining to herself. She likes to eat well, and dress well, and this house is certainly beautiful. But when I asked for the afternoon off, to go with Tom to meet his brother, she was very short with me, as if I hadn't a right to a few hours away from the kitchen. It's not that I'm not

grateful to be given a roof over my head and my meals, you understand, but it's customary to pay wages to a cook and housekeeper.
She's asking me to take on quite a few chores and to date she hasn't
said a word about any cash changing hands. I'll keep my eyes and
ears open, that I will."

"Are you going off with Tom after lunch, then?" I felt a moment
of envy that Phoebe was young and carefree and could spend some
time with her young man. A young man who'd be content reading
Black Beauty or *Oliver Twist* instead of a dull tome on the battles of
Napoleon.

"For a few hours, yes. His brother's at home today."

"I see. Phoebe, will you ask Tom if he's going to be seeing that
Mr. Rohann? I've discovered I don't have the Jaubert ring, and I
think that either those bandits got away with it or he still has it and
doesn't know who it belongs to. I'd like to have it back."

"I'll ask him," Phoebe promised.

Once more Alfred refused to allow me to use the back stairs, and
this time not even the promise of a bit of bread would lure him away
from his self-appointed post.

"He's spoiled rotten," Phoebe said. "It'll take meat, and I don't
have any. I guess you'll have to use the other stairs."

Mrs. Fox did not approach me for a decision on the vital question.
She did enter the sewing room when both Dodie and I were there
and tell us which of the bolts of cloth might be used for our own
needs, and to have a fitting on the suit we were making for her, expressing herself as being well satisfied with our progress.

I was sitting near the front window and saw Tom when he approached the house, and on impulse I put down the chemise I was
stitching. "I'm going down to talk to Tom, Dodie. I don't know when
I'll be back."

She looked up at me, surprised, but offering no protest. My feet
clattered on the upper stairs until I encountered Estelle on the second-floor landing.

She was, as usual, inappropriately dressed for a young woman
spending an afternoon at home. There wasn't a line of her thin body
that wasn't clearly outlined under the flame-colored silk that would
only have been suitable for evening wear. Yet I felt a fleeting moment of envy, for it was a beautiful dress and I'd never in my life had
anything made from such a piece of goods.

My need to escape suddenly expanded. I wanted to be out of the
house, out of anything connected with the place, and I suddenly
knew where I wanted to go.

"It's dangerous to run on the stairs," Estelle observed. "You'll fall
and break your neck."

At the moment I couldn't have cared less; it would have solved all my problems in one quick moment. I sounded a bit breathless. "Where did you say Papa was buried?"

She regarded me coolly, as if assessing the reason for my wanting to know. "I didn't say, did I?"

"Well, where is he buried?"

"In the cemetery, naturally."

"Which one?" In a city the size of San Francisco, I knew there must be more than one.

Her hesitation was brief. "Calvary. Why?"

"Where is it?"

It seemed to me that alarm flared in her eyes, but then she shrugged and I decided I must have imagined it. "Up that way. There are half a dozen cemeteries over there, big ones. Thousands of graves."

I turned away from her and went on down to the lower level. I would go and visit Papa's grave, and maybe, sitting there and trying to think what sensible advice he would give me if he could, I could come to some sort of reasonable decision. At the very least, I would have had a few hours away from the oppressive atmosphere of the house.

Tom had come, as was fitting, to the back door. I caught them just as he and Phoebe were about to slip out again.

"Tom, will you be seeing Mr. Rohann?"

He was looking fit and content, except that his arm was still in a sling; it didn't appear to bother him. "Not for a day or two, miss; I spoke to him this morning."

Disappointment silenced me, although I couldn't have said why this should be so. If he had the ring he would return it when I made contact; if he didn't, it was lost to me forever. Either way, there was nothing urgent about it.

"He was in a tearing rage, he was. I was surely glad it wasn't *me* he was wanting to tear limb from limb."

Mildly distracted, I asked who he was angry with.

"I couldn't get the gist of it, really. Family problems of some sort, I guess. Anyway, he was packing his bags and moving to the Palace Hotel. You remember, the one across from the boardinghouse where you went when we first got here? Cursing and swearing, he was, and he threw a hairbrush through a window just before I got there, I heard tell."

So I wasn't the only one with problems. Well, I'd trade mine for his, sight unseen, I thought wryly. "Well, when next you do see him, would you ask about my ring, Tom? He may still have it."

He promised to do so, and then after taking a minute or two to tell me about their proposed outing, during which they would take a cable car to the rooming house where he was staying with his brother, they were off.

I had come down without a shawl, but I decided that while the sun was shining I could get by without one. I had only the vaguest of directions to the cemetery, but I knew that the ocean was off in the direction Estelle had indicated, so the cemetery couldn't be so terribly far away.

I walked briskly for some three blocks, welcoming the strain on my muscles after too many hours sitting over my sewing, and then I saw the grassy expanse behind a wrought-iron fence, and the marble of tombstones.

When I reached a gateway, however, it was to find that the cemetery was the wrong one. Calvary, Estelle had said. Well, she'd also said there were a number of graveyards, and there were, all clustered together in one area.

When I located the proper one, I came to a halt, leaning a hand across the fence, staring at the sign.

Papa, although he said he considered himself a Christian, had never belonged to a denominational church and had seldom gone to services with Mama and me as Methodists.

And in Mrs. Fox's house I had not seen one single thing to indicate that she had any religious affiliations at all.

Yet the sign clearly stated that Calvary was a Catholic place of burial. I stared at it, uneasiness combining with my exertions to make me feel strange, half ill.

Why should Papa have been buried in a Catholic cemetery, I wondered?

◇◇◇◇◇◇

Instead of finding his grave and sitting for a few quiet moments to attempt to commune with Papa, I walked until my legs were trembling and I talked to the grounds keepers at five different cemeteries. What I learned was bewildering.

There was no one on any of their lists by the name of Edward Marshall Hunter. Of course if he'd been buried recently his name might not yet have been entered, they admitted, but they thought that anyone who had died two months ago must surely have been on it even though his tombstone might not yet be affixed to the grave.

And I was assured most emphatically that no one who was not a Catholic in good standing could possibly have been interred at Calvary.

❖❖❖❖ **15** ❖❖❖❖

I walked more slowly returning to the house on Fell Street, wishing that the cable cars ran north and south in this section of the city rather than only east and west. I tried to think how Estelle could have been mistaken about Papa's burial place. Granted, there was a wide choice of cemeteries, but how could one mistake the name of the proper one when one had presumably attended a funeral there only a few months earlier?

A cable car clanged toward me on McAllister Street, heading toward Market Street, and on impulse I stepped to the curb. "Sir, does this car go anywhere near the Palace Hotel?" I demanded.

"Within a block of it, miss," the motorman said, and following what I knew to be an absurd whim, I dug out a nickel and climbed aboard.

The moment I had taken my seat I knew how ridiculous I was being. To go to a man's hotel alone, even in midafternoon, would scarcely be considered proper conduct for a young lady. If Mr. Goodwin were to learn of it, he might even reconsider the propriety of marrying me. And I could imagine Mrs. Fox's reaction.

Yet I did not want to return to the house. I was perturbed and upset, and perhaps outside counsel would be of considerable benefit. Not that I had any reason to think Mr. Rohann would offer his services in this regard, but he had been kind to Tom, and he was a native of San Francisco. Perhaps in addition to returning my ring, if he had it, he would also give me some advice. Not about my own personal circumstances, I could never confess such a thing to him, but about Papa and the oddness of Estelle's pronouncement that he was buried in a Catholic burying ground.

When I got off the cable car, the Palace was pointed out to me, in case I should be so blind as not to be able to see it. By this time I was having second thoughts about the entire matter, and it was getting late enough so that I really could not afford to spend much time before catching a second cable car home. Had it not been for my frugal soul insisting I could not waste ten cents on an aborted errand, I might well have simply caught the next cable car going in the right direction and forgotten all about Mr. Rohann.

The desk clerk gave me a rather sharp look when I asked for Mr. Rohann's room number, and then apparently decided that anyone so shabby and insignificant-looking must be there on legitimate business. "Up the stairs, and to your right," he directed.

The stairs were nearly my undoing, after all the walking I'd already done today. I had to pause to rest, and then I went on down the carpeted corridor, watching for the correct number.

When I found it I hesitated, for clearly Mr. Rohann was not alone. I could hear voices, male voices, and at least one of them sounded angry. I seemed always to be inadvertently eavesdropping these days, I thought. Yet I had no choice but to interrupt if I hoped to accomplish my mission, although there was slight possibility of discussing anything with Sebastian Rohann if he were not alone.

I swallowed hard, inhaled, and knocked sharply on the door.

The voices ceased.

I waited, but no one came, and I rapped again.

A moment later the door was jerked open with almost enough violence to take it off its hinges.

For a few seconds I did not recognize the former second mate of the *Gray Gull*.

He had shaved off his beard, leaving the mustache, and trimmed the auburn curls into a semblance of a proper haircut. And his clothing was quite different from the rough seaman's clothing he had worn then, being a well-tailored suit of dark broadcloth and a flowered vest of embroidered satin with a silk tie.

He stared down at me, puzzled, and then enlightenment cleared his expression. "Oh, it's Miss . . . Hunter, isn't it?"

"Yes, sir. Excuse me for disturbing you, but I wonder if you might have gotten my ring back from those bandits? I've only just realized that I no longer have it, and . . ."

He stepped backward into a large and lavishly appointed room. I might have hesitated to enter, but the other occupant of the room, a tall thin gentleman leaning against the mantelpiece smoking a cigar, looked most respectable, and I wanted my ring.

"A heavy gold ring with a black stone and an odd monogram on it? JS or some such thing?"

"Yes, that's it. Do you have it, then?"

"It's here somewhere. Come on in, I'll have to look. I thought it was funny nobody claimed it, but I never figured it belonged to you It's a man's ring."

"Yes, it belonged to my grandfather." I shifted my weight uncomfortably when he closed the door, but did not feel brave enough to protest this.

He rummaged in a dresser drawer, where he had obviously simply dumped the contents of his suitcase, and came up with the ring. "Here. I was tempted to wear it myself, but it's too tight for anything but my little finger." He dropped it into my hand and scrutinized my face intently. "How are you getting along? Found a position yet?"

"No, I . . ."

He didn't wait for my reply, however, but spun back to face his companion, who was moving toward us with purpose. "Where are you going?"

"Off. I've told you everything I know, Sebastian. I don't know what you'll want to do, but whatever it is, it will have to be fast, I'm afraid, or it's going to be too late."

"Wait a minute. Wait a minute." Sebastian Rohann poked at the other man's shirt-front with a hard forefinger, and then he turned quickly back to me. "How'd you like to be a lady instead of a wait-ress or a scrubwoman, Miss Hunter?"

A small surge of indignation brought my voice up to an audible level. "I have no desire to be either a waitress or a scrubwoman, sir."

"Aha!" He said it with an air of triumph that struck me as both theatrical and absurd. "How about it, Cromwell? Won't she serve as well as anyone? Get me a magistrate or a preacher, and we'll tie the knot right now!"

I took a step backward, uncertain as to what he was getting at. The man addressed as Cromwell favored me with a sympathetic look, I thought, which did nothing to clarify the situation.

"I'm afraid, Sebastian, that you haven't made yourself clear to the young lady. I don't believe she's assented to your proposal."

"Haven't you? I distinctly heard her say she had no desire to be ei-ther a waitress or a scrubwoman."

"Mr. Rohann, I haven't the slightest idea what you're talking about. I have never had any intention of either scrubbing floors or waiting tables, unless it should one day be in my own establishment."

"Ah, you see, Cromwell, she is ambitious, she envisions an estab-lishment of her own. Well, Miss Hunter, we can do better for you than waiting for you to work up to owning your own restau-rant . . ."

"Sebastian, stop and listen to yourself, and then listen to Miss Hunter. You're talking at cross purposes. She doesn't know what you're getting at, she's just said so. You'll have to make it clearer."

I edged a bit nearer the door, hoping that he hadn't somehow managed to lock it. The Jaubert ring, its chain lost, had been dropped into my purse. I had what I'd come for, and although nei-ther of these gentlemen appeared to have been drinking it occurred to me that I would be wise to leave before the conversation became any more peculiar.

Sebastian Rohann's hand shot out and grasped my arm, just above the elbow. "Am I not making myself clear, Miss Hunter?"

"Excuse me, I must catch the next cable car or I won't get home in time to dinner, and then Mrs. Fox will be vexed with me even more than she is already," I said.

"Who the hell is Mrs. Fox?"

"My . . . my stepmother. Please, Mr. Rohann, if you'll release my arm, I'd like to be on my way."

He sighed. "You're right, Cromwell, she doesn't know what I'm talking about. I thought she looked reasonably bright, but what the hell, in a situation like this one can't be choosy. Sit down, Miss Hunter."

Against my protests, I was forcibly directed to a chair and pushed into it. Rohann took another chair and sat facing me, leaning forward as if to instruct me in some important matter. I was beginning to think that perhaps he *was* drunk, after all, although I could detect no odor on his breath. Behind him, the tall Mr. Cromwell smiled wryly.

"It isn't her intelligence that's at issue, Sebastian. You simply aren't expressing yourself well enough to be understood by anyone who hasn't the facts of the background."

Rohann scowled. "Are you saying I can't speak intelligible English? Never mind, I'll start over again. Please, my friend, get me a magistrate, someone who can perform a legal ceremony, while I make myself clear to Miss Hunter."

Cromwell hesitated, then shrugged. "All right. I'll get one. But I'm not at all sure Miss Hunter's going to go along with it."

Rohann waved an impatient hand at the door. "Go! Go!" Then, his eyes boring into mine, he demanded, "You aren't married, are you?"

"No, I'm not married. Mr. Rohann, please, I really must catch the next cable car . . ."

"Or Mrs. Fox will be vexed with you. Yes, I heard you say that. Forget about Mrs. Fox and listen to me very carefully." His eyes, of that strangely light yet penetrating blue, bored into mine. "I need a wife. Immediately. I am asking you to marry me. Mr. Cromwell has gone to find a magistrate, and when he comes back with one you have only to say 'I do.' Do you agree to that?"

I started to stand up. "You're not drunk at all, you're insane."

He pushed me back into the chair. "Maybe you're right. If you'd been through what I've been through the past couple of days, you'd be insane, too. Obviously you have led a more sheltered life than I thought, or I'm more repulsive than I thought, or something. I'll try again. I have returned home after a two-year estrangement from my family, which consists of my grandfather, Caleb Rohann, and my cousin, Roderick. My grandfather has control of the family fortunes, a sizable portion of which should be mine, since it belonged to my father. However, it is in the control of my grandfather, and because we had a violent disagreement about how the business should be run I left San Francisco to think about it. I came back convinced even more firmly than ever that I am right, but I was prepared to let matters ride, if necessary, until the old man died. The trouble comes in two parts. One, he is now ailing and at the age of eighty-six is not expected to live much longer. The second part is the worst. While I was gone, my cousin Roderick persuaded him to make one of the most asinine wills anyone ever thought up, and unless I can persuade the old man to change it before he dies, that bastard of a Roderick will inherit the entire business. The entire business!"

By this time I was listening to him, although it had been difficult not to bog down on what appeared to have been a genuine proposal of marriage some minutes back.

"You . . . you have to be married . . ." I ventured hesitantly, "in order to inherit the money your father intended you to have?"

"Ah!" He gave a cry of satisfaction. "You're not stupid, after all. Precisely. I have to marry a decent woman and settle down . . . meaning to establish my own home and behave myself. Once the old man's gone they'll play hell dictating as to my behavior, but while he's here Cromwell says I'll have to demonstrate that I'm grown up and responsible . . . and that includes getting married at once."

"But why me?"

"Because I've been gone for two years, and the females I've encountered in the few days I've been back are not the sort who would qualify as respectable wives. I haven't time to go looking for a proper lady. You're here, you aren't married, and if you marry me you won't have to worry about finding a position as a maid, or whatever it was you were looking for. There is plenty of money . . . and as soon as I got in touch with Cromwell . . . he's my lawyer . . . he saw that the trust fund left to me by my mother was made available. But that's a drop in the bucket compared to what's left to be tapped in the family business. And if the old man dies before I can convince him I can handle the responsibility of the presidency of the firm, which as the oldest I'm entitled to, I won't have more than a miserable little allowance, and Roderick will be in control until he runs the entire shebang into the ground. Which, if I know Roderick, will take about six months. Now, will you marry me?"

"The whole idea is the craziest thing I've ever heard of," I said, but my pulses had accelerated and I was looking at this man in a new light. Perhaps he was wild, perhaps he was unstable . . . but he was far younger and more attractive than Alastair Goodwin.

"That only proves you're exactly the sort of wife I need. A good, sensible woman. You mentioned a stepmother. Are you living with her? Happy with her? Satisfied to go on under her thumb until you find some middle-class lout who'll expect you to be his own private housekeeper and maid?"

The thundering in my ears was the result of a pounding heart, I knew, yet it seemed almost to drown out the sensible responses I should be making to such an outrageous and unorthodox proposal.

He leaned toward me, putting a hand on my wrist as it lay on the arm of the chair. It was a hard hand, firm, eager and young; I sensed no gentleness in him, but purpose and resolve . . . and excitement. Sebastian Rohann was everything that Alastair Goodwin was not.

"I'll tell you what. I promise you a marriage settlement, a substantial bank account in your own name, if we can win the old man over in time. I'll instruct Cromwell to draw up the papers and make it legally binding, so that you'll have the protection of control of your own funds. That in addition to what I would normally provide for my wife, of course. What do you say?"

I needed a husband. Though I had been fighting the idea of marriage with Mr. Goodwin, I had begun to give in to it somewhere deep inside, as proved by my deep sense of despair.

And here, seemingly from out of nowhere, had come an alternate choice. I had a moment of guilt, knowing that this man would be much harder to fool than Mr. Goodwin about a "premature birth." Yet he wasn't asking for any affidavit of my innocence and purity, was he? A respectable woman, a decent woman . . . well, I was both of those things.

If I didn't take this man, I would have to take the other. It was not likely that a third choice of action would become open to me, unless I chose to bear a child that might well be regarded as illegitimate and attempted to support it by myself.

It must have been clear that I was wavering, for otherwise I would have rejected the proposition vigorously and at once.

Rohann began to smile, so that even the glacial blue of his eyes took on warmth. Oh yes, much more exciting than Alastair Goodwin! "Is it a go, then, Miss Hunter?"

I was spared having to reply because the door opened and Mr. Cromwell walked in, followed by a round little man in clerical garb. Rohann rose to his feet, drawing me up with him. "Well, that was quick."

"I found Reverend Tallinger here in the hotel," Cromwell said. His gaze settled on me, curiosity in his eyes. "Have you explained the situation to Miss Hunter? Is she agreeable?"

"Yes." He said it with as much assurance as if I had indeed replied in the affirmative. "Let's get on with it. What's your first name? I can't go on calling you Miss Hunter."

"Saunielle," I murmured, causing the Reverend Mr. Tallinger to look from one to the other of us, seeking an explanation for a man not knowing the first name of the young woman he intended forthwith to marry.

"Saunielle Hunter. And I am Sebastian Rohann, and we would like to be married at once, sir."

The minister spoke to me. "Are you agreeable to this, Miss Hunter? You are not being . . . coerced, in any way?"

If I were coerced, it was by circumstances, not by anyone here. I had the sensation of being swept along on a tide beyond my control, and while it was rather frightening it was not exactly unpleasant.

"She is definitely not being coerced," Sebastian spoke for me. "Shall we begin?"

Reverend Tallinger moistened his lips. "At once?"

"At once."

And so I stood with Sebastian Rohann in a hotel room, and the clergyman recited the service . . . without music, without flowers, and with only an attorney who was a stranger to me as a witness, and I was married.

There was a sense of repetition when the ring was called for, but Sebastian's hesitation was brief. "My mother's wedding ring is there in that mess of junk, somewhere, Cromwell. There, with my studs. That's it. Here, will it do for size?"

It did, a narrow band of gold that quickly warmed on my finger. And several bills exchanged hands, and the clergyman was gone.

"I must . . . I am expected for dinner at Mrs. Fox's," I said, coming as it were to my senses at last.

"Where does she live? Does she have a telephone?" Sebastian demanded.

"I don't know . . . I haven't seen one. It's Mrs. Belle Fox, on Fell Street."

"Cromwell will take care of it. Tell them she's been delayed, that possibly she will be able to get there tomorrow. If not, she'll send another message."

"But my things . . ."

The look he gave me was eloquent: that my "things" were not worth picking up. "You won't need them tonight; they'll keep until tomorrow, also."

"No, please, I must get a message to Phoebe, at least. Is there some way to send a note?"

"Cromwell will take it, won't you, Cromwell."

Cromwell's lips twitched, but it seemed to be more from amusement than annoyance at being ordered about this way. "Certainly, miss . . . Mrs. Rohann."

Hotel stationery was produced, and Cromwell was found to have an excellent fountain pen, and I was given five minutes to produce something that would not send the household into fits. I decided to explain as little as possible and trust that my assurance that I was all right would keep them from sending for the police.

Cromwell accepted it gravely. "Will there be anything else, Sebastian?"

"No. I believe we'll go over to what's her name's, on Powell just off Market, Miss Ninvetti?"

"Will you be wanting a carriage?"

"We'll make do with a rental hack, it's not very far. Thank you, Cromwell. I'll be in touch."

"I'm sure you will be," Cromwell said, and the amusement had deepened.

It was with a sense of complete unreality that I descended the stairs with Sebastian and was handed into a carriage for the short drive to Miss Ninvetti's, whoever she was. He made no attempt to explain anything to me, and I was too numbed to think up the proper questions.

Miss Ninvetti had a dress salon.

She swept forward, smiling, a woman built somewhat on the proportions of Belle Fox, but I knew immediately that she was much more tastefully dressed and that her pearls were genuine.

"Miss Ninvetti, good afternoon."

"Mr. Rohann. What a pleasure to see you again. It has been a long time. What may I do for you?"

"Quite a lot, I hope. It may involve keeping your shop open after hours, if that's possible. It's an emergency."

"In an emergency, one always attempts to cope," Miss Ninvetti said. She retained her smile but could not hide the curiosity in her dark eyes nor refrain from scrutinizing me.

"Good. This young lady has recently arrived from Virginia, and all her luggage was lost," Sebastian lied glibly. "She needs to be completely outfitted, head to toe. Morning dresses, afternoon dresses, evening dresses, lingerie, shoes, nightgowns, everything."

Miss Ninvetti sucked in her cheeks. "That will indeed take some time. Please sit down while I speak to my assistants. And then we will see what we can do."

The unreality increased from that point on. I was measured and turned this way and that, undressed to my chemise and petticoat so that various costumes could be tried on; these then were whisked away to be quickly altered.

No one asked me if I liked anything. It was, "Do you care for this, Mr. Rohann?" or "Perhaps in gold, Mr. Rohann," and Sebastian said yes or no and we went on to the next garment.

I had eaten very little that day, and I was beginning to feel faint from hunger. Somewhere along the line the seamstresses were allowed to have coffee and food brought in from a nearby restaurant.

Sebastian and Miss Ninvetti seemed impervious to the demands of the body, and again no one asked me if I cared for anything.

I had been sewing to earn my living for a number of years, but I had never seen such fabrics as these. Nothing that was brought out could have been bought for less than fifty cents a yard, as compared to the five to fifteen cents the women at home would have paid for dress materials.

They were soft and rich and came in the most varied array of colors. I ought to have been in mourning for both Francis and Papa, but even the black frocks scarcely looked as if they were an expression of anyone's grief unless it were the person who had to pay for them.

Paying for them did not appear to be a problem, however. Sebastian did not ask the price of a single item. There were stockings, gloves, hats, purses, and wearing apparel of such an intimate nature that it was embarrassing to see it paraded before a male.

Even the fact that I was not wearing a corset had been made public from the first, and I was allowed to be fitted for one before the dresses were brought out. It was while I was being pinned into a soft rose-colored silk evening gown that the new corset and the hunger together combined to make me sway dizzily and almost pitch off the low stool on which I was standing.

Sebastian was there immediately, taking my arm, helping me down. "What's the matter, aren't you feeling well?"

"I'm . . . I haven't eaten for so long, it's made me giddy."

"Why didn't you say so?" He turned to Miss Ninvetti. "Put her back into that blue crapon, it's a good fit as is, isn't it? Can you do something with her hair, nothing elaborate, just something quick? And I'll get her out of here and off to dinner."

"Of course, Mr. Rohann," the woman murmured, and for a few more minutes I was manipulated as if I were a doll. My hair was loosened and combed out and redone, so that when at last I was returned to Sebastian I scarcely recognized the girl in blue who was reflected from half a dozen mirrors.

He stood looking down at me, critical of every detail, and then the smile broke over his features and he tugged at one end of his mustache and pronounced judgment.

"I'll be damned if you aren't a raving beauty. I think you'll do, Saunielle, my dear, I really think you'll do." And then, over my shoulder to Miss Ninvetti, "Everything that's passable as is, send it over to my suite at the Palace Hotel. When may we expect the rest of it?"

"I'm sure we can have it all ready by tomorrow afternoon, sir," Miss Ninvetti said, and I wondered if those poor creatures in the back of the establishment would have to work all night to accomplish that.

No money changed hands. If he could manage this sort of thing now, I wondered how rich he would be once he'd inherited the anticipated share of the family business.

I would have been less than human, even under circumstances such as these, if I had not responded to a dress such as the one I was wearing. It was a beautiful thing, by far the finest I had ever had, and I gloated over it even as I speculated on just how difficult it would be to earn it.

A brief carriage ride took us back to the hotel, where arrangements were made for supper to be served in our suite.

I do not remember what we ate. I do remember that there was wine and that it was not the deliciously sweet stuff I was used to but what Sebastian referred to as "dry." I didn't care for it, but sipped obediently when he urged it upon me.

"Now," he said when we had finished, leaning back in his chair and smiling. "Let's see how Mrs. Sebastian Rohann impresses the old man."

I stared at him, momentarily befuddled. "You mean now? Tonight?"

"Tonight, indeed, my love. Who knows whether he'll still be functioning tomorrow? Let's go." He stood, pulling back my chair, and I rose as if in a dream . . . or, more accurately, in a nightmare, biting my lip but prepared to earn my keep. If nothing else, I should be able to convince "the old man" that I was a lady.

◇◇◇◇ 16 ◇◇◇◇

I had thought Belle Fox's house to be enormous. It would have fitted easily into one wing of the house on Taylor Street where old Caleb Rohann lived.

"What do you think of it?"

"It must be impossible to heat," I observed, sounding more composed than I felt.

He laughed. "That it is. It's a mausoleum. Takes about twenty servants just to dust. Ah, here's Marlon."

Marlon I took to be a butler. He was formally dressed, austere, and carefully allowed no expression on his ancient face.

"Good evening, Mr. Sebastian."

"Good evening, Marlon. We'd like to see the old man . . . my wife and I. May we go up?"

Not by so much as a flickering eyelash did Marlon reveal that he was surprised that Sebastian had taken a wife in the interval of a few hours since he'd left this place. "I will inquire, sir," he said.

We were ushered into a foyer nearly as large as the one at the hotel. It had some sort of tiled floor that echoed hollowly under our feet and it was cold enough to make me draw my wrap more closely around me. I stared at the light fixture high overhead. "Is that electric light?"

"Yes. Damned nuisance. He had among the first ones installed in San Francisco, and they were always blowing out or setting a fire at the most inopportune moments. How do you like my ancestors?"

The portraits lined the walls, dark, somber pictures. "None of them look anything like you."

"No. I'm a throwback to my maternal grandfather. That's the old man, there. Caleb III. It was painted twelve years ago."

I stepped closer to this one. The subject was an elderly man, tight of lip, firm of jaw, even more austere than Marlon. "He looks charming," I murmured.

Sebastian cast me a startled look, and then a wariness came into his eyes, as if he were wondering if there might not be more to me than he had supposed.

"Mr. Rohann will see you, sir," Marlon said from behind us.

I had assumed we would climb the stairs that curved gracefully up from one side of the foyer, but my legs were to be spared that further indignity. For there was an elevator, electrically powered, that would take us to the second floor. We were allowed to go up on our own.

I had never ridden in an elevator, and the unexpected sensation in the pit of my stomach nearly made me cry out. I was glad when the gates slid open and we stepped off, and decided I would have preferred the stairs.

The corridor was much wider than the ones at Mrs. Fox's, and carpeted so as to muffle our footsteps. There were more portraits up here, in the same drab colors. They were all male. It would appear that the Rohanns didn't count their womenfolk important enough to bother painting them.

Sebastian opened one of the darkly varnished doors and stood aside for me to enter. My heart in my throat, I did so.

It was the most massive bedroom I had ever envisioned, and since there was only one light burning beside the bed the corners of it were in darkness.

I wondered if Sebastian had intentionally chosen this dress for me to wear tonight because of this room. For it was done entirely in deep blue, not navy but a midnight blue . . . the carpet, the velvet drapes, the bed covering, the upholstered chairs. All the woods were dark.

I alone, in pale blue, provided contrast.

"Good evening, sir. I hope we aren't disturbing you."

The old man in the bed reminded me of nothing so much as a bald gnome. He had thick eyebrows, as if to make up for the lack of hair on his head, that jutted over sharp, dark eyes.

"Marlon said you'd brought your wife."

Sebastian's hand touched my elbow, guiding me to stand beside the bed where the light from the lamp fell upon all our faces, and I was subjected to the most exacting scrutiny of my life. I tried to remember Mama's poise in awkward situations, and I stood quietly, examining him as he examined me.

"My wife, Saunielle. My dear, my grandfather."

He put out a hand and I took it. It was cool enough to suggest poor circulation, boney, and without strength.

"Saunielle. An unusual name. Sounds French." It was almost an accusation.

"My mama was French," I admitted.

"You are not a San Francisco girl."

"No, sir. I was reared in Virginia."

His dark eyes probed at me with the cutting edge of a knife. "How old are you?"

"I will be eighteen the twelfth of October, sir."

His sudden movement was startling; I thought at first that he was grabbing at me, but it was an opened book that lay on the night table beside him. He thrust it into my hands. "Can you read that?"

I lowered it to catch the light, and read aloud.

> *"My hard fortune*
> *Subjects me still to your unkind mistakes,*
> *But the conditions I have brought are such,*
> *You need not blush to take: I love your honour,*
> *Because 'tis mine; it never shall be said*
> *Octavia's husband was her brother's slave.*
> *Sir, you are free; free, even from her you loathe;*
> *For, though my brother bargains for your love,*
> *Makes me the price and cement of your peace,*
> *I have a soul like yours; I cannot take*
> *Your love as alms, nor beg what I deserve."**

The old man grunted and removed the book from my hands to place it, still open, on the bed beside him. "You read well." It was a grudging admission.

"My father was a schoolmaster."

* From *All for Love,* by John Dryden

"You have the speech of a lady."

"My father's family were the Hunters of Hunter's Hill, Virginia. My mother was one of the Jauberts, from Limoges, in France." There was nothing in my family background to be ashamed of; the unsteadiness had left my legs and I felt less gauche than I had a few moments earlier.

"Do you by any chance play the piano?" he demanded.

"Yes, sir."

"Well?" Again it was as if he dared me to meet his exacting standards.

"Yes, sir. Well enough to give advanced lessons to students. My mama was an accomplished pianist."

He grunted once more. "What the devil have you married my grandson for?"

I swallowed against sudden nervousness but my voice did not change. "Why does any woman marry any man, sir?"

"Was it for his money?"

"When I met him," I said truthfully, "I did not know he had any money."

He had been sitting propped among his pillows. He suddenly flopped backward, as if exhausted by the effort of speaking. "Will you come tomorrow and play for me?"

"If you like," I agreed, then looked to Sebastian. "If I may, sir?"

"Certainly. Why not?" There was something new and strange and exciting in Sebastian's eyes.

"At two," the old man said. He closed his eyes, and I knew that we were dismissed.

Sebastian didn't speak until we had closed the old man's door behind us. He paused long enough to light up a cigar and inhale of its smoke before he turned his full attention to me.

"Who the hell are you?"

"Saunielle Hunter, of Virginia."

"You didn't come to San Francisco looking for a position as a housemaid."

"No. I never said I had. You were the one who kept assuming it."

"Why did you agree to marry me?"

"Because I came expecting to meet my father, who would have made a home for me. I found instead that he had died, and I was literally destitute, with several other people to provide for. A woman in my position has few choices, Mr. Rohann."

When he grunted he sounded much like his grandfather. "And I was better than starving to death, eh?"

I couldn't seem to stop swallowing when I was nervous. "I thought so, yes."

For a moment longer his visage held, and then it cracked open in a silent laugh. "Oh, I have done well today, I do believe. I've got me an educated lady, with not only intelligence but spunk. You may be more than I bargained for, Saunielle."

I made no reply to that. And when, back in the suite at the Palace Hotel, he brought out a bottle of brandy and proposed a nuptial toast, I drank with him and felt the warming liquor spread through my system and thought that this must be infinitely better than having married Alastair Goodwin.

◇◇◇◇◇◇

I woke in the morning with a feeling of well-being such as I had not experienced in some time.

Sebastian was already up and dressed, fitting cuff links to his white shirt. He smiled at me. "Good morning. I'm going down for a news-paper and to order breakfast. Take your time, have a bath, if you like. You have half an hour, at least."

But when he had gone I made no move to get out of bed. I lay there with my eyes closed and relived the previous night.

No doubt the brandy had contributed to my acceptance of the inevitable. Like any other well-bred young woman of my generation, I was aware of the evils of alcohol. Many a girl had been led down a wayward path because she allowed herself to be first seduced by drink. Yet in my own case I could not but feel that it made things easier for me.

A major part of the inevitable, of course, was my comparison of Sebastian with Francis. When tears wet my cheeks as I thought of that other wedding night, so short a time ago, Sebastian found them in the dark and kissed them away. And when his passion finally roused mine, and I no longer thought of Francis but gave myself up to the fervor of the moment, I learned that Belle Fox had been at least partly right.

Not that I was not still convinced I could never have so responded to Alastair Goodwin. But I had never anticipated that another man would send the flames through my body as Francis had done, and now I knew that Sebastian was more skilled a lover, as firm yet gen-tle, and I even began to wonder if Phoebe might have been partly right, too.

Where had she come by her reasoning, this little country girl who had never done anything but work in someone else's kitchen, whose grand romance was with a penniless young would-be sailor? Touch-ing could be exciting, Phoebe had said. Oh, I would have to admit to Phoebe that she had been right about that!

I tried again to conjure up Francis' face, but the visage that formed behind my eyelids was a different face, with curly auburn hair and a large mustache and eyes that could be either a warm or a glacial blue, depending on the owner's mood.

Was it possible that Phoebe was right about that, too? That I had been the victim of a girlish infatuation, flattered beyond words when an attractive man showered me with attentions? Had my relationship with Francis continued, would I have discovered that what we had was purely physical? If, as Phoebe claimed a good many people thought, Francis *had* stolen money from the bank, was he the sort of man I could have loved?

To my astonishment, I discovered that I did not want to think about Francis. He was dead, and I would never know the truth about him. While I had a long time to live, and a new husband who was so much an improvement over the one my stepmother would have wished upon me that I must make every effort to build a good marriage with him.

This resolve was strengthened when Sebastian returned, not half an hour but an hour later. He arrived at the same time as the waiter, who wheeled in a little cart and began to lay out our breakfast. I thanked God that my morning sickness seemed to have abated, since I was in no way prepared to explain it to a bridegroom.

"Sorry I took so long, I hope you aren't starved," he said, ignoring the waiter. "I had to wait for a man to arrive to open the vault. I brought you these. Hold out your hands."

I did so, quite unsuspecting, and he emptied the contents of a brocaded bag into my palms.

"They were my mother's. Not many, but all fine things, I think. There's nothing here suitable for daytime wear, but you can play with them until we have an evening out."

I stared at them wide-eyed. A sapphire brooch, surrounded by tiny diamonds. Earrings and a matching pendant that might be either garnets or rubies; I didn't know, but they were exquisite. A single long strand of pearls. A gold and enameled locket containing a wisp of red-gold curl.

"Clipped from my head when I was four, I believe," Sebastian said in wry amusement. "Fancy her having kept it all these years!"

Over scrambled eggs and tender ham I learned a little bit about my husband. That he had had two older brothers, both of whom died in accidents, one with a horse and one at sea. That his father had expired of a lung ailment some four years previously, his mother six months later of a tumor similar to the one that had taken Mama from me.

"Then your grandfather and your cousin are all the family you have?"

"Yes. And Rohann Textiles. In a way all the people who work there are my family. I grew up working in the place, because both my father and my grandfather believe in the heirs learning the business from the ground up. It's a pity they didn't also believe in my ability to think, to learn and grow."

"What did you want to do?" I asked, intrigued. Textiles . . . that meant fabrics, dress goods. No wonder he had been so knowledgeable last night at Miss Ninvetti's.

"I wanted to manufacture ready-to-wear dresses and other items. The old man says that a lady of taste will not wear clothes she buys off a rack. I insist that she will. The modern woman is too busy to do all her own sewing, and not wealthy enough to hire it all done. Besides, by mass-producing common wearing apparel we can provide jobs for more of our people, and it will encourage women to buy things they are now doing without or give them leisure for other things when they don't have to spend half their lives plying a needle. I'm convinced that ready-to-wear clothes can be of good quality and that we'd make money creating them."

It sounded reasonable to me. "Then why won't your grandfather let you try it?"

"Because it would cost a lot of money to set things up in the first place, and he's not convinced that ladies used to quality clothes will support such an industry. He's a pig-headed old goat." Sebastian looked at me speculatively, a smile returning to his lips. "But I think he liked you."

"What am I to do when I return there this afternoon?"

"Read to him. Play the piano for him, if that's what he wants."

"I don't know how well I'll manage if I have to talk to him."

"You did all right last night. Say what you think. Don't try to impress him; he's a shrewd old devil, and he sees through fraud in a second. That's one reason I couldn't fool him into thinking I thought differently than I do, even if I wanted to. Suppressing my opinions and anger is like trying to hide the chicken under the egg; they're just too large to make it possible. So all you have to do is be what you are: a respectable woman. I can't image how I came to be so lucky as to find you this way. If I'd settled for a woman off the streets he'd have known in a minute."

I had an uneasy moment wondering how Sebastian and his grandfather would feel if they knew I was carrying a child, but there was nothing I could do about that.

"I'll have to see about finding us another place to live. A hotel suite is all right for a bachelor, but scarcely the thing for a married couple. I take it you feel the same way I do about the family home; it makes a nice museum but it's hardly a place we'd want to live, even if the old man weren't in it. The sensible thing is probably to build a house to our own specifications, but that takes time. So I'll see what might be available in a town house to rent."

I cleared my throat. "Does it have to be an entire house? I mean . . ."

"Yes? What? Do you have something in mind?"

"Mrs. Fox . . . my stepmother . . . has this lovely big house. She has suffered some sort of financial reverses, and for the time she's taking in guests. Right now there are four elderly gentlemen." I saw the furrow forming on his brow. "But she has a suite of rooms on the second floor . . . a beautiful lady's room done in pink and white, and a gentleman's bedroom and study. I should think it would be most comfortable while other arrangements are being made."

"A rooming house?"

"It's not a proper rooming house," I assured him earnestly. "It's a lovely private home, and . . . and there's an enormous library and a music room with a piano. It's exactly the sort of house I would have designed for myself if I'd had a free hand."

The furrow smoothed itself out. "And you'd like to live in the pink and white room."

"It's quite the prettiest room I've ever seen."

"Well, let's go take a look. On Fell Street, you said? We can go on the dinkies, then. I dislike getting out a carriage if I can travel by cable car; they're so damned much safer, especially on the steep hills. Have you finished eating?"

I had, and we had only to find a hat to go with my dress, the same pale blue one I had worn last night, since the rest of the things had not yet been sent over from Miss Ninvetti's, and we were ready to go.

I knew that Phoebe would have had my note, but as it had explained virtually nothing I was nervous at arriving at the house on Fell Street. Belle Fox would not be happy that I'd taken such a step as marriage without her knowledge, I thought. However, with Sebastian there beside me I didn't think her tongue-lashing would be too severe. I did not have the impression that Sebastian had been subjected to many such, nor that he would tolerate them.

The day was one of the city's best, brisk and sunny under a cloudless sky. I could tell that Sebastian approved the neighborhood when we got off the cable car.

He gestured with one hand. "Have you been to the park yet?"

"No. I haven't been anywhere, except to the cemetery, trying to find Papa's grave."

"I'll take you there one afternoon, it's only a few blocks. Golden Gate Park is very pretty, it's over a thousand acres and many people spend their Sundays there. If you like flowers you'd enjoy the Conservatory, and they also have outdoor concerts and baseball games and various wild animals in fenced areas."

I agreed that I would look forward to seeing it. And then we had reached the house, and we went up the steps and rang the bell.

It was Phoebe who opened the door, her eyes wide and then astonished when she saw Sebastian. "Oh, Miss Saunielle, you can't imagine the commotion you caused by not coming home last night! Mrs. Fox was most upset, she was! Mr. Rohann, sir. Come in, come in."

"I'm sorry I couldn't have explained, Phoebe, but there was no time. Mr. Rohann and I were married yesterday afternoon."

For a moment it seemed that her eyes would bug out of her head. She was taking in my new clothes, and the gold wedding band and I thought it might be too much for her.

"Oh, miss! Congratulations! Oh, I hope you will both be very happy!"

"We have that intention," Sebastian said casually. "Now, if you'll be so good as to call Mrs. Fox."

Belle came from the back of the house before Phoebe had time to summon her. From her expression I think I might have been in for it, but she was stopped cold by the assured gentleman beside me even before he said a word.

"Saunielle, my dear. We were concerned. Your note to Phoebe was scarcely reassuring." She looked questioningly at Sebastian.

"Since Miss Hunter and I were married yesterday afternoon and had a number of things to attend to, the note was the best that could be managed," he said, with a tone indicating it was of little importance to him what she thought about the matter.

It would be accurate to say that this news was a shock to her. I saw the color go out of her face, but she recovered quickly. "I see. I had no idea. Saunielle did not mention to me that she was acquainted with . . . anyone. I am Mrs. Fox, and you are . . ."

"Sebastian Rohann." I could tell by the way he said it that he took it for granted the name would be recognized, and I also felt that it *had* been, for her eyes dilated in what might have been grudging respect. "My wife tells me that you have a small suite of rooms available to rent that might do for us until we can find a house of our own."

She recovered fairly quickly. "Why, yes, ah . . . I do have two bedrooms and a study . . ."

"Could we see them?"

I didn't understand why she was suddenly so flustered. I had not so far observed that she was a woman who flustered so very easily, not on a minor matter such as the renting out of a suite of rooms. "Why . . . why, certainly. I will show them to you myself."

I was not certain, either, why I did not want to leave this house. Perhaps it was the ties with Dodie and Pity and Phoebe, although I could probably have taken them with me if my husband continued as indulgent as he had so far proved to be. And I did not much care for either Belle Fox or her niece, Estelle. I thought it was the house itself, which had a good air about it . . . a welcoming house, as if I had come home to it, even though I had never in my life lived in a place half so grand.

It was vastly different, climbing the stairs this time, than it had been on our arrival at this house. I was no longer a frightened girl without funds, dependent upon whatever charity my stepmother might see fit to bestow.

We looked at the study first, with its shelves of books and a smoking stand and comfortable leather-covered chairs, and then the adjoining bedroom, equally masculine and elegant. I could tell nothing from Sebastian's demeanor; his scrutiny of the rooms was casual, almost disinterested.

"And here," Mrs. Fox said, opening the door that joined this room to the next one, "is a lady's boudoir, of course."

Sebastian's cool blue eyes swept across it appraisingly, and then, to my relief, he nodded. "It suits you," he said to me. "Very well. We'll take it. Is there a telephone in the house? I'll arrange to have our belongings brought over."

There was a telephone, in a sort of closet under the stairs on the first floor. While Sebastian and Mrs. Fox went to it, Phoebe and I remained behind in the pink room. The moment the others were out of sight, Phoebe hugged me with a squeal of delight.

"Oh, miss, I don't know how you did it, but it's marvelous! Mrs. Fox is furious, though, and since you put me up to listening I can tell you why. She like to had conniptions when you didn't show up at dinnertime last night, and poor Mr. Goodwin was asking about you and she didn't know what to tell him. I sort of hung around the back parlor when they thought I was washing up, and I heard them talking. I got the impression real strong, miss, that there was money changing hands between them if you married him, because it sounded like he didn't intend to pay unless you were a decent girl, and he couldn't understand why a decent girl wouldn't come home at night."

"Oh, Phoebe." This confirmed my suspicion, but it was incredible, all the same. "That's the same as selling me into slavery! How could she do such a wicked thing?"

"That isn't all, miss. I listened around several places while you were gone. That Estelle and Mrs. Fox had a regular row later, upstairs, and Estelle said it was a good thing you were gone and she hoped to God you'd not come back at all, there was more important considerations than money! Now what do you make of that?"

I didn't know what to make of it. Perhaps it had been a mistake to return, but if that was the case we could always leave. Sebastian was accustomed to finer accommodations than these, and he was only indulging me, I thought.

I remembered, then, that Estelle had told me Papa was buried in the Calvary cemetery. "I'm going to find Mrs. Fox and ask her, perhaps Estelle was mistaken. Because it's a Catholic cemetery, Phoebe, and the grounds keeper seemed quite certain they would never have accepted anyone who wasn't of that faith."

"It does seem odd she wouldn't get it right," Phoebe agreed. "Still, I don't think Estelle is all that bright, and she doesn't care much about things of concern to other people, only herself. I don't know what she's got against you, though; you've done her no harm."

"Well, it's not likely she'll do me any now. I'm going down to speak to Mrs. Fox, Phoebe. Oh, wait until you see all the clothes Sebastian has bought for me! I know I ought to be in mourning, but truly I don't want to wear black for months and months, not when I've all these lovely things. I don't think Papa would mind, he didn't want me in black after Mama died, no more than for a few weeks."

Phoebe looked into my face. "You're finding Mr. Rohann not so hard to take," she said knowingly, and laughed when I blushed. "Ah, I'm teasing, miss, you know I wish you well! And I'm glad you're back, maybe you can do something with Miss Pity. She kicked up a dust at dinner last night again, she did. Insisted there are rats up on the third floor, and got Mrs. Fox quite red in the face. I've not seen any sign of them, I think she's only getting old. Maybe you could talk to her."

I promised to do so, and went quickly down the front stairs. Sebastian was still engaged with the telephone; I could hear his voice, so I went on until I found Mrs. Fox in the dining room. She and Estelle were doing something with the silver, sorting it into a special box.

They had been quarreling, as was obvious from their flushed, angry faces, but they ceased when I entered the room. Estelle cast me one quick, inexplicably hostile glance, and went on jabbing knives into the proper place in the silver chest.

Belle, too, was angry, but she forced a smile for my benefit, a smile that went no further than the grimace on her lips. "My dear, you have done very well for yourself. Mr. Rohann! He's a very wealthy man, I believe."

"Yes, I believe he is. Mrs. Fox, I wanted to ask you about Papa's grave. I think Estelle made a mistake when she told me he was buried in Calvary Cemetery."

"In Calvary?" Belle's eyebrows rose. "Did Estelle tell you that?"

"Yes. Only it's a Catholic burial ground, and Papa was not Catholic."

"I must have made a mistake. I didn't go to the funeral," Estelle said very quickly. "I thought you said it was Calvary, Belle."

"No. No." Belle ran a hand under her chin and down her throat, resting it on her bosom. "It was Laurel Hill. Why . . . why were you asking about that, my dear?"

"Because I wanted to visit his grave. Only I couldn't find it. I went to five different cemeteries, and no one knew anything about an Edward Hunter being buried in any of them."

The moment of silence stretched a bit too far, and then Belle said, "I suppose that's because the headstone isn't there yet. It's been ordered, but it takes time to make up a really nice tombstone. Estelle, if you've finished with these things, you might take some towels up to Mr. Quayle; if you'll excuse me, Saunielle, I want to give Phoebe orders regarding dinner."

Neither of them looked directly at me as they left the room. I stood looking after them and thought that it wouldn't matter about a tombstone, the records kept must be of the *graves*. I didn't know why they were being deliberately evasive, but I was sure they were, and I felt chilled without quite understanding why.

❖❖❖❖ 17 ❖❖❖❖

Although I had dreaded my visit with old Caleb Rohann, it developed that I did not even see him. Sebastian took me to the house on Taylor Street, leaving me in the custody of the ancient butler, Marlon, at the appointed time. He himself had some affairs to take care of with his lawyer; he would be back within a few hours, he promised.

The house was no more inviting in the daytime than it had been at night. Its elegance and richness had no warmth, offered no welcome. I heard no voices save my own and Marlon's, no sounds other than the mechanism of the elevator as we were lifted to the second floor. Everything was padded, carpeted, insulated against the outside world. Even the windows seemed too few, so high up and so far away that little of the bright sunshine penetrated them.

I cleared my throat as we stepped off the elevator. "Will Mr. Rohann want me to read to him, Marlon?"

"Not today, madame. He is not feeling well."

"Oh! Well, perhaps it would be better if I came back . . ."

"He has requested that you play for him, madame. Miss Lucy's piano has been moved into the room next to his bedroom. He asks only that you play. Perhaps he may see you the next time you visit the house."

Somewhat startled by this arrangement, I followed the man into the private sitting room. It was less soberly decorated than the other rooms I had glimpsed; although there was nothing gay about it, it did have the look of having been lived in, for there were books and several comfortable chairs and a good reading light and footstool.

The piano was a recent addition, standing in the middle of the floor, a magnificent grand.

"You will find music in the piano bench," Marlon informed me, lifting the lid. "I believe the instrument is in good tune."

It wouldn't dare not to be, I thought irreverently. "Is there any particular piece, any special sort of music, that Mr. Rohann would like to hear?"

Marlon's face was impassive. "He simply said for you to play, madame."

And so I played. Hesitantly, at first, because I was somewhat out of practice and I was getting the feel of the instrument. But it was a fine one, and in tune as promised, and gradually I forgot the man I was playing for and simply lost myself in the music, selecting favorites of my own as I came to them.

Since my parents had loved the classics, and that was the type of music I found, this was what I played. Handel, Beethoven, Vivaldi, Mozart, Fibich, Liszt, Scarlatti, Krebs, Purcell . . .

I didn't hear Sebastian enter the room; only gradually did I become aware that I had a listener other than the sick old man in the next room. As the last notes of the final melody died away Sebastian put a hand on my shoulder.

"You play very well indeed. I doubt that he's heard anyone play since my grandmother died. This was her piano. Had she been a man, she would have been a concert pianist, I suspect. Aren't you tired? You've been playing for well over two hours, without a break."

I flexed my hands. "Yes. I am tired, I'm out of practice. Do we . . . do we say good-by before we leave?"

"Marlon says not, which is just as well. I'm in no mood to talk to the old bastard; I've just seen a copy of this infamous will of his. Slightly irregularly, I may add, so don't mention it anywhere."

He put the shawl around my shoulders, and I realized that I was cold. How did a sick man bear it in a house so cold?

"How did you manage that, if it's supposed to be a secret?"

"Didn't I tell you? Cromwell is a junior partner in the law firm that serves my grandfather and Rohann Textiles. He first came across the will some eight months ago, quite by accident. He was curious, so he read through it, and then he was appalled, as any thinking person would have been, at the conditions in it. He tried to contact me, sent out messages to half the hotels in the Western Hemisphere. The only trouble was, I wasn't at any of them. It's a lucky thing I came home when I did, or Cousin Roderick would have cut me out completely, damn his eyes. Cromwell thinks Roderick used considerable influence against me, which he might have, living here where he was in constant contact with the old man."

We were entering the elevator by this time, and it struck me that the atmosphere of the house was subtly altered when Sebastian was in it. He seemed to fill a good deal of the space, for all that he was not a large man, and one was no longer oppressed by the silence.

"Anyway, Cromwell didn't hear that I was back in town until yesterday. When he did, he came directly to me to inform me of the absurd conditions of that will. I'll have him to thank . . . and you . . . if we've pulled this off."

"I don't understand why you signed on as a second mate of the *Gray Gull,* and why you had to play cards to win passage money home. It seems that you are not without funds in your own right."

"There's a trust fund left by my mother. However, I wasn't to touch it until the age of thirty. That was set up on the assumption that I would be drawing a salary for my work at Rohann Textiles; Mother didn't foresee that the old man and I would clash and I'd go off on a rampage around the world for two years. Since I had reached the rather advanced state of maturity set by the trust a few months ago, Cromwell saw to it that it was turned over to me at once."

Marlon was there to open the front door for us, and we bid him good-by and continued our conversation as we waited for the returning cable car.

"You speak about Mr. Cromwell as if he were a friend . . . and he calls you *Sebastian*. Yet you refer to him by his surname as if he were an inferior."

He gave a short bark of laughter. "Inferior! Cromwell is inferior to no one, I assure you! His first name is Cedric, but ever since he was seven years old he has made it a practice to bloody the nose of anyone who so addresses him. It was worth it a few times, but he was always taller than I and had a longer reach, and I got tired of having my nose bloodied. Ah, here's our car."

It was amazing what a difference it made, to be escorted about the city by a gentleman. Everything was easier; even the skies seemed brighter and the breezes balmier. Sebastian had lived in San Francisco since he was a boy. He knew people everywhere and called them by their first names . . . waiters, policemen, bankers, business people, the cable-car conductors, old women who sold flowers on the street corners.

He not only knew the city, he loved it. Here he had played ball as a boy. There he attended school. He pointed out Westminister Presbyterian Church, where he had attended services with his mother as a child. He told me who lived in various grand houses, and all about their families and their businesses, and about an old man who sold newspapers at the corner of Market and Powell streets, and about San Quentin, the grim state prison across the bay in San Rafael, and of the army disciplinary barracks on Alcatraz Island, from which it was said to be impossible to escape.

I was astonished at how much I learned on that ride back to Fell Street, both about San Francisco and about the man I had married. More about Sebastian, I thought, than I had learned about Francis in the weeks we had met furtively and briefly. Had Francis been the man I thought him to be? Or was Phoebe right? Had he been no more than a thief who would have brought me grief had he lived?

We arrived at home to learn that all our purchases from Miss Ninvetti's had been delivered, and Phoebe had been putting them away for me in the tall wardrobe in the pink room.

"They won't all fit, miss!" she greeted me enthusiastically, her cheeks bright. "I never saw so many clothes in all my life!"

"Do you think it's wrong of me to wear them, so soon after . . . ?"

"No, and Mr. Sebastian don't think so, either. It's up to a woman to do what her husband likes, isn't it?"

"So long as it's what she likes, too," I agreed, and we laughed and put our minds to deciding what I would wear down to dinner.

"It seems I'm to be maid of all work, as well as cook," she said as she was dressing my hair. "The missus put me to running the carpet sweeper and using a dust rag this afternoon."

"Oh, Phoebe! That is too much of her! Cooking for a household the size of this one is enough for any one person to do!"

Sebastian appeared in the doorway and stood watching, his glance approving the soft rose-colored bengaline he had selected. "Who's this? Mrs. Fox, the slave-driver?"

"She hasn't said a word about paying Phoebe anything above her room and board, and she's cooking for nearly a dozen people, and now she's expected to scrub and clean as well! It hardly seems fair."

He smoothed his mustache along his upper lip. "Why don't we tell her you have need of the services of a full-time maid, and you'd like Phoebe. Let her find herself another cook and maid."

I saw Phoebe's face reflected above my own in the mirror. "Oh, sir! Do you mean it?"

"I'll tell her. Can you get that hair styled within another twenty minutes? Or must I go down to dinner alone?"

"Oh, I'll have it done, sir! Indeed I will!" Phoebe assured him, and

I could tell by her face that my new maid had succumbed completely to Sebastian's charms.

"Oh, Lord, I'd like to see her face when he tells her! But maybe she'll be angry enough to throw me out."

"How can she, if we're living here and you're to be my personal maid?"

"That's right. He won't let her, will he? What do personal maids do all day, Miss Saunielle?"

"I have no idea," I admitted, and when we both began to giggle, Sebastian shook his head and retreated to the study.

Phoebe abruptly stopped laughing. "But I started out to tell you, miss. She told me to run that sweeper thing in her room, Mrs. Fox's. I knew she was going out, I even stood on the second-floor landing and watched her go. So then I took it on myself to look around a bit while I was in her room."

I spun around on the stool. "Phoebe! What did you find?"

"Well, I remember you said she couldn't find that marriage certificate when you asked about the papers. And I remembered too you told me she didn't seem the sort of person your papa would have taken for a wife, not after your mama. So I thought it wouldn't hurt to see what I could find."

"And?"

"And I found what looks like a genuine marriage paper. Not that I ever saw one, but it's sort of official-looking, has all sorts of signatures on it. Hers, and a clergyman's, and one that says Edward Marshall Hunter."

I don't know what I felt, whether the news pleased me or not. "Then she was telling the truth about that."

"She strikes me as one who would lie if it was to her advantage, miss. And that Estelle . . . well, never mind her, it's Mrs. Fox we're talking about. But it looks real, like I said. It was buried at the bottom of a dresser drawer along with some other papers."

"What did the signature look like? Papa's, I mean?"

"How do I answer that? It was like he'd signed his name, that's all I can say."

I sprang up and found my purse, the shabby, pathetic little thing which had carried my few dollars all the way across the country. I'd never have need of it again, for Sebastian had bought me a selection of much finer ones, but it still held Papa's last letter. I brought it out and spread it for Phoebe to see.

"This is his handwriting. Did it look like this?"

She studied it, frowning, then nodded. "I think so, miss. Something like, anyway. Although maybe it was . . . not quite so firm. Still, I suppose a man might be nervous at his wedding, mightn't he?

I don't remember your Papa all that well, but he seemed to me a real gentleman. I don't think Mrs. Fox is a real lady, miss."

"I don't think so, either. Yet she says she married him, and if there's a paper to prove it . . ."

"To tell the truth, Miss Saunielle, I don't think I like her all that much, her nor that Estelle, either. I'm sort of surprised you wanted to come back here and all, when Mr. Sebastian would have found you a house of your own if you wanted."

"He still will, Phoebe." I spoke slowly. "I'm not sure why I wanted to come back, except . . . I love this house. Isn't that odd, when we've been here such a short time, but it's as if . . . as if it were *my* house, my *own* house. It couldn't be more to my taste if I'd done it all myself. Look at this room . . . it has everything in it I ever wanted, and the colors were intended for a brunette, and I feel . . . at *home* here. Even the library and the music room are so perfect, it's as if whoever chose the books chose them just for *me,* all my favorites, all the ones we used to talk about getting one day, when we could afford them . . ."

"Seems strange," Phoebe observed, recapturing my hair with the comb, "that Mrs. Fox would invest so much in books when she doesn't read, and that fancy piano, when all they want to do is listen to the gramophone . . ."

I swiveled again, once more disturbing the effect she was trying to create. My chest felt odd, as if something had clamped around my lungs so that they couldn't fill.

"Phoebe . . . Phoebe, this house is just what Papa would have bought, if he'd been buying a house for us to live in. If he'd had lots of money, I mean . . ."

The comb was suspended in midair. "And he said he was going to have lots of money, didn't he? And he was going to send for you . . ."

We stared at each other, almost forgetting to breathe.

"Oh, miss! What if . . . what if your papa did buy this house? Only if he married Mrs. Fox . . ."

"Whether he married Belle Fox or not," I said in a fierce whisper, "he would never have failed to make provision for me! I know it, Phoebe! If he had married, he expected me to come and live with them. And he would have . . . have set up a trust fund, or something, the way Sebastian's mother did for him, I know he would have. What were those other papers you found in her dresser drawer?"

"I don't know, I didn't look at them all that close," she confessed, "except to see they weren't marriage papers. I would have brought that one for you to see, but I was afraid I wouldn't be able to do it and get it back without her missing it. Maybe I can try again. Miss

Saunielle, you don't think she's only pretending she married him, to take possession of the house?"

"I shouldn't think she could hope to get away with that, not indefinitely, not unless she really did marry him. But there must be a deed to the house somewhere. And he'd have made a will. The moment he came into the money, however much or little it was, he'd have seen a lawyer and made a will. He was that sort of man, Phoebe, always did things sensibly and properly."

"Well," Phoebe said, "then we'll have to find the deed, and the will."

I nodded, then held still so that she could comb the last curl into place. "I think we'd better try," I agreed. "Because if Papa *did* buy this house, then I'm sure I have a right to at least a portion of it."

"Hey, in there! Are you ready?" Sebastian called, and there was no more time to talk.

During the evening, in the light of our conversation, I looked at the house with new eyes. And the conviction strengthened that Papa had had something to do with the furnishing and the decorating of it. So many things beyond those we had thought of reminded me of our own home in Virginia, when Mama was alive, or of the homes my parents had described from their youth.

And here and there was a touch that was pure Belle Fox . . . a picture, an art object that clashed with the taste of the rest of the place, as her personal quarters were at variance with ours. Belle Fox, I thought with growing certainty, had put only a few touches to this house; it had been created by someone whose tastes were totally different from hers. And I vowed that I would not rest until I knew the truth.

It wasn't until we had completed dinner and the gentlemen were to be left for their cigars and brandy that another thought occurred to me. I had not been able to locate Papa's grave. Did that mean that it was not in one of the five cemeteries at all? Was there not only no tombstone but no grave to mark with one?

And in that case, exactly what *had* happened to my father?

◇◇◇◇ 18 ◇◇◇◇

Sebastian declined an invitation to stay with the lodgers, saying that he would take his cigar on the front porch and didn't need the brandy, and that once he'd finished his smoke he would rather like to familiarize himself with the house.

My impression was that neither Belle nor Estelle was exactly happy about this prospect, although they offered no specific objections. Was I, in the light of my admittedly wild new suspicions, imagining things?

There was nothing we could do tonight, but tomorrow . . . tomorrow, there would be an opportunity for either Phoebe or me, when Mrs. Fox was safely engaged elsewhere. I wanted a look at that marriage certificate myself and the other papers as well. It speaks for my frame of mind that it did not even occur to me that what I proposed was probably both illegal and unethical, as well as violating all the rules of behavior in which I'd been indoctrinated. As soon as possible, I was going through Mrs. Fox's papers.

Ten minutes of the gramophone was once more enough for me. I wanted to know what Sebastian thought of the house, and I wanted to talk to Phoebe. Dodie sat listening to the music and repairing her shoe as best she could in preparation for a trip to the store to replace her footwear, and Belle Fox rocked with the bulldog in her lap, relaxed and listening to the latest tunes.

I didn't know where Aunt Pity was, but I found her in the back of the house with Phoebe, getting a drink of water.

"Well, you've done yourself proud, Saunielle," she greeted me. "That's a fine, strapping man, and Phoebe says he's bought you all sorts of pretty things."

"Yes, he has."

"Not a bit intimidated by that Fox woman," Pity said, handing Phoebe her glass to wash. "I was watching her face when he told her you wanted Phoebe for your maid. She was furious, but she didn't say much. He's a man used to doing what he pleases without too much interference, I'd say. That's not a bad thing in a man."

Not unless he happened to marry a woman who was carrying another man's child, I thought uneasily. That was something he'd have trouble doing anything about, and I wasn't at all sure how he'd react. In spare moments, what few of them there had been, I had been trying to think of a way to broach the subject, to explain to him before the fact became evident. So far I had rejected at least a dozen approaches and was no nearer a solution than when I'd started.

"I think I'll go up the back stairs if that nasty little dog isn't guarding them tonight," Pity said. "I wonder how he decides who to allow to use them? That Estelle is running up and down all hours of the day and night, and he never seems to bother her. But he lies up there on either the second- or third-floor landing, wherever I want to go, and refuses to let me by. I'm tempted to hit him with something, but I'm afraid he'll bite me."

"He's not so bad," Phoebe said. "I'm getting a bit friendly with him since I've been in the kitchen. I slip him a bite now and then, although it's probably the worst thing I could do for him. He's already so fat he has to be carried up and down stairs, poor thing."

Pity snorted. "Poor thing, indeed! He's a vicious little wretch!" And then, in one of the sudden change-abouts that were becoming common with her, she added, "It's a wonder that Estelle isn't as fat as the dog, the way she eats."

Phoebe and I looked at one another. "I hadn't noticed that she eats a lot, Aunt Pity," I said finally.

"Oh, all the time. Constantly. No more than the rest of us at meals, but in between times . . . oh, my. Seems to me every time I slip out of my room to go back to the bathroom . . . and at my age that's every few hours, even during the night . . . that girl is going up or down stairs, carrying something to eat or the dirty dishes, and then that nasty little beast growls at me as if I had no right to use the passageways. I suppose"—and she looked at me wistfully—"that your young man will be moving you out of here and into a home of your own? And you won't want an old lady along if he does?"

I grasped her hand and squeezed it. "Of course I'd want you, Aunt Pity. I don't know about a home of my own, how soon there will be one, but if I can possibly take you all with me I'll do it."

She nodded rather absently, as if the possibility were a remote one, as perhaps it was. And then she started up the back stairs. I watched her with compassion, thinking that anyone seventy years old shouldn't have to climb to the third floor of a very tall house every time she went to her room.

"Is it true?" I asked when she had gone. "'About Estelle eating all the time?"

Phoebe shrugged. "I don't know. Certainly there are dirty dishes in the sink sometimes when I come down, but not very many. If Estelle was eating something she didn't want anyone to know about, she's only to wash up after herself. As much food as there is in this house it'd be hard to tell what's missing. And whatever else you may think of Mrs. Fox, she's not stingy with the food. She's never told me what I can or can't eat, not yet, anyway." She grinned. "Maybe she will, now that I'm to be your maid instead of the kitchen help. Miss Pity was right about that, she didn't like it a bit when Mr. Sebastian said she'd have to get herself another cook."

"Phoebe, I've been thinking and thinking about Mrs. Fox and this house. You've been in her room, and it's different from the rest of the house, isn't it? I mean, she's filled it with a different type of furnishings . . . the *taste* is not the same, I suppose I mean."

She considered. "Her room is certainly nothing like the one you're in now. I'd even prefer the one she's assigned to me . . . the furniture's not so heavy, like. Is that what you mean, miss?"

"Yes. And things like the library . . . it's as if Papa had picked out every book in there, just for him and me. All our old favorites, all the books we ever talked about wanting someday, if we could ever afford them. And the piano, in that beautiful room they don't go into at all. I have to find out, Phoebe. I have to be sure if it's *her* house, as she says, or if Papa bought it. If he *did,* I won't believe that there isn't somewhere something saying it's at least part mine, even if he did marry her. And I'm not so sure of that, either. Tomorrow, when Mrs. Fox is busy downstairs, will you keep watch while I go into her room and look at that marriage certificate myself? And anything else I can find . . . if it's her house she must have the deed to it somewhere." I drew in a deep breath and continued, "And another thing I must learn is the truth about Papa's death. Estelle told me he was buried in one cemetery, and Mrs. Fox said she was mistaken, that he was in another one, but the keepers at both places said they didn't have any record of an Edward Hunter being buried there. So there are all those things I must find out, if you'll help me."

"Of course I'll help you, Miss Saunielle," Phoebe promised. "It won't be so hard, now that I don't have to be down here in the kitchen. We'll manage it tomorrow."

Sebastian found us there, talking in low voices as Phoebe washed the dishes and I wiped them, as we had often shared the tasks back home in Virginia. He stood in the doorway, his voice bringing us around guiltily.

"What's all this? I thought we were getting Phoebe out of the kitchen, not you into it."

"I . . . we were talking, and it was just habit to pick up the dish towel," I admitted. "Is everyone listening to the gramophone yet?"

"I guess so. I didn't go in. You're right, this is a lovely house, most of it, although there are a few incongruous touches. The entry hall is quite lovely except for that monstrous coat rack and that terrible picture. Do you suppose they'd all be annoyed if you played the piano for me? I'd much rather hear that than records."

However, by the time we retraced our steps toward the front of the house, the gramophone had run down and no one got up to rewind it. A glance into the back parlor showed only Belle Fox and Mr. Goodwin, deep in a conversation that seemed unsatisfactory to both of them.

Fearing that I might be the subject of that conversation, I was only too glad to hurry on past to the music room, where Sebastian moved about, lighting a few lamps and then settling himself in a comfortable chair with his feet up.

"Play," he commanded, his smile making it a request rather than an order.

And so we spent the second evening of our married life together in the beautiful music room, shut away from the others, forgetting them. I could even allow myself to imagine that this was our house, that we were alone in it except for the people we wanted to be there, and that we had no problems other than what we might care to do to entertain ourselves tomorrow.

It was a false picture, of course. As we went up the stairs, late in the evening, Sebastian reached out and took my hand, smiling at me. *Oh, yes, Phoebe,* I thought, *you were right. The touching is exciting.* And my heartbeat quickened, because although I was installed in one bedroom, and he in another, I had no doubt that he would come to me. I knew that I could love this man, that there was more than the touching. And the small beginnings of happiness bubbled within me, tempered only a little by the knowledge of what I had concealed from him.

He did not have to come to me; he never left me in the first place. He stood in the doorway, looking down on me, and I hoped that I correctly read what I thought I saw in his eyes.

"I never thought it would be like this," he said.

The breathless quality of my voice was caused by the constriction in my chest. "Like what?" I asked.

"Being married. Spending an evening listening to my wife play the piano. Watching her in the lamplight, the sheen of her hair, the curve of her cheek, the grace of her hands. And thinking what it would be like, later, in the dark, when I could only see her in my mind."

Color flooded my neck and face, but he bent to kiss me on the lips. "Saunielle. Saunielle, you are so beautiful, and so sweet, and so innocent . . ."

His voice was husky, and when his mouth closed again over mine I stiffened momentarily, because it was impossible not to remember why I had married him, and then his urgency was communicated to my body so that I must respond, I must put away any thoughts I did not want to have . . .

Only later, lying beside him in the darkness, listening to his regular breathing, did the thoughts come back, and refuse to be put down. I must tell him. I must tell him as quickly as possible, tomorrow.

Tomorrow, I promised myself. Tomorrow, I would tell him.

◇◇◇◇◇◇

The following day dawned wet and cold. The wet was not rain, however, but fog: fog that packed itself between the houses and filled the strip of parkland between Fell and Oak streets as solidly as bolls of cotton.

I woke late again to find that Sebastian was nearly finished dressing, and when I turned my head I was appalled at the wave of nausea that swept over me.

I had thought the morning sickness had ended, but it seemed this was not so. I closed my eyes, waiting for the unpleasant sensation to subside, glad Sebastian had not noticed my waking. I lay still, fighting the nausea until he had left the room, and then I barely made it to the commode and the basin there.

Dear God! Thank heaven I hadn't sat up before it struck me, or there would have been no way to keep it from him. Would he have guessed the reason for my illness?

When I was sure Sebastian had gone downstairs, I made my way alone to the third-floor bathroom since the second-floor one was occupied. I rinsed my mouth and made my morning toilette, grateful that once I'd thrown up I usually felt better fairly quickly. One of my cousins had been sick all day, unable to eat except late at night, for months of her pregnancy.

I met Pity when I came out of the bathroom. She looked older, almost shriveled, this morning.

"Oh, it's you, Saunielle. I wondered who was in there for so long."

"Was I? I'm sorry, Aunt Pity." I took a closer look at her. "Aren't you feeling well?"

"I'm tired. I don't know how a person is supposed to sleep around here," she said, drawing her wrapper more tightly across her chest.

"Oh? Why? Did we disturb you, coming upstairs just before midnight? I guess we didn't try to be especially quiet, but I didn't think . . ."

"You didn't bother me. I didn't even hear you. It's that *girl*."

"Estelle?" The glance at Estelle's door was eloquent enough. "Why, what was she doing?"

"Talking to herself. Half the night."

"Talking . . . ? Are you sure, Aunt Pity?"

"Sleeps half the day, talks to herself half the night. I've seen newborn babes get their days and nights mixed up, but not grown women. How's a person supposed to sleep through that?"

"Can you hear what she says?" I asked, intrigued.

"No, except that she sounds cross. I've noticed she's cross when she speaks to the rest of us, but why would a person be cross with herself? And she opens and closes her door . . . I don't know how many times."

"Maybe she wasn't feeling well and she was going to the bathroom."

"I wouldn't feel well, either, if I ate all that food in the middle of the night," Pity proclaimed.

"Did she bring up food again last night?" I wasn't sure whether or not Pity was confused, but for whatever reason, she certainly didn't look as if she'd slept, just as she said.

"Whole tray full. Quarter past one in the morning, mind you. I never wanted to get old and deaf, but there might be advantages, having a room next to that one." She went in the bathroom and shut the door, but I stood for a few seconds, listening to the gush of water into the marble wash basin.

Mrs. Fox had said something when we first came about Pity being hard of hearing. I hadn't given it any thought until now, but was that why she'd put Pity in the room next to Estelle's? Did she know Estelle's nocturnal habits would disturb anyone with normal hearing?

I was concerned but couldn't immediately see anything I could do about the situation.

I got dressed, looking out into the street at the sound of carriage horses to see Sebastian disappearing into the fog. My spirits dropped. I hadn't had a chance to say anything to him, and I didn't even know when he would be back. *This evening,* I thought. *After dinner, I'll suggest that instead of music we retire to our own study, where we won't be disturbed, and I will tell him. I will explain how desperate I was, and he will surely see that I had no real choice, that I could not have allowed myself to be sold to Alastair Goodwin as if I were a slave on the block. And if he is beginning to fall in love with me, as I think he is, then he will forgive me for deceiving him, and everything will be all right.*

If I believed that, why did my fingers tremble on the buttons of my dress and why did my lips in the mirror look bloodless?

I started downstairs, only to meet Phoebe coming from the floor above. She peered over the railing, then hurried to join me.

"Oh, miss, I thought you were still sleeping. Mr. Sebastian said not to disturb you."

I lowered my voice. "I woke up, but I was afraid I'd be sick if I moved before he left the room. Did he say where he was going?"

"He called for a carriage and said to tell you he had more business with the lawyers and would be back by dinnertime, miss."

Dinnertime! How the hours stretched ahead of me without the prospect of seeing him. Phoebe read my face rather accurately.

"You're falling in love with him, aren't you, miss? It's what I've prayed for, and I think he's . . . it's happening to him, too, from the look of him."

"Maybe. I hope so . . . only he doesn't know yet, Phoebe. I'm going to tell him, tonight, about . . . you know. And then maybe it will all be over." I swallowed hard, painfully. "Maybe he'll throw me out in the street when he knows. And Mr. Goodwin won't want me, either, and then where will I be? Where will we *all* be?" It was bad enough that my own fortunes rose or fell by what Sebastian decided about me; it was worse that Dodie and Pity and Phoebe would also suffer if I did.

"He won't throw you out, miss. I'd take any sort of odds on that," Phoebe assured me, but I wasn't nearly as sure as she was.

"Why are you going down so early?" I asked. "You aren't cooking today, are you?"

"No. Estelle is, and quite a fuss she made over it, too. I heard them yowling at one another like a pack of cats when I came up last night," Phoebe said, "I can't for the life of me understand why they're living together, since they don't seem to like each other much."

"Estelle is probably dependent upon her aunt for support. I suppose we ought to feel some sympathy for her."

Phoebe made a snorting sound. "I'll save my sympathy for somebody more worthy. Heaven knows what sort of breakfast you'll get with her fixing it. Would you like me to fix something just for you and bring it up?"

"No. It would only be cold by the time you got it all the way up here, anyway. Let's both keep an eye out for Mrs. Fox, and if she goes out we'll get upstairs and see what we can find in her papers." I said it without a single qualm, so convinced was I by this time that something was amiss.

"We'll have to watch out for Estelle, too. She's a sneaky one, and I've caught her watching us, different times."

Startled, I paused in my descent of the stairs. "What do you mean?"

"She stands where she won't be noticed, like in a corner or just inside a doorway, and she watches. All of us. It's sort of creepy."

"It sounds creepy. Like this day. I've never seen such fog in my life. When Sebastian left I could scarcely see the carriage at the curb for it, although I could hear the horses as they moved away. I wonder if Mrs. Fox is likely to go out if it stays like this?"

"Dodie's going out, to buy her shoes, she said, whether it's foggy or not, although she's hoping it will lift. Did she tell you she telephoned about that position in the paper? Imagine, Miss Dodie using the telephone! I think it scared her half to death, and her voice squeaked, but she did it. She's to be interviewed tomorrow, so she said she simply had to buy her shoes today, first, fog or no fog."

"Well, I expect she'll find her way all right. The cable-car men will know where they are and give her directions; they must be used to this. Wouldn't that be something, if Dodie got a position that enabled her to support herself! It's so cold . . . tell her she can take my shawl if she likes, I think it's heavier than hers."

"Yes, miss," Phoebe said, and we were downstairs, and we could smell burning toast. Phoebe grinned. "Yes, it's Estelle cooking, all right," she said.

It was a dreary morning. The house felt strange to me without Sebastian in it, which was absurd, since it had felt perfectly all right before he had come here to live. And while I longed for his return, I also dreaded it, and what I must tell him.

Estelle carried in platters of fried eggs, swimming in grease and most of them with their yolks broken, and bacon that had not been cooked quite crisp enough. Everyone ate without enthusiasm, it seemed to me, and I noted that there were a number of charred crusts left on various plates.

I watched Belle's niece with more than my previous interest, wondering about her. She did look tired, very tired, and very thin for a person who was supposed to be eating extra meals in the middle of the night. I was on the verge of summoning up some of that sympathy I had mentioned when I met her gaze, and that killed anything I might have been feeling. For her eyes flashed at me in what I could only interpret as a venomous resentment, perhaps because I had usurped Phoebe's services.

Having those services, I had no idea of what to do with them. She had already found places to put away my new belongings, I had made my bed myself from force of habit, and until we could begin our illicit search of Mrs. Fox's room there was nothing special to do.

All four of the elderly lodgers had declined to go out into the unattractive day. They sat in the back parlor, reading the *Chronicle* or smoking or shuffling through the corridors on undefined errands of their own. I met Mr. Goodwin, who gave me a most reproachful look and was unable to bring off the smile he attempted.

Embarrassed, I nodded and kept on going. I had no desire to be alone with Mr. Goodwin. Whatever happened with Sebastian, I told myself, I was better off than I would have been married to Mr. Goodwin.

The ringing telephone was startling enough to bring us all to a halt. Everyone stopped whatever he was doing, and for a moment no one made any move toward the instrument hidden away in the closet under the stairs.

Then Belle Fox came, moving majestically in her emerald wool serge, chosen for its welcome warmth today, and disappeared into the closet. I couldn't hear what she said, although I frankly lingered in the hallway in the hope of making out what it was.

When she came out, she moved with the briskness of purpose. She ignored me, and the elderly lodgers, and made her way back to the kitchen where Estelle was clearing up.

Not until Phoebe came along with a small tray bearing a teapot and two cups did I learn that Belle was going out. Phoebe smiled slyly at me, speaking for my ears alone.

"You asked me for tea, miss. I'm bringing it to your room."

"I did? Oh yes, I did. Did they say anything worthwhile?"

"They talked in that sort of cryptic way they have when other peo-

ple are around. Is that the word I mean? They don't quite come out
and say what it is, they sort of hint at it, so no one else can tell what
they're talking about? Anyway, Mrs. Fox is going out for a short
time, she said. And Estelle is very much out of sorts. When her aunt
told her to keep an eye on things," Phoebe altered her natural tone
of voice, imitating the significant tone used by my stepmother, "Estelle informed her that she'd had a bloody rotten night and she
needed some rest, and she'd damned well better find a cook if we all
were to get any dinner. What do you think of that?"

"She actually swore?"

"Did she not. As if she's used to doing it, too. I knew she wasn't
any lady, right from the first, I did." We were now climbing the stairs
with the tea I had supposedly ordered. "Let's watch from the front
windows, we can see from your room when she leaves. And then
once Estelle goes upstairs it ought to be safe to move. One of us can
stand guard to make sure she doesn't start down the stairs, while the
other one looks through the lady's dresser drawers."

"We'll have to be quiet. Mrs. Fox's room is right under Estelle's."
I was shivering a little, my hands cold. The tea would be welcome, at
that.

"I don't think you can hear much from one floor to the other, not
unless somebody drops something heavy, and even that wouldn't
make much noise, not on carpets. Would you get the door for me,
miss?"

She poured the tea while I stood at the front window, waiting for
Mrs. Fox to appear. There was no lessening of the fog, in fact it
seemed even more intense than it had been earlier. I stood sipping
from the thin china cup that looked like something Papa might well
have purchased if he remembered the ones Mama had had, and
thought that if Sebastian did not throw me into the street when I told
him about the baby, perhaps I would tell him all the rest as well. All
the things that frightened and puzzled me. I suspected that he was far
better qualified than I to get at the root of all the disconcerting matters. I could imagine him simply demanding of Belle Fox that she
produce all relevant documents and reveal to us the exact circumstances of Papa's death and his burial place.

And what Sebastian demanded, Sebastian would undoubtedly get.

Phoebe had joined me at the window, and we both breathed a
small sigh when at last Belle appeared below us. She wasn't squan-
dering money on a carriage; she was either walking to her destination
or taking a cable car.

"There she goes. Let me check on Estelle, miss. And I'll get a tid-
bit of some sort for Alfred, in case he's guarding the queen's jewels
again, or whatever it is he does."

That hadn't occurred to me. "What if he won't let us in her room?

She might have planted him there in front of her door, and he seems to understand what she wants him to do."

"Don't you worry. That bacon wasn't cooked fit for human consumption, but Alfred doesn't know that. What was left over was stuck into that icebox thing to be cooked up later with a batch of beans. I'll bring along enough of it to take Alfred's mind off his guard duties."

Outside, Mrs. Fox had vanished into the thick mist. I turned from the window, the teacup clattering in its saucer as I replaced it on its tray.

"All right. See if you can find where Estelle is. Then you can watch while I take a look in *her* room."

Phoebe was trembling, too, but I thought it was more from excitement than any fear of being caught.

Actually, I realized, I wasn't afraid of being caught, not with Mrs. Fox out of the house, not with Phoebe making sure Estelle didn't walk in on me.

Maybe what I was afraid of was what I would find in Mrs. Fox's room.

◇◇◇◇ 19 ◇◇◇◇

Belle Fox's room held its own special scent, too heavy for my taste. Heaviness extended to almost everything in it, for the furniture was massive as opposed to the more graceful items in the rest of the house.

Phoebe had posted herself in the corridor outside, where she had a good command of the back stairs and the second-floor hallway, and she could step into the bathroom to rap on the wall in warning if anyone should appear to pose any danger. We had decided that this would not include anyone other than Estelle and Mrs. Fox, since no one else was likely to enter the room where I was.

I worked quickly, because I had no way of knowing how long Belle would be gone. Phoebe had told me where she had found the papers, and it was the work of seconds to have them in hand.

Many of them were letters, and I glanced over them quickly, finding nothing significant. She apparently had a friend in Santa Rosa, and a sister in Santa Barbara, with whom she carried on a sporadic correspondence. I put them to one side for further perusal if there should be time, and went on to the other papers.

The marriage license was there. I read through it in seconds, feeling a tightening of the abdominal muscles. For it proclaimed that Belle Engadine Fox and Edward Marshall Hunter had been married on the ninth of August, 1895, in the City and County of San Francisco. Each of the participants had signed the document.

It was my father's name that I studied. As Phoebe had remarked, it seemed somewhat less clear and less firm than the signature on my letter, but perhaps that was only a natural nervousness of a bridegroom. Certainly the handwriting was quite different from that of either the bride or the clergyman who had performed the ceremony.

It could have been forged, perhaps, but only by someone who had a genuine signature at hand to copy; I had no real reason to think that had been the case, except for wishful thinking.

I turned my attention to the clergyman's signature. It was written in such tiny, cramped letters that I had trouble making it out, but I thought it was Wm. Gerriger. There was nothing to announce either his denomination or an affiliation with a specific church.

William Gerriger. I said it aloud, to set it in my mind. Then the certificate went back into the drawer, and I turned to the remaining papers.

There were only a few, and none of them was a deed to the house. There was a bill of sale for another piece of property, however, and I copied down the particulars on a sheet of the scented pale green notepaper from Belle's desk. On the fifteenth of August of this year, Belle had paid for a house at an address on Grant Avenue a sum of six hundred dollars. For the balance owing, the statement said. Did that mean she had previously paid part of the purchase price and this was the final payment?

◇◇◇◇◇◇

There was no deed to this property, either. Perhaps she kept the deeds in a box at the bank, or perhaps her lawyer kept them. Hadn't they told me Papa had died on the twelfth of August? Was it significant that only three days later Belle had bought, or finished paying for, a house? And if she'd bought a house on Grant, why was she living in *this* house?

I found out a moment later, at least a part of what I wanted to know. The final document in the collection was a copy of a legal agreement concerning the sale of a property on Grant Avenue to one Emily James for the consideration of one thousand dollars, five hundred being hereby paid, the balance to be paid at the rate of . . .

I stopped reading the particulars and went back to the previous document to compare the property descriptions. On August 15 she had paid for the house, on September 22 she had resold it?

"Miss Saunielle?"

I jumped, emitting a stifled squeak. "Phoebe! Is someone coming?"

"No, miss. I just didn't hear anything and wondered what was happening. I can see from here, and hear, both. We're perfectly safe, I think. Have you found anything?"

I told her.

"Why would she do a thing like that?"

"If she bought it and then found she could make a profit by selling it right away, she might have done that. Since she must have been living here then and didn't buy it to live in," Phoebe suggested.

"Or she needed the money, although I guess that doesn't make sense, does it? If she was rich enough to buy a house one month she wouldn't be in dire straits a month later so she'd have to sell it. Except that she did say some of her investments hadn't turned out, or something, that's why she had to take in 'guests.' Oh, Phoebe, I don't see that I've discovered anything important, not really. See, here's Papa's signature, and it *looks* like his. Either that or it's a fairly good forgery, and I don't even know why I think it might be that. She *was* seen with Papa, in a carriage, by Mr. Johansen, and he thought they were quite friendly and Papa seemed happy. And if she'd . . . *contrived* the marriage proofs, why wouldn't she have shown this to me, instead of saying she'd mislaid it?"

"We might learn something by talking to this . . ."—Phoebe consulted the paper—"Emily James. If we copied down the address . . ."

"I have it. And the name of the clergyman who married them. I wonder if he might be the same one who . . . who conducted the funeral service."

"Well, maybe that's something. But if she was really married to your papa, even if he's the one who bought this house, I don't see how you're going to claim a share of it, miss. Not unless there's a will."

I didn't, either. Discouraged, I began to replace the papers. I hesitated over the letters; was it likely there was any thing of value in them? None of them was *from* Belle, after all, and they seemed to be concerned with clothes and domestic matters. I put them back in the approximate order I'd found them.

"All right. That's all, I guess."

We closed the door and for a moment there was absolute silence in the big house. And then from the top of the back stairs we heard Estelle's voice.

"*Stay,* you little wretch. Don't let anyone pass, do you understand?" And then, in a different tone of voice, as she started down the stairs, "It's going to take more than a fat, ugly little dog to stave off disaster if I can't talk some sense into her pretty soon, but you might as well do what you're here for."

Phoebe and I stared at one another, and then by unspoken consent stepped into the bathroom, pulling the door closed behind us. A moment later Estelle's feet sounded on the landing and then going on down to the kitchen.

"Well," Phoebe murmured when she had gone, "what did *that* mean, do you suppose?"

"It meant there is something for us to learn, if we probe deeply enough," I said. "Why is Alfred posted at the top of the stairs? What is he guarding?"

Again we did not need to speak. Phoebe opened the door, and very quietly, so as not to be heard from below, we began to climb the stairs.

Alfred lay on the third-floor landing. He pricked up his ears and growled at our approach, but Phoebe didn't hesitate.

"Hello, Alfred. How'd you like a nice piece of bacon, eh?"

He still looked menacing, but he'd stopped growling. He accepted the first bit of bacon and licked at Phoebe's fingers. She was braver than I, for I wouldn't have trusted mine that close to his teeth.

"What are you guarding, old boy? What's up here that we aren't supposed to know about?"

He rose on his stubby legs as we gained the top step, but was diverted when Phoebe offered another bit of meat. I stood looking down the long passageway toward the front of the house.

"You and Pity and Dodie are all sleeping up here, and I did, to begin with. Estelle's room is there, and there's the locked storage room and the one empty room. Why would they have put us up here if there were something they didn't want us to find?"

"There wasn't much other place to put us," Phoebe pointed out. "Not unless she just didn't let us come in the first place."

After the briefest of hesitations, I turned the knob of Estelle's door and looked inside.

"Whew! Easy to see she doesn't like housekeeping," Phoebe observed. "She's got as many clothes as Mr. Sebastian bought for you, miss, but they won't last long if she never hangs any of 'em up. What a mess! She'd never know if a dozen people searched her quarters. What's that scent?"

"Nothing I care for. Look, there's a key on the inside. If she had anything to hide, she'd lock the room, wouldn't she?"

"Seems like it. What are you to keep us out of, Alfred, love?"

I made a movement toward the bathroom. Alfred watched impassively. He hadn't blocked my way to Estelle's room, either, once he'd tasted the bacon. He was watching Phoebe, his pink tongue hanging out.

My gaze fixed firmly upon him, I took two quick steps toward the locked storage room directly across the hall.

Alfred showed his fangs and growled.

It seemed prudent to stop. Phoebe tried it, and also came to a halt. "I haven't any more bacon. But it seems clear enough. He doesn't want us to go near that room. Now why should that be, when it's supposed to be locked? We couldn't get in it, anyway, could we?"

Defeated, we withdrew. But not forever, I vowed. Something was very strange in this house and I was determined to know what it was, because I was convinced that for some reason I was at the very center of the maelstrom.

◇◇◇◇◇◇

Belle returned in time to prepare a noon meal for all of us, and to announce that she would be interviewing women for the position of cook on the following day. She seemed, I thought in my newly perceptive state, to be tense and preoccupied.

Estelle served, and it was impossible to miss the fact that she was tired and irritable, which seemed to confirm Pity's claim that she had been awake a good deal of last night.

My speculations as to why this should have been were pointless, and I forgot about them both. The Reverend Mr. Quayle was ahead of me when we left the dining room, and I scurried to catch up.

He stopped, blinking, when I spoke his name. He was not much taller than I, and he looked as if all the juices had long since been drawn out of him. I wasn't sure he even remembered who I was.

"Eh? Were you speaking to me?"

"Yes, sir. As a clergyman, I thought you might be able to help me."

He straightened slightly, smoothing a sparse strand of white hair over his pate. "Be glad to, if I can."

"It's important that I locate another clergyman by the name of William Gerriger. All I know about him is that he was in San Francisco about two months ago."

"Gerriger? Can't say as I place him, miss. But I'm not too active any more, could be I've only missed meeting him."

"Is there any way you could suggest that I could locate him?"

He scratched his head, so that the hair smoothed only a moment earlier stood up in peaks. "Well, I might try calling around, see what I can learn."

I assured him that I would be most grateful for this, and he immediately trotted off toward the telephone closet. While he was so engaged, Dodie came along into the entryway, wrapping my shawl tightly around herself.

"It's still very foggy, but I've got to go. Mrs. Fox gave me a map of the city, so I can find the shoe store. I hope this shoe holds together until I get there."

"Wait a few minutes, Dodie. I'd like to see your map, and maybe Phoebe and I will go with you," I suggested. This she was only too glad to do, for the mists were enough to make anyone welcome company. I fetched my own wrap, a repped silk jacket with feather trimming made me feel quite elegant. It might have seemed rather elaborate for afternoon wear, except that both Belle and Estelle dressed far more elaborately.

By the time Phoebe appeared to join us, Mr. Quayle had the information we wanted.

"Billy Gerriger, they say it is. I've written down the church where you'll find him. Trinity Episcopal, it's just off Union Square."

I thanked him profusely and tucked the paper into my handbag. And then, after a consultation with Dodie, we mapped out our itinerary.

We had all looked out the windows, but I had not truly believed the density of the fog until we descended into it. It closed around us, blotting out the house and the shrubbery; we linked hands, fearful of getting lost from one another if we did not.

At the corner where we must cross Hayes Street, we came to a halt on the curb, listening for the sound of a vehicle which might run down the imprudent.

There was no sound of wheels or horses, but in the stillness we heard quick footsteps, which stopped a moment after our own.

"We're not the only idiots out in this," Dodie said nervously. "I wonder if that person is heading for the cable cars too?"

We crossed the street and went on to the car stop, seeing no one else. The bells of the little car were welcome, indeed, and we climbed aboard, with me digging for a few of my remaining coins.

The car was surprisingly full by the time we reached Market Street; two women had gotten on at the stop after ours, so it appeared that this was an acceptable method of travel for unattended females.

We left Dodie at the shoe store, taking a different cable car for which we obtained a transfer. We decided to try for Reverend Billy Gerriger, first, and then walk the few blocks to the Grant Avenue address; this would put us in a position to catch a return car with a minimum of walking once we'd concluded our investigation.

Billy Gerriger invited us into a chilly, somber little office. He was about the same age as Reverend Quayle, but round and plump where Mr. Quayle was thin enough to show bones. He wore thick glasses set so far down his nose I couldn't imagine how they could be of any use to him.

"I'm only the assistant pastor, you know. It isn't Father Chelsea you want, is it?"

"No, sir. I'm looking for the minister who married Belle Fox and Edward Marshall Hunter on August 9 of this year," I told him.

He had stubby eyelashes that fluttered rapidly when he thought. "August 9?" he said at last. "My . . . do you have reason to think I might have done that?"

"I saw a marriage certificate with what purported to be your signature on it. Don't you remember the wedding, sir?" I wondered how he could bear to work in a place that was so cold.

"Can't say that I do. But then, since I can't see well enough to write out sermons any more, I do a lot of weddings. Not the fashionable ones, you see, but the . . . ah . . . ordinary ones. Especially among people who are not of our parish." He glanced around as if to make sure he was not overheard, as if such weddings were something illicit.

I struggled with disappointment. "It was only two months ago! Mrs. Fox is a rather tall woman with a full figure, and bright auburn hair. Quite an attractive woman, most people would probably say, and she'd have been stylishly dressed. My . . . Mr. Hunter was a tall man, handsome, dark-haired, probably also well dressed."

He shook his head. "My eyes, you see, I'm very nearsighted. Have trouble finding the spot to sign my name, actually. But I know the ceremony by heart, no problem there. I married a couple just an hour ago, and I couldn't tell you what either of them looked like, really. They had very nice voices." He added that last hopefully, as if that might comfort me.

"Then . . . there's no way of telling whether or not you *did* marry this particular couple?"

"Oh, I didn't say that! I keep a record, of course. Always keep a record. We can go look at the book."

He might have made the entries in the book, but he had a great deal of difficulty in reading them. It was I who finally found it, right where it was supposed to be. *Belle Fox and Edward Hunter. August 9, 1895.*

There was also an illegible notation. "What is this, sir?"

He squinted at it, both over and through his spectacles. "Ah . . . yes, that indicates they were not married in the chapel here. That's not unusual, especially if the parties are not members of the church. I often go to their homes."

"Do you think you did, in this instance?"

"I'm afraid I wouldn't remember, miss. It's possible, but I couldn't say for sure."

"I see. And I suppose you wouldn't remember, either, if you conducted a funeral, on August twelfth or thereabouts?"

"Funeral?" He was disconcerted that we'd switched from weddings. "Ah . . . well, I *do* conduct burial services, of course. Who . . . what would be the name of the deceased?"

"Edward Marshall Hunter."

"Ah? Oh, the same . . . oh, my, that's too bad. No, no, surely I'd have remembered *that,* if I'd buried a man only a few days after I married him. Oh no, I'm sure I didn't do *that.*"

He let us out, rubbing his hands apologetically because he hadn't been of more assistance.

We walked on in silence for a time, somewhat depressed by our inability to come to grips with anything tangible. I was roused from my own reverie by Phoebe's hissed, "Miss Saunielle."

"Yes?"

"Have you noticed the writing on the shop windows, miss? It *is* writing, isn't it, even if I can't read a word of it?"

Only then did I become aware that the character of the city had changed as we walked. Not only were the signs very strange indeed, but a good many of the people on the street had yellow skins and oddly slanted eyes.

"They're Chinese, I think. What was that address, again? Do you think we've made a mistake?"

We had not, however. On the outskirts of what we learned to be Chinatown, we found the house Belle had first paid for and then sold, in rapid succession.

It was a large house, almost as large as the one on Fell Street, but much more ordinary and in poor repair. It was overdue for both cleaning and painting, except for a sign that proclaimed it to be a "Boardinghouse, gentlemen only, reasonable rates by week or month."

We climbed the steps and rang the bell, Phoebe keeping a sharp eye out behind us at the Chinese, who had so far paid us no attention whatever.

The woman who came was in her forties, blowsy, not too clean, but cheerful-looking. "Yes?"

"Mrs. James? I wonder if I might talk with you for a moment."

"Come on in, I'm about to have a cuppa tea. Miserable day, ain't it?" She ushered us through an entryway crammed with potted plants into a dining room where half a dozen men sat around waiting their tea. They looked at us curiously but inoffensively. "I only take gentlemen," Mrs. James informed us. "Much less trouble that way."

"We aren't looking for lodgings. We're looking for information."

She poured tea into chipped cups, all different, and urged us to sit down. "Well, I don't know much about anything, but I can see, now I take a better look at you, you wouldn't be wanting to live in this part of town. What is it you want?"

"You bought this house from Mrs. Belle Fox, did you?"

"That's right," she said promptly. "Give her a thousand dollars for it . . . or will, when I get through payin' for it."

"Were you aware that she had paid for it herself only a month earlier?"

"I weren't aware of nothing except that she give me a clear title to it. I been saving, and my husband agreed it would be a good investment, give us a place to live and make a little money on the side. Good thing I got it, because poor Henry died shortly after we moved in, and I got a way to keep myself without his paycheck. Got nearly a full house, only two empty rooms."

I hesitated. "Were any of your roomers here before you took over?"

"Most all of 'em," she agreed. "Mr. Stokes, Mr. Blum, there, Mr. Sade. Everybody here now except Mr. Looper was here when Mrs. Fox run the place herself."

I stiffened, sitting up straighter, my tea forgotten. "Mrs. Fox operated this as a boardinghouse herself?"

"Sure did," one of the men piped up. "I lived here two years, while she owned the place. Wasn't as good a cook as Mrs. James, but she run a good house."

"And she ran the place until she sold it to Mrs. James in September?" I didn't know what it meant, but it meant something. How would Papa have met her, living in a place like this? And how had she managed to pay for it, after what must have been years of making monthly payments on it?

"Did that," the man nodded. "Then she met that rich dude, and said she didn't have to run no rooming house no more, she was going to be a lady. Come back here a few times, and she was sure dressed like one." He nodded his head again, remembering.

I leaned toward him, warming my hands on the thick china cup. "This rich man, do you remember his name?"

The man looked around at his contemporaries, and they all shook their heads. "Nope, don't remember. Never saw him."

"Did she ever say his name? Could it have been Hunter? Edward Hunter?"

"Hunter? Yeah, that might have been it. Fella with a soft voice," Caxton said. Caxton met him once, not here, somewheres else when Mrs. Fox was with him. Said he had a soft voice, with a sort of southern accent, like."

"Mr. Hunter was from Virginia," I said, aware of a fine tremor in my limbs.

"Yeah, that could be it."

"And did she say she was going to marry him?"

"I don't know if she said *marry*. Not to me, she didn't. She just said she didn't have to run no rooming house no more. But I reckon it's possible."

"Do you think she got the money to pay for the house from this Mr. Hunter?"

They consulted among themselves, and then allowed that it was possible. They were reasonably certain she'd paid for the house *after* she met the gentleman.

We talked for a few minutes more, without gleaning anything else. But both Phoebe and I were in an excited state as we prepared to depart. For if Belle had obtained the money from Papa to pay for this house, had it also been his money that paid for the house on Fell Street, which had obviously been far more expensive? And if so, how could we determine what I might be entitled to?

We took our leave, with Mrs. James cautioning us as she peered into the foggy street. "Gets darkish early when the fog hangs in like this. Get you along to the car stop right away; this ain't exactly the sort of neighborhood where young ladies wanders around alone once it gets dark. Good luck to you, dearie!"

I was to need it. For a moment later, as we descended the front steps into the eddying mists, I felt a stinging sensation at my left temple and staggered sideways in an undignified sprawl.

Phoebe cried out, as did I, and a moment later a more searing pain ripped through my shoulder. I stared down in shock and amazement to see blood soaking the front of my new silk jacket before the reddish haze obscured my vision and Phoebe's screams faded, as well.

◇◇◇◇ **20** ◇◇◇◇

My fainting spell could scarcely have lasted for more than a moment, and was due more to the tightness of my stays than to my injuries, for Phoebe was still on her knees beside me, eyes wide, begging me to speak.

The old men and Mrs. James had come out of the boardinghouse and clustered thickly around, the woman taking the initiative and peeling back my jacket for a look at my shoulder.

"She was shot! I heard two explosions, and she just crumpled up and fell down," Phoebe said, relief evident in her face when I struggled into a sitting position. "Oh, miss, are you all right?"

"Bloody lucky," one of the old men commented. "Just grazed her head, didn't do much harm there. How's the shoulder?"

"Lucky there, too, no thanks to those hoodlums, whoever they were," Mrs. James stated dourly. "No more than flesh wounds, either of them, but she could well have been killed. Come inside, miss, and I'll put a dressing over that until you can get home. Your lovely dress and jacket are ruined, I'm afraid."

"It's them rascally Chinese, I'll bet. That Chee Kung Tong killed three people right up the block only a week ago, they say. Them Chinese secret societies don't care who else they kill, long as they get the ones they want."

"The Tongs use hatchets," someone else protested. "I never heard of 'em shooting anybody."

"It's the Tongs, you can bet on that," a third voice asserted. "Best get a carriage to take you home, miss, you won't be in any condition to walk to the car stop."

But when a dressing had been placed over the shoulder wound (the one above my ear was so minor it needed no more than to be washed off) I realized that I hadn't enough money to hire a carriage. No doubt if Sebastian was home when I got there he would take care of it, but I couldn't depend on that. The only person who would certainly have the money would be Mrs. Fox, and I had no intention of asking her for anything, not in my present frame of mind.

"I'm sure I'll manage all right on the cable cars," I assured them, and so a pair of them agreed to see that we got there safely, for which we were most grateful.

I had thought my injuries relatively insignificant, which they were, but I hadn't counted on my own reaction. Huddled in my share of the seat aboard the "dinky" I began to shake uncontrollably until Phoebe took off her own shawl and wrapped it tightly around me, and then sat chafing my hands until we reached our stop.

We still had two blocks to walk, and the fog was incredible, thicker than ever. Once inside the front hallway, I sank onto the nearest chair, legs trembling, unable to take another step. Perhaps I even blacked out for a moment or two, for the next thing I knew half the household was there.

Mrs. Fox brought brandy, and Sebastian came, shouldering the others aside, his face showing concern. In the background Phoebe was giving a fairly lucid account of the affair, and Estelle said sharply, "But where *were* you?" which no one answered. And then, the brandy warming my gullet and spreading in lovely ways through my body, I was lifted in Sebastian's arms and carried up the stairs.

He wasn't satisfied until he peeled off jacket and dress, tossing them aside as of no consequence, and removed the bandage to check the shoulder himself.

"It looks all right, but we'll have a doctor over to make sure. You came home on the dinky after this? Why didn't you call for a cab?" he demanded.

"I didn't have any money . . . or not enough. We'd planned on the cable cars . . ."

In a savage movement, he drew out his own purse and withdrew a roll of bills, stuffing them into my handbag. "For God's sake, you've only to tell any driver that you're Sebastian Rohann's wife and he'll know I'll take care of the tab! What in heaven's name were you doing in Chinatown?"

I could have told him, only it was all so involved and I was very tired. "We'd left Dodie off, to get her shoes, and we . . . just walked. It looked . . . interesting."

"It's interesting, all right. Next time let me know and I'll show you around, but it's no place for women alone. Why in the hell anyone would be shooting at you I don't know, but you'd best check with someone who lives here before you go exploring again, make sure it's safe."

"The men . . . an old man said it was the Tongs, the Chinese secret societies."

He made a scoffing sound. "They're mostly concerned with killing off one another. And they chop each other up, or use a garrote, nice and quiet and inexpensive, not like using guns."

He knelt at my feet, slipping off my shoes, and leaned forward to cup both hands around my face. "Saunielle, do you know how I felt when I heard Phoebe's voice saying you'd been shot? Dear heaven, how could I have become so attached to you so quickly?" He stood, drawing me with him and into his arms. His kiss, at first gentle, increased in passionate intensity until he left me breathless, and nothing to do with my stays at all.

There was something different in his blue eyes when he finally looked into my face. "I'm just realizing what a very wicked thing it was that I did to you, Saunielle."

"Wicked?" I echoed, bewildered.

"Marrying you simply as a means to get the old man to release my rightful inheritance. I never thought about you as a person at all, you were no more than a convenience. And now, God help me, I'm . . . I think I'm falling in love with you." He said it in a tone of wonder, as if it were an astounding thing.

Now was the time for me to make my own confession, for I had used him fully as much as he had used me. "Sebastian," I began, but he was still speaking.

"I think we've won Grandfather over. Or, I should say, you have. Because he called his lawyers in this morning, and just a few hours ago Cromwell got a look at the changes in his will." He kissed me again, in sheer exuberance of spirits. "Since I have undertaken to be a responsible family man, I'm qualified to return to my position with the company. And when the old man dies, I'll take over the running of it. Not Roderick, the little sneak, but me!" He laughed into my face. "What would you like, love? Diamonds? Furs? Carriages and servants? A mansion overlooking the Golden Gate? Name it, and it's yours!"

"Sebastian, there's something . . ."

Someone knocked on the door.

"Oh hell," Sebastian said, and strode to pull it open. "Yes, Estelle, what is it?"

"There was a telephone call, sir. The gentleman said his name was Marlon, and he said to tell you that old Mr. Rohann is dying. He wants you to come at once."

"Oh hell," Sebastian said, in a totally different voice, and I could tell that for all his battles with "the old man," there lingered some memory of the better times, when there had been friendship and even love between them. "All right. Thank you." He turned back to me, ever so briefly. "I'll have to go. There's no telling when I'll be back." His smile flickered. "Don't get mixed up in any more family fights or Tong wars, or whatever the hell it was."

And then he was gone, and I had not told him about the child I carried. But, whether from the brandy or from his kisses and his words, I felt warmer and calmer and almost happy. For if Sebastian loved me, as I knew now that I loved him, then everything would fall into place and be all right too.

◇◇◇◇◇◇

How naïve we can be, when we are raised on fairy tales! They fell into one another's arms, or they married and lived happily ever after! How little relationship those stories had to real life.

Phoebe joined me with a tray for supper, which was very simple, consisting of thin slices of bread and butter, cold ham, and canned fruit. Dodie came with her, bearing her own similar tray.

"There's no regular dinner tonight. I guess Estelle is getting up something for the old gentlemen, but the rest of us are shifting for ourselves, miss. It seems that both Estelle and Belle expected the other to do the preliminaries, but they both went out and didn't get back until shortly before we did. Then the fuss over you slowed things down a little more, and Mrs. Fox has a headache, so here we are."

"It's been a horrid day, all around," Dodie contributed. "I was afraid I wouldn't be able to find my way home in that dreadful fog, and then someone followed me, and I was so frightened I ran the whole way from the car stop. My heart was pounding so I could scarcely breathe."

"Followed you?" I paused in the act of placing a slice of ham between my slices of bread. "Who was it?"

"I don't know. I never saw him, I only heard him. Footsteps on the sidewalk, and when I stopped he'd take one step, and I'd hear him, only then he'd stop too. As if he didn't want to get close enough so I could see him."

"But you're sure it was a man?"

"Yes, I think so." She sipped at a spoonful of peach juice. "You remember, when we left the house earlier we heard someone behind us, too, only it was lighter, and the heels sounded the way a woman's does. But this was heavier, like a man's. Once when I stopped I thought I could hear his breathing. Isn't it odd how the fog seems to sort of carry the sounds? Anyway, it scared me half to death. But I did get my shoes." She stuck her feet out to show me the shoes of black Dongola kid with soft white glove leather tops. "I got a free buttonhook, too, because of the sale. Now I can go for my interview with Mrs. Salisbury without looking a complete frump. I wish my navy wool was a bit more stylish, but I suppose it isn't necessary for a seamstress to be a fashion plate herself."

That set us to looking through my new wardrobe, looking for something that might be suitable for her to borrow for the occasion, and we forgot about the man who had followed Dodie in the fog.

Sebastian did not come home. At ten o'clock I prepared for bed. Phoebe and I had been reading aloud, and she went along to her own room, only to return a few minutes later with Aunt Pity. It was only too clear that Pity had come against her will.

"You talk to her, miss, she won't listen to me!"

Pity cast her a scornful glance. "You act as if I'm in my dotage! Well, I'm not, Phoebe my girl! And I'm not having hallucinations! There's something mighty peculiar going on up there, and I'm going to tell that girl she's got to stop whatever she's doing so I can sleep! How's a body supposed to stay up days when she can't sleep at night, I ask you?"

"We're already . . . what's that phrase?—*persona non grata*—in this house. If you get everyone angry at you, Miss Pity, they may make it very unpleasant for you," Phoebe warned.

Pity's nostrils flared. "Well, it's very unpleasant for *me,* not to be able to get any sleep for that girl running around at all hours and talking, and now I know why! She's got someone locked in that room at the head of the stairs!"

Behind the old lady, Phoebe made a helpless gesture, but I was no longer so sure the problem was one of senility. "What did you hear, Aunt Pity?" I asked quietly.

"I heard her talking to someone, someone she doesn't like, from the tone of it. I couldn't make out all her words, and no name, but I think she was urging someone to eat. So it isn't her that's consuming all that food, but whoever she's got locked up in there!"

"It's that room that Alfred guards," I reasoned. "Phoebe, where do they keep the keys to the doors that are locked?"

"They each have a bunch of 'em, miss, on a ring and a chain. I never saw any anywhere else. Do you think there really is someone in that room? Kept prisoner, like?"

"I think it's time we found out." I had an overwhelming sensation of drowning, of being unable to breathe, and I wished that Sebastian would come back. I would tell him everything we knew, and I was sure he would help us learn everything else. Suspicions rose like wraiths of fog in my mind, but when they had almost assumed recognizable shapes they twisted and faded and took on new dimensions, leaving me more confused than before. "We need those keys, Phoebe. There must be times when Estelle doesn't carry hers . . . like when she takes a bath, for instance. When does she usually bathe, Aunt Pity?"

Pity sniffed. "Haven't heard her but once since we've been here. Staying clean's not one of her strong points, she just covers it all up with powder and perfume."

"Miss Saunielle, who . . ." Phoebe began, but I shook my head. I wasn't ready to put those nebulous suspicions into words yet.

I walked to the door of my room and withdrew the key in the lock. "In our house back in Virginia you could open any door with almost any key. Remember, Phoebe, the time I locked myself in after a shouting match with Aunt Rachael, and she got the key to her own door and worked it around until it opened my door? I wonder if the keys in this house have any duplicates?"

Without waiting for a reply, I walked to the door into the study, and tried my key there. It fitted into the lock all right, but did not lock the door, so I strode through and tried it in the door into Sebastian's room, and then on his door into the hallway. On that one, it worked.

Excitement was a thin, hot trickle of electricity in my system. "Let's go see if it works."

Alarm flared in Phoebe's face, but she didn't argue. "Alfred's up there. He may not let us near the door to find out."

"Then we'd better have something to give him to draw his attention. Will you get something?"

She vanished without a word. "Where's Estelle now?" I asked.

"Went into her room just before Phoebe dragged me off down here. I was going to bang on her door and tell her what I thought about people making noises all night."

That complicated the problem. For if Pity could hear the girl talking in her own room . . . or in the room directly across the hall . . .

then Estelle would hear us. Unless we made some sort of cover sounds of our own, something she wouldn't find odd enough to investigate.

"When Phoebe comes back, Aunt Pity, would you go in the bathroom and run a tub full of water? Run it full open, so it will make as much noise as possible."

"But the heater's not lit, and it takes ages for the hot water to rise from the furnace," Pity protested. "They told us not to waste water that way."

"Nobody's going to take a bath in it. I only want to make enough noise so Estelle won't hear us trying the key in that lock. Oh, and get the key from your room and Phoebe's, and I'll take all the ones from here, just in case. Let's go."

We made our way up the front stairs. At this hour the elderly men were all in their rooms, most of them probably already asleep. The stairs were unlighted except for lamps on the various landings, and tension added to the pain I already felt from the injuries I'd suffered earlier.

Even so, it did not feel like a sleeping house. I cautioned Pity to silence, and she nodded without speaking.

Alfred was there, at his post in front of the storage room door. He must have been getting used to us, because he didn't get up to growl but did it lying down, displaying his wicked little fangs when he curled his lip.

We stopped at a reasonable distance, wondering if the dog would rouse Estelle. Her door was closed and there were no sounds behind it.

Alfred heard Phoebe coming before we did, turning his head toward the stairs, his growl subsiding although he made no move to abandon his post.

Phoebe was panting a bit, and she carried a saucepan of milk. "It was on the stove, someone's made an evening drink and left it with the skin forming on it. So I just brought it the way it is, since there wasn't any meat left from supper. We don't have to worry about Estelle, she's sitting with her aunt in the back parlor and they're having a row about something. I thought it might be interesting to listen to it, but maybe it was more important to tend to this, first."

Alfred sniffed gingerly at the milk, then looked at Phoebe, obviously thinking she ought to have done better than this.

"Go on, it's nice and warm, you'll like it," Phoebe urged, and he lapped at it, at first without enthusiasm, and then more quickly, cleaning it up.

While he was doing that, I approached the door behind him with my collection of keys. It took only a few moments, however, to realize that none of our keys would even fit into the keyhole. It was an entirely different type of lock.

"Well, maybe she's left her keys in her room this time of night," I said without much hope. But this time Estelle, too, had locked her room.

Pity put her ear to the panel of the door, listening intently. "I don't hear anything now. I say, is anyone in there?"

She had raised her voice enough so that Phoebe and I made shushing motions at her, which she ignored. "He doesn't answer, if he's in there."

"I remember Papa said at Hunter's Hill the household keys were often hung on a nail in the kitchen. Do you suppose there's any chance we could find such a place here? Keys to everything would be rather heavy, and I've never noticed Mrs. Fox carrying hers. Let's see if we can find them. You stay here, Pity. You can be a sort of guard, only stay inside your room with the door ajar and just watch. If you leave your lamp out no one will notice."

We skirted Alfred to reach the back stairs, but it was clear now that it wasn't the stairs he objected to our using, he was trained to keep casual wanderers away from the locked storage room.

Phoebe was right about the row; we could hear it all the way back in the kitchen, although when I closed the door at the bottom of the stairs the sound must have carried to them and their voices were lowered at once.

We set about quite methodically to search for keys, looking into the pantry, inside of cupboards, in the broom closet. There were no keys. We went on to more unlikely places: drawers, odd nooks and crannies.

We didn't find the keys, but we did find something else.

In the umbrella stand in the front hallway, I found a gun.

◇◇◇◇ 21 ◇◇◇◇

Why had I looked in the umbrella stand for the keys? I had no reason whatever to think anyone in their right mind would have hidden them there. But I was looking into every aperture where a sizable collection of keys could be put, and that was one of them.

At first I didn't credit what I was seeing, and when I did I was afraid to reach in and draw it out.

Phoebe, whispering because we didn't want anyone to know where we were or what we were doing in the dimly lighted hall, demanded upon hearing my indrawn breath, "What is it? Did you find them?"

"No. Phoebe, there's a gun in there. It's a pistol, isn't it? Papa used to have one that he used for target practice."

She reached in among the umbrellas and drew it out. "A pistol," she confirmed, and then she held it to her nose and sniffed. "I don't know a lot about guns, but I know you can smell them right after they've been fired. Smell, miss."

I swallowed hard, fighting the compulsion to sit down on the hall chair. "Phoebe, you don't think . . ."

"They said it was the Tongs . . ."

"But Sebastian said the Tongs don't shoot guns, they use hatchets. Oh, my God, Phoebe . . ."

We stared at each other and then at the weapon. It was not very large, nor very heavy, weighing less than a pound, but it looked much like the one Papa had had, which was capable of firing six shells, one after the other.

Some of the wispy suspicions suddenly took on new life, more definite form. There had been someone behind us in the fog when we left the house, someone who stopped when we stopped, someone who might have been following us. A woman, Dodie thought, because of the sound of the heels, although I hadn't paid that much attention. And then Dodie had been followed from the cable-car stop to the house by someone . . . a man? . . . who had been careful not to approach close enough to be seen.

Belle and Estelle had both returned to the house very shortly after Dodie, not long ahead of Phoebe and me. When we came in, I trembling so that I had to sit down, who all had been there? I tried to remember and couldn't say for sure. Had someone followed us to Grant Avenue, fired the shots, and taken a "dinky" home while I was being cared for by Mrs. James? And then, because there were so many people around, hidden the pistol in the easiest place, to be retrieved later?

It seemed altogether too much of a coincidence to think otherwise. The gun *had* been recently fired. And if it were kept for legitimate purposes, which was quite possible in a household of women and elderly men, it wouldn't be hidden in an umbrella stand.

Phoebe ran her tongue over her lips. "What'll I do with it?"

"Maybe we'd better put it back. Until we know what we're going to do, it might be better if they don't know we've found it. Do you know how to unload it?"

She shook her head, and I was no more knowledgeable than she, so we had to leave it as it was.

"Sebastian will be back soon," I said in a voice that Phoebe leaned forward to hear. "Let's leave it . . . everything . . . until he comes. And then I'll tell him all of it, and he'll know what to do."

She nodded, sliding the weapon back into its nest of umbrellas. "That's it, miss, Mr. Sebastian will take care of it."

But Sebastian, when he came, was in no mood to listen.

I heard him coming up the stairs shortly after midnight. I had undressed and gone to bed, but not to sleep, listening for the sound of horses and the carriage he would surely take this time of the night.

His steps were heavy and slow, much slower than usual. I had left a light burning so that it would show under my door, fearing that if he believed me asleep he would go on to his room. I slipped out of bed and reached for the dressing gown that lay across the foot of the bed, my heart beginning that now familiar pounding. I had gone over the words so many times in my mind, and this time I would do it properly, I would start with the last letter from Papa . . . no, with my meeting Francis . . . and go on to the end, so that he would understand why I had had to do what I did . . .

The knob turned and then stopped as if he'd changed his mind.

"Sebastian?" I had kicked my slippers under the bed and I felt for them, then gave up and moved toward the door, opening it myself. "Sebastian, I'm so glad you're back . . ."

My words faltered and died, for he looked terrible. In a matter of hours his eyes seemed to have sunk into his skull, and his mouth was a grim, flat line.

"Sebastian . . . ? Your grandfather . . . ?"

"He died half an hour ago." His mouth twisted in what I thought was pain, and then he drew in a deep breath and stepped into the room, closing the door behind him.

"Is it true?" he demanded, and now there was ugliness in his tone, in the lines of his face.

Involuntarily, I took a step backward. "Is what true?"

"That you're *pregnant.*" His hand came out and grasped the neck of my gown, so quickly that even as I flinched he had ripped it downward, exposing me. "Answer me! *Are you?*"

He must have read the reply in my face even as I struggled to find the words to tell him that it was not the way he thought. His gaze raked over me with the cutting edge of a razor; I felt as if I'd been slashed, a wound far more painful than being grazed by a bullet.

"Sebastian, I was going to tell you as soon as you came home . . ."

"I'll bet you were!" He was trembling in a fine, controlled rage. Controlled, except for the fact that his hands had formed fists. To have been struck by them would have been less agonizing than to look into his eyes and see the rage, the humiliation, the suffering there. "Well, I won't wait around to listen to your story, whatever it is. I'll spare us both that, Saunielle. You've served your purpose, and

I've served mine, haven't I? Your child will now be *legitimate*. So that makes us even. Cromwell will be in touch with you about the legalities, and I'm enough of a gentleman so I won't betray you. But I never want to see you again as long as I live, because if I do, I'll probably kill you."

He turned on his heel and strode out of the room, leaving me clutching the shreds of my nightdress.

My paralysis lasted only seconds, but by the time I'd found another wrap to cover my nakedness and run after him, he was nearly at the bottom of the stairs. I called his name, but he did not turn, did not reply, and the reverberations from the slamming door echoed through the silent house with enough force to waken everyone in it.

Stricken, I could only cling to the banister with hands gone icy. What had happened? How had he found out? And then, long after the sound of the horses' hoofs had died away in the street outside, I thought, *What am I going to do now?*

Phoebe found me there, my tearful face pressed against a newell post, crouched in much the same position as the child within me must be.

"Miss Saunielle! What is it, what's happened?"

I told her, in so incoherent a fashion that it's a wonder she made it out. She led me back to my room, making no effort to curb my sobbing, only providing me with a square of linen to cry into.

When the worst of the outburst was over, we looked wanly at each other in the lamplight.

"You don't think he'll come back, miss?"

"No. Oh, Phoebe, he said he never wanted to see me again as long as he lived, and that he'd probably kill me if he did!"

"He's badly hurt, because he loves you, and what he thinks isn't what really happened. When he knows that he'll come back, miss, I'm sure he will."

I would have liked to think so, but I didn't. "I waited too long, Phoebe. I should have somehow managed to tell him sooner, myself. I think then he'd have understood, but . . ."

"But someone else told him. There's no way anyone could guess by looking at you, miss, so someone had to tell him."

Having to think had a calming effect on me. "Yes. You're right. Who would have done that, and why?"

"Who knew? Me, and Mrs. Fox, and Estelle."

"Why, Phoebe? Is it me they're quarreling about? Estelle wants me out of this house, and I don't know what Mrs. Fox wants. Why did she let me come here in the first place if she didn't want me? What are we going to do, Phoebe?"

Poor Phoebe was spared having to come up with a sensible reply to the unanswerable by a tap on the door, and then Pity's white head appeared in the opening.

"I heard you talking . . . Phoebe, I think you'd better take a look at that dog."

"Alfred? Why? What's he doing?"

Pity edged into the room, not appearing to notice my sodden condition. "He's not doing anything, that's the trouble. He kept on guarding that room for a while, and then I think he died."

"Died!" That was enough to take my mind off my own troubles, at least momentarily. "What makes you think he died, Aunt Pity?"

She gave me a look such as one bestows on a not-too-bright child. "Because he sort of fell over and he's just lying there, not doing anything. Even when I prodded him with the toe of my slipper, he didn't move. If he'd just gone to sleep he'd move if I poked him, wouldn't he?"

It seemed important enough to find out. We went up the stairs together, being quiet so as not to wake anyone, in case there were any lucky enough to have slept through Sebastian's exit. I was surprised that Belle Fox, at least, hadn't turned out to see what was going on, for she was closer to the front door than Phoebe was, and Phoebe heard it.

We found Alfred much as Pity had said, lying with his head on his front paws, unmoving. Phoebe sank to her knees, putting a hand on his flank, and then leaning to lay her ear against it.

"He's not dead, but he's certainly sleeping hard. There must have been something in the milk."

In the gloomy passageway, I felt the hair rising on the back of my neck, something I had previously experienced only in a pleasurable way when reading a particularly frightening story late at night. This time there was nothing pleasurable about it at all.

"I wonder who got the rest of it?"

Phoebe turned and looked at the locked door. "If there is someone in there, and Estelle wanted him . . . or her . . . less restless at night, she might have brought up the milk with some sleeping medication in it."

"We've got to get into that room. There must be some way to lay hands on the keys. And we'll have to do it ourselves, because . . . because Sebastian won't help us, now. Pity, is Estelle in her room?"

She shook her head. "No. I think she went out a bit ago."

"Out?" Phoebe and I were a chorus of astonishment. "At this time of night?"

"Well, she had on a wrap, and she went down the stairs. I assume she went out; it wasn't the sort of thing one wears in the house unless the heat is off in midwinter. I don't understand. What's going on?"

"We don't understand, either, Aunt Pity. But we're going to find out. Is her room locked?"

It was, but it yielded to the key to Phoebe's room. We were past the point of being cautious. I felt that if I survived this night . . . and I was not sure I cared, one way or the other . . . I would have to take on Belle Fox and Estelle in open confrontation simply because I could no longer bear to go on the way we were.

We charged into Estelle's room, lit lamps, and began to go through her belongings with a carelessness that was immaterial, since they were strewn everywhere.

"If she went out, she'll have taken her keys so she can get back in," Phoebe guessed.

"Maybe. And maybe, if it's a sizable bunch of them, she'll have left everything here except the one to the front door. Ah!"

And there they were, tossed into the drawer in the little nightstand beside her bed.

There were a lot of them; it looked as if she carried duplicates to all of ours, as well as the general household keys. It wasn't even necessary to try all of them on the door to the "storeroom," because it was so different from the others that it was immediately apparent.

My hand only trembled a little as I inserted the key in the lock and turned it, but apprehension recalled the nausea of my morning sickness.

The room was dark, and it took us a few minutes to fetch an oil lamp from Estelle's room.

And there he was, and I knew why there had been no grave for Edward Marshall Hunter.

◇◇◇◇◇◇

He lay in a drugged sleep, but Papa was alive.

The first few minutes in the room were rather wild ones, for me. I flung myself across the bed, imploring him to wake up, until Phoebe tugged at my shoulder.

"Miss, he's had some of that same milk as Alfred. You won't wake him until it wears off."

"What if she's given him too much? What if he doesn't wake up?"

"If she'd wanted to kill him I'd say she's quite capable of doing it, miss. They've kept him locked up here for some time, it would seem. No wonder Estelle didn't want us here! If they hadn't thought Miss Pity was deaf, they wouldn't have put any of us close enough to notice anything amiss. Well, there's your 'rats,' Miss Pity."

She stood beside the bed, looking down on him. "Poor Edward. He's been very sick, I'd say, from the look of him. More than just being given drugged milk. I don't understand. Why is he locked up here?"

"No doubt when he wakens he'll be able to tell us," I said, gradually regaining control of myself. "But we've suspected, Phoebe and I, that Papa bought this house, for himself and me. And then somehow he seems to have married Mrs. Fox, unlikely as that seems, and rather than acknowledge him as her husband, who was ill, she simply appropriated all of his belongings. She didn't expect me, and she was shocked when I turned up. I don't know why she admitted she'd been married to him; if she hadn't I'd have simply gone away."

"Would you?" Phoebe asked shrewdly. "When that Mr. Johansen had seen them together? Wouldn't you have kept searching until you found out what had happened to him?"

I had to admit that I would have. All the implications of this monstrous hoax hadn't quite caught up with me, but some of them had. She had tried to force me . . . no, *sell* me . . . into what could only have been a disastrous marriage, perhaps to get me out of this house in an acceptable fashion.

And Estelle . . . from the beginning Estelle had been hostile. She had not wanted us here, for she had feared exactly what had happened; that we would discover Papa.

"I ought to find a doctor for him," I said, touching the hand that lay limply atop the sheet. He had lost a good deal of weight and aged far more than the five years we had been apart; there was a lot of gray in his hair and his beard. But he was living, breathing, and tomorrow he would wake up and know that I had found him.

"Doubt if a doctor would do much, except to let him sleep it off naturally," Pity said. "We used to give laudanum to the soldiers during the war, and sometimes it was frightening how long they would sleep. But when they were in pain they would move and moan, even under the drug. Edward's not in pain, he's sleeping peacefully."

"Yes. But I won't, not while he's here. I'm going to wake Dodie and look at that map of hers, see if there's a hospital near. Or . . . maybe it would be enough just to get him out of *here*. We could take him to Mrs. Morton's. She liked him, he had a friend there. I wonder if it's possible to summon a conveyance of any sort, this late at night?"

They looked at me dubiously. "How would we get him downstairs, miss?"

"Look at him, he's lost pounds and pounds! Surely if we made a stretcher of some sort we could get him down, the four of us."

"Down three flights?" Phoebe asked, but she'd already peeled back the covers to look at the wasted form in the nightshirt that needed changing.

"You rouse Dodie," I said. "And I'll go downstairs and use the telephone, see if I can call up a carriage."

Phoebe turned from the bed to call after me. "I know what we can do, Miss Saunielle. There's a ladder in the pantry. We can pad it with blankets and tear up a sheet to fasten him on it, and then I think we can maneuver around the turns in the stairs, even."

I ran. The ladder came out and was leaned near the bottom of the back stairs, ready to go up. And then the telephone. I'd only used one once in my life, but I knew one cranked the handle to get the attention of the operator and then told her either a number or the person one wanted to call.

Before I got to the telephone, however, I found Belle, and I saw why she hadn't been investigating. She was sprawled in her chair in the parlor, in what could only be described as a drunken stupor, for the brandy bottle stood open beside her, much depleted, and her glass had fallen from her hand onto the carpet.

Good. Let her sleep, and she wouldn't bother us. I hurried on past to the telephone closet.

The operator was an alarming time coming on the line, but when she did she was helpful, to the extent of telling me that she had no way to contact any of the drivers of the cabriolets still working at this time of night. They'd be in the theater districts, or around the good restaurants.

I thought furiously, and then did the only thing I could think of. I called Caleb Rohann's palatial home on Taylor Street, frightened when the butler came on the wire but even more determined. Chances were he didn't know anything about Sebastian's repudiation of me, not yet.

"Marlon, this is Mrs. Sebastian Rohann," I said, and felt my mouth go dry and my chest ache with the effort of trying to breathe naturally.

"Yes, madame," he responded immediately.

"Marlon, I'm very sorry about Mr. Rohann. And I have an emergency for which I need a carriage. Is there any possibility that a family conveyance would be available?"

His voice was strangely distorted but recognizable. "Certainly, Mrs. Rohann. Where would you like me to send it?"

I gave him the address, considerable warmth in my voice, and then dared to ask. "Mr. Sebastian hasn't returned there, has he, Marlon?"

"No, madame. Is there a message if he should do so?"

I swallowed hard, blinking back the maddening tears. "No. No message. Thank you, Marlon."

When I had hung up, I became aware of my own dishevelment. I would have to dress before I could go anywhere. How long did we have before Estelle came back? And what would she do when she did?

I remembered the gun and knew that it was too dangerous to leave it where it was. The last thing I wanted was to confront Estelle with a loaded pistol just as we were trying to leave the house.

I paused, thrusting one hand deep into the umbrella stand, then wildly pulling out the umbrellas even as I realized the truth. The pistol was gone. Estelle must have taken it with her. Well, there was nothing I could do about that now but to hurry, and hope we could be gone before she returned.

The ladder was awkward to handle, and before I got it to the second floor Phoebe joined me to help, having heard it bump against the walls. I hoped Belle had drunk enough brandy to incapacitate her for hours.

"Miss Dodie's getting dressed. I had a little trouble explaining things, but I think she's all right now. Did you see anything of Mrs. Fox?"

I told her, and also about the pistol. We climbed the rest of the way in silence.

In our absence Pity had undertaken to get poor Papa into a clean nightshirt. She was muttering angrily about the way he'd been taken care of, for he had not been bathed regularly and he had bed sores.

"You shouldn't have undressed him, Aunt Pity," Dodie said, somewhat shocked and no more than barely awake. "You're a maiden lady, and you know what Mama would have said!"

"Pish," Aunt Pity said flatly. "I dressed and undressed more than one man during the war, and made them all feel the better for being clean. Though the poor man needs more than a nightshirt to achieve that."

We set to work, padding the ladder and tearing up a sheet into wide strips, and then we secured Papa to it, as on a stretcher, and wrapped him warmly with another blanket, and secured that, and we were ready to go.

Poor Papa was so pitifully thin that we had no trouble lifting him, Phoebe and I, although she was worried that such a strain might be very bad for me. A miscarriage was the least of my worries at the moment; if being upset would bring one on I must have lost the infant long since, and might yet, I told her, from the sheer horror of remaining another night in Mrs. Fox's house.

"All right, let's go," I said, and reached for the bar at one end of the ladder when what we had been dreading happened.

There was no warning. We heard nothing until Estelle appeared in the doorway, her thin face flushed and angry, still in her outdoor clothes.

"How did you get in here?"

"Does it matter?" I turned to face her, noting that she did not carry the pistol, at least not in sight. "We're taking him out of this house, Estelle, and you can't stop us. Your aunt is passed out in the parlor, and there are four of us to your one."

"I don't think you're going anywhere at all," Estelle said, her face mottled and ugly, and there was conviction in her tone. "Because the odds are better than that, *Mrs.* Rohann. There are *two* of us, and we have a loaded gun that's the equal of several more."

I would have sworn Belle was in such a deep stupor she couldn't possibly have come out of it, but I was ready to fight the pair of them with every means I had. And when I'd rescued Papa, I thought in determination, I would find a way to reach Sebastian, too. If he loved me, there would be some way I could make him listen to me . . . and if he listened, he would understand. Estelle and Belle Fox be damned, I was taking Papa out of this place.

But it was not Belle who stepped to the doorway beside Estelle.

It was someone I had thought never to see again. I felt as if the blood had drained from my body, taking with it my strength and my wits as well.

For I was staring into the mocking face of Francis Verland.

❖❖❖❖ 22 ❖❖❖❖

It was Phoebe who cried out. Speech was beyond me, for the moment.

He looked no different. Tall, elegant, with his diamond stickpin, a cruel amusement in his half-smile.

"Hello, Saunielle. You didn't mourn for me very long, did you?"

My lips formed his name, but no sound issued from them. He was a stranger, even his face seemed sharper and different now.

Estelle drew his attention from me. "What are we going to do now?"

"The same thing we were going to do before. Nothing's changed, there are only more of them to get rid of. You're sure this Rohann isn't going to come tearing back to the rescue?"

"He won't be back," Estelle said, and there was malice in the bitter smile she bestowed on me. "Not the way he went out of this house!"

I inhaled deeply enough to force the necessary air into the words. *"You* told him."

"Somebody needed to. Belle wouldn't, the fool. She wouldn't tell him, she wouldn't get rid of you, and now see what's happened. If you hadn't come here it would have been so simple." She cast a contemptuous glance at the unconscious man on the improvised stretcher. *"He* couldn't do anything. He's had two strokes, and eventually he would have died a natural death. Only now we can't wait for that, thanks to you."

Her meaning was only too clear. I realized that Francis carried the gun, and I had no doubt that he'd made sure it was loaded. That meant at least five, possibly six shells. Plenty to go around for all of us. Yet I could not give up, not when we'd just found Papa, sick, but alive. Not when Sebastian was thinking the worst of me, when he didn't know I truly loved him.

"It was you who followed us today," I said to Estelle, "and shot at me." Unconsciously, my fingertips brushed the dressing on my shoulder.

Francis laughed. "If she'd been a decent shot, a major share of the problem would have been solved. *He's* no threat, she'd only to leave him alone until he died. Incidentally, *I'm* an excellent shot, so don't get any ideas, ladies."

Dodie and Pity stood, frozen-faced, probably not understanding any of this. Phoebe understood all too well, and she put in her own two cents' worth. "A fine man you are, Mr. Verland. Stealing from your employer, making it look as if someone else had done it . . . it was *him* found with the ring on him, wasn't it? That poor Mr. Erquart? I suppose you killed him, too."

"I hadn't much choice, as a matter of fact," Francis said, with an appalling lack of concern. "The damned bank examiner came a month early. I expected to have the funds and be well on my way to California with my bride before he came, and even if they ever came after me, my rich father-in-law wouldn't have let them jail me. Your letter came so opportunely, my dear, and it was too tempting to pass up. Only once they knew the money was missing from the bank I had to disappear, in such a way that they wouldn't look for me. I was sorry to give up the Jaubert ring, but I understand they gave it back to you. Where is it, Saunielle?"

Though it was painful, I couldn't stop swallowing, which left my mouth dryer than ever. "Where is what?"

"The Jaubert ring! The constable took it off the body from the river and gave it back to you, I know that."

Why did he want the ring? My mind raced, but to no avail; I could make no sense of his demand.

He took a step toward me, and I saw the viciousness in his dark eyes. "Where is it?"

"It . . . it was stolen. On the train trip, on the way out here."

His left hand came up in a brutal swing, nearly jarring me off my feet. "I don't believe you. Where is it?"

I had no idea why the Jaubert ring was of any importance, but it might possibly give me a bargaining point if it were valuable, if he wanted it badly enough. "I told you. It was stolen."

"I told you I hadn't seen anything like that," Estelle put in. "Not since she's been here. If they'd had anything that was worth money they'd have converted it; you ought to have seen them! Shoes and clothes worn out, looking as if they'd just made the trek by covered wagon!"

Francis looked speculatively at my present attire, one of the traveling suits Sebastian had bought for me. "It looks as if this new 'husband' has taken care of that. Did he give you jewels, too?"

I said nothing, but he must have read the affirmative in my face, for he smiled. His smile was nothing as I remembered it, no warmth, no beauty, nothing human or humane. "Well, we'll have time to check on that later. It's too bad there isn't some way to cash in on everything, including the Rohann fortune, but I can't figure out a way to do it. We'll have to settle for the Jaubert one, and let it go at that. But I need that damned ring. If anyone of you knows where it is, if she's lying about it being gone, you'd better tell me."

No one said anything. Phoebe was the only one who knew I'd gotten it back, knew that it lay in a drawer in my dresser with the pieces Sebastian had given me.

"No? Well, all right. I have a valid marriage certificate, and maybe that will be enough, although the ring would have been very convincing. The man wasn't in Virginia long enough to learn anything about me, at least I don't think he was. So when he shows up here in San Francisco, as he will eventually, I've only to produce the proof of our marriage and that ought to make me your heir."

In spite of my shock, I was beginning to make sense of the entire thing. I knew my mother's family had had wealth, and although she had been estranged from them for many years before her death, it was quite possible that my grandfather, before dying, had relented in his anger. Relented enough to leave his fortune to Mama, or, since she had died, to me.

I wet my lips. "Did you know . . . about the Jaubert fortune . . . when you married me?"

"Oh no, I didn't learn about that until the little lawyer came looking for you. If I'd known earlier I'd have done things very differently, maybe managed to put back the funds from the bank and left town an honest man. Luckily he didn't stay around long enough to learn much except that you'd taken a ship for California. And I had friends who reported back to me and helped me get out of Virginia. By the time I learned about the ring and the fortune, it was too late to reappear and take my place as your husband. There were too many things I couldn't explain, such as how the ring came to be on a dead man in the river. So the only thing to do was to vanish and surface later as your widower . . . and heir."

Oh yes, it was getting clearer all the time. Clearer and muddier, all at the same time, because the clearest thing of all was that he couldn't allow me to live if he expected to get away with any of this. Me . . . or anyone else in this room.

"And Estelle? How does she come into this?" I was amazed that I'd been able to keep them talking; their confidence must be immense, that they would not be interrupted, that they would be able to carry out their plans with us. I no longer cared about the details, all that mattered was staying alive, but so long as I could keep them talking there was a chance . . . a faint one, but a chance.

Francis laughed. "An amateur, but not a bad one, if only she were a better shot. I followed you today, and your visit to Chinatown was perfect for my purposes. If young white women were attacked and killed down there everyone would say it was their own fault for being so foolish. People die there every day, and no one ever knows who killed them. Sometimes, I understand, they simply disappear, but I couldn't have that happen to you, because I needed proof of your death so that the Jaubert fortune would then come to me. So I followed you, thinking to do you in in an alley, somewhat in the manner of the Tongs who are experts with the garrote. Only Estelle got to you first, and when I observed *that*, I was very curious and decided to wait. I wanted to know why she wanted to kill you. Once I learned that, it seemed logical to join forces, since we both had a good deal to gain from your death and two of us could accomplish this more easily and with less risk."

"We're wasting time. Belle may wake up," Estelle interjected uneasily.

"I don't understand." I had tried to glance unobtrusively around the room, seeking a weapon, but there was nothing. "What had Estelle to gain?"

"Why, this house and home, of course. You mean you haven't figured that out? That your darling papa had hired Mrs. Fox as a housekeeper in his grand new home, and then only two days after he moved in he had a stroke! What a marvelous bit of luck! He was virtually helpless, and Mrs. Fox persuaded him that it would be wise to marry her if he wanted to be fed and cared for until he died. Estelle told me all about it, it was quite a bold and clever plan, except that they had no idea you were coming to California. He'd neglected to mention that. They even found a clergyman who was half-blind and senile to perform the ceremony, what could be better?"

I saw that Phoebe, too, was casting about for some means of disarming the man, for between us we could handle Estelle and possibly even Francis, for all his superior strength. If only he didn't have that pistol!

On the ladder-stretcher, Papa groaned and rolled his head.

Francis immediately lost his good humor. "For God's sake, he's coming around already! You didn't give him enough of the stuff!"

"I told you. He refused to swallow, and even when I held his nose he struggled and spilled a lot of it." Estelle was sullen. "I've suspected he was getting better and was keeping it hidden, and tonight I was sure of it because he was awfully strong for a man who's had two strokes and not enough to eat since the last one!"

"Two strokes?" I said quickly. "Did you have a doctor for him?"

"A doctor? And let him tell the man we were keeping him prisoner? I wanted to stop feeding him and let him die, but Belle wouldn't let me, she was sure she could force him to tell where he'd hidden the rest of the money. She wouldn't have had to sell her old rooming house or take in lodgers here if she'd had it. And see what that's gotten us! We haven't found it, and she let you stay in the house until you discovered he was here, and now we've no choice but to get rid of the lot of you!"

"And you think that will solve your problems?" I feigned astonishment. "Francis', maybe. If I'm found dead, and there's no evidence indicating he did it, he'll get what *he* wants. Is that the way you're going to do it? I'll be killed in some way that can't be traced to Francis? When he has witnesses to say that he was elsewhere, perhaps? Is he going to let *you* do it, Estelle? But what good will that do you? At the moment you can't be charged with anything but holding a sick man prisoner"—I conveniently forgot her attempt to murder me—"but if you go through with this you'll be guilty of murder. I'm not sure what the penalty is for murder in California . . . hanging, or do you have that new gas chamber here? Either way, an unpleasant way to die. And if Papa's hidden the money, and you haven't located it in the two months you've been in this house, what makes you think you'll ever find it? How will you keep the house, you and Belle, without funds to run it? There will be taxes, and someone sooner or later will demand proof that you own it, won't they? Belle may pass herself off as his widow, but without legal proof of Papa's legitimate death she's going to have a time convincing anyone who really gets curious. She can't sell this place, she had to dispose of her own house because she hadn't funds, and she must be desperate indeed to take in a houseful of roomers when she was keeping Papa locked up here. Have you thought about it, Estelle? What he's asking you to do? Don't you see he's using you, as he used me? And if you're depending upon that pistol to do the job, you'd better think again."

There was a startled silence, and I saw a leaping flash of understanding in Phoebe's eyes.

"We found it this evening," I said deliberately, "in the umbrella stand, and took the shells out of it."

I had thought surely Francis would have checked it himself when Estelle handed it over to him. A look at his face convinced me that he had not; that he was, at least briefly, unsure if what I said was the truth.

Estelle believed me. She gasped, uncertain what to do, poised for flight.

And her belief convinced Francis. He swore, flinging what he thought to be a useless weapon away from him. I heard it land on the bed behind me with a muffled sound, but there was no way I could reach it, for Francis launched himself at me, hands closing around my throat as he carried me backward.

His fingers cut cruelly into my flesh and I knew that his strength was so superior to mine that even a knee brought up sharply, my only weapon, wasn't going to be enough.

I heard Phoebe's yell of unladylike anger, and realized vaguely that she was struggling with Estelle in an attempt to come to my assistance. My vision was fading away into a reddish haze as my breathing was cut off, and I fell backward onto the bed, arms flailing wildly and without purpose.

And then my fingers touched metal. Metal, on the bed. It could only be the pistol, and with a supreme effort, consciousness failing, I grasped it and brought it up.

If Francis had not been so furious, so intent on throttling me, he could easily have taken the weapon away from me. As it was, I do not think he was aware that I'd found it.

I brought it up into the space between us, where he knelt on one knee over me in a grotesque mockery of the love-making that had once been between us, and I pulled the trigger.

For a few seconds his hands did not loosen, and then he withdrew enough so that I could see his face. His mouth went slack, more from surprise than pain, it seemed, and then he slid sideways onto the bed and then onto the floor.

Everyone else in the room was poised as if playing the old game of Statues. I gasped painfully, the pistol forgotten as I brought my hands up to my bruised throat. Estelle was the first to move, darting toward the bed and the pistol, but Phoebe was only a second behind and shoved the other girl off balance to capture the prize herself.

I pushed myself into a sitting position, chest heaving, but Estelle was no longer threatening. Phoebe spoke coldly.

"Two this afternoon, and one now," she said. "That should leave three more. I'd suggest you stay where you are, miss, unless you want the rest of them."

For a moment no one moved, no one spoke, except Estelle, who was cursing in a helpless, tearful manner. I moved so as to avoid touching Francis, who lay as he had fallen, blood spreading on the back of his coat where the bullet had passed through his body.

There was blood all over the front of me, and my throat hurt abominably. I croaked, "Is he dead?"

"Oh, I should think so, miss." Phoebe's face was very white, her freckles starkly visible across her nose. "Oh, miss, I think I'm going to be sick!"

And my sturdy, pragmatic, brave Phoebe thrust the pistol into my hands and fled for the bathroom.

We heard footsteps on the stairs, and I thought for a moment that the coachman from Rohann's had arrived and let himself in. Dear God, what would he think of the carnage, the blood . . .

But it was Belle.

She stumbled a little, her eyes bleary as she struggled to make out what was going on in the crowded room. "I thought I heard a shot . . ." she began, and then stopped, pressing both hands against the door frame as if to keep from falling. "Who's that?"

It hurt to speak, and the wound on my shoulder was aching as well, but I wanted this to come to an end as soon as possible, and I got the words out. "Francis Verland. The man I married back in Virginia." I looked down on him, and I ought to have been horrified and shocked beyond measure, and all I felt was detachment, as if he were a perfect stranger who had invaded my home and attacked me. "I had to shoot him. We'll have to call the police."

Belle was breathing heavily, moving her head slowly from side to side as if by not believing she could make it all untrue. "Is he dead? In my house?"

Talking was somewhat easier with practice, although I suspected my throat would be sore for a long time. "I think you are in error, there, Mrs. Fox. *Papa's* house, not yours."

She began to believe, then. That it was all over. That she was defeated. "I didn't hurt him," she said defensively. "I never did anything to him. I took care of him."

"By not calling a doctor for him? By letting Estelle feed him on starvation rations? By not letting him know I was here, when I could have helped just by being with him?"

"He knew you were here," Estelle said. "I don't know how, but he knew. Belle was a fool. I never dreamed she'd let you stay more than a day or two. If she'd simply sent you away none of this would have happened."

"I'm going downstairs," I said unsteadily, "and call the police and a lawyer. And then, since this is *our* house, I think you'd better pack up your things and leave it. Unless the police take you into custody, of course."

I stepped over the drugged dog as I left the room, and Belle saw him for the first time. With an outraged cry, she dropped to her knees and cradled him in her arms, sobbing over him as one would over an injured child.

A woman who could cry over a dog, when she'd kept my papa a prisoner in his own house for over two months and cared not a whit what happened to him, was beyond my comprehension.

I went down the stairs, feeling nothing, not even, for the moment, joy in the knowledge that we had found Papa in time, nor in the confirmation of our suspicions that this house belonged to him, for Sebastian was gone and he had sworn he would never come back. But there was no time to think about Sebastian . . . Sebastian, who was not and never had been my legal husband. He was free, if he wanted to be. When this was over I would tell him that. And then, if my courage lasted that long, I would tell him that I loved him, as he had once told me.

Someone was at the door, and I answered the bell like a sort of automaton, letting in the coachman. I must have been a sight, my hair loose and streaming as it had been when I got ready for bed, carelessly dressed in the dress I had worn on the journey West, which was the first thing that had come to hand, blood on my hands and skirt.

"Mrs. Rohann?" he asked with incredulity.

"Yes. Please come in and wait. I must make a telephone call, and then . . ." I didn't know whether I wanted to leave now, or not. Thinking was almost more of an effort than I cared to make.

I left him standing there, bewildered and alarmed, to open the door of the telephone closet.

It took five minutes, but the operator was able to locate Cromwell. When I explained the circumstances, he asked no questions but promised to be there directly. He would notify the authorities himself.

As I replaced the receiver on the hook, Belle came downstairs, her face swollen with crying, carrying Alfred under one arm and an old-fashioned carpetbag under the other.

"I did the best I could for you, my dear," she said, with some remnant of dignity. "And I meant none of you any harm."

I could not find it within myself to reply. She rested the bag on a chair and stroked the head of the ugly little bulldog, who was limp and unresponsive. "If there is a conveyance available, I will go to a hotel," she said.

The coachman, who must have been quite amazed at the state of this household at two o'clock in the morning, stepped forward. "Would you like me to take the lady to a hotel, madame?"

"Yes. Yes, please do. And I don't think I'll need you myself, after all. Thank you for coming."

I didn't wait to see them gone. Belle Fox was of no concern to me any more.

Upstairs, we moved Papa into the room that had been Sebastian's, and left a light burning beside him so that when he woke up he would know he had been rescued. And then I went back down and let in Mr. Cromwell, who took over as if the occurrences of this evening were no more than routine.

Policemen came, and wiped their feet before crossing the front hall carpet, and spoke in hushed voices. Estelle, who had evidently planned to slip quietly away, was once more trapped by her own greediness, for she tried to load up and take as many things as she could carry. They found her in her room, loading suitcases. I stood to one side, ignoring her invective, as one of the policemen led her away.

Mr. Cromwell urged us all to try to get some rest, assuring us that everything would be taken care of and that an officer would be posted on the second floor and another in the entryway until morning. We were in no danger and we should sleep if we could.

Dodie, who had quite remarkably restrained herself from having hysterics throughout the ordeal, offered to share Pity's bed for the remainder of the night. Phoebe asked if I would like her to use the chaise in my chamber, but I shook my head. All I wanted was to be alone for a time, to sort it all out in my mind.

"Then maybe I'll just keep Mr. Hunter company. Be there if he wakes up," she said, and I made no objection to that.

It would be an exaggeration to say that I slept, but I did rest somewhat. When Phoebe tiptoed to the doorway that connected my room with the study, I was instantly awake, however.

"What is it, Phoebe?"

"He's waking up, miss. He's asking for you."

I hurried through to him, falling on my knees beside the bed, and I daresay we cried together a bit, although that is not quite clear to me now. And then we talked until dawn, and I learned how it had all come about.

He had had no intention of marrying Belle Fox. He had only thought to hire her as a housekeeper, and he had penned the letter asking me to join him, when he was stricken the first time.

"It was relatively minor, as strokes go, but I couldn't get out of bed, not even to reach the telephone downstairs. And then she got the idea that if I married her, when I died the house and my fortune would be hers. It wasn't true, because the first thing I did was to make a will, leaving everything to you, the house *and* the money. She was convinced the rest of the cash was hidden here in the house, and I couldn't speak, at first, to tell her the truth. When I could, I was so angry and alarmed at what they might do that I thought the best thing to do was to pretend to be helpless and keep working in secret to regain my strength. I don't know what would have happened if you hadn't come into the house. I might have been able to reach a point where I could overpower her and get out of that room. Or she might have decided to be rid of me once and for all before I was strong enough to prevent it."

"I think that's what they planned," I said soberly. "That you should die, and then I should, so that Francis would then inherit from me."

He was weak, and he had to rest frequently, but already, only hours after he was released, Papa was looking better and stronger. His fingers curled round mine on the edge of the bed.

"Poor Saunielle. You've had a dreadful time, haven't you? But it's all over, and on a reasonable diet I'm sure I'll get well again. There is plenty of money now for everything we want or need."

"No one said where the money came from, Papa."

"I wasn't at any pains to tell them, so undoubtedly they didn't know. It was an investment, you might say." He paused to sip at the glass of milk Phoebe had left beside his bed. "Five years ago, when I first came to California, I met a man in Sacramento. He was a man like me, dispossessed by the War Between the States, a man who had known fine things and been totally stripped of them. He wanted to try his hand at mining, was convinced there was a wealth of gold and silver out there in Nevada that still hadn't been discovered.

"Well, you know me. I'm not much of a gambler. I liked the man, but I declined to go with him. But, more or less as a joke, I offered to grubstake him, because he was even more broke than I was. I matched the hundred dollars he already had, and he said that would get him started, and would entitle me to half of whatever he turned up.

"As you can imagine, I never expected to see him again. Nor to earn any return on my money. He went to Nevada, I traveled about California and eventually wound up here in San Francisco, where I secured a position that enabled me to make ends meet, but not much more. And then a few months ago I learned that my 'partner' was trying to locate me, and I wrote a letter to the town I'd heard he was in.

"Saunielle, don't let this experience with Belle Fox and her niece sour you on humanity. Because this man I'd grubstaked, not even seriously, had hit it big, really big. When he couldn't locate me, he opened an account in my name in a Sacramento bank. And half of all the proceeds from his mine went into that account! It had been accumulating for over four years, and when I identified myself it was all turned over to me and transferred here to San Francisco. The mine is still producing, although there's no telling how long that will continue, but even if it ran out of ore tomorrow we'd still be well fixed. And now you tell me this young man, this Francis, says there is money coming from your mama's family, as well." His smile was warm. "So everything's fine, isn't it, my dear?"

Everything except me, I thought. I hadn't told him about Sebastian. I had left messages with Marlon at the Rohann house, only to be told that they would be delivered if and when Sebastian returned there.

Cromwell came to the house during the day to inquire after me. There was no telling how much he guessed of what had happened between Sebastian and me. But he treated me with the deference he would have shown his friend's wife in the best of circumstances and assured me that we had nothing to worry about. With Papa's evidence, as well as that of the others who had witnessed the shooting, the police were convinced that it was an act of self-defense. While I would have to appear before the authorities to present my testimony, I was assured that no action would be taken in the matter of Francis Verland's death.

He had taken preliminary steps to invalidate the forced marriage between Papa and Belle, only a technicality, he said, since it had not been a legal union to begin with.

My marriage to Francis, so far as he had been able to determine from the document Francis carried, was quite legal and binding, but of course dissolved upon his death. And since my wedding to Sebastian had taken place while I was legally married to Francis, *that* had not been valid, either.

I penned a dozen letters to Sebastian, to be sent to the only address I knew, for Cromwell did not know where Sebastian had gone any more than I did. I told him that he was quite free from all legal responsibility for me, stating only that I had not known my first husband was alive when I undertook a second marriage. In each of the letters I ended by saying that I loved him, until the final one, and then I couldn't bring myself to send any of them.

Cromwell did not tell me what had happened to Belle and to her niece. I didn't ask.

Dodie went to her interview for the position as resident seamstress, although I told her there was now no need for that, and returned triumphant. I had never seen her with so much color in her face, and it was most becoming. She appreciated our offers, she said, but felt that it would be best if she were self-sufficient, and she would be moving into the Salisbury home.

We sat in the parlor, drinking tea and eating the tiny sandwiches Phoebe had prepared to hold us over until dinnertime, and Dodie told us about the Salisbury family.

"Mrs. Salisbury is a very quiet, lovely woman, who wears beautiful clothes. Very kind and sweet, not at all demanding. There are four daughters, from twelve to eighteen, all of them quite pretty, with long blond hair. Only the oldest has her hair up yet. They're all in need of everything, Mrs. Salisbury said, so there will be plenty of sewing to do. Mr. Salisbury owns a foundry, whatever that is, and seems to make a good income."

"It sounds a nice family," I said, nibbling the bread I didn't want.

"There's also a son." Dodie's color heightened, so that I perceived at last the real reason for her pleasure in securing the position. "His name is Charles, and he's nearly twenty-three. He's also fair, and quite good-looking. He said that he might be in need of some shirts, as he has trouble getting ready-made ones to fit. He offered to bring the family carriage around to transfer my belongings and his mama agreed that it would not be unsuitable." She blushed even brighter, and though fighting my own depression, I felt good for Dodie.

That same afternoon, the little man in the dark suit came to the door. I knew at once who he was, for several people had described him to me, the man we had thought to be a tax collector.

"Miss Saunielle Hunter?" he asked politely when I opened the door.

It seemed strange to be addressed once more as *Miss Hunter,* when I had been, in such rapid succession and for such a short time, *Mrs. Verland* and *Mrs. Rohann.* I did not feel like anyone, and certainly not *Miss Hunter* again. I felt as old as Aunt Pity.

Still, I murmured, "That is correct, sir."

He produced his credentials and passed them over for my perusal. "I am the attorney for your late grandfather, Jean Claude Jaubert. I would like to speak to you, if I may."

Since he had followed me halfway around the world, it seemed only civil to usher him into the parlor and offer him a cup of tea. He accepted it gravely, sipped, and put it aside. "Monsieur Jaubert left a rather large fortune, Miss Hunter, and since you are his sole surviving grandchild, all his children being deceased, you are the recipient of it. I must ask for proof of your identity, of course, but I'm sure that is merely a formality."

"Papa has his marriage papers, with Mama's signature on it," I offered. "And the other family papers, as well."

He inclined his head. "I will be happy to examine those, if I may. Before he died, Monsieur Jaubert expressed a wish that his representative ascertain whether or not you had in your possession a ring that he had once given to his daughter, Angélique."

"The Jaubert ring. Yes, I have it," I said. Phoebe was sent to fetch it, and he examined it with what appeared to be gratification.

"Yes, indeed. The Jaubert ring. This alone would convince me that I have found the proper heir. Perhaps you have a legal representative with whom you would like me to discuss the transfer of funds to this country?"

I gave him Cromwell's name and he departed, a small man who could have saved me a good deal of anguish had he arrived in Virginia a few days earlier.

"Imagine!" Phoebe said when he had gone. "You're rich, Miss Saunielle! You won't have to worry about money ever again, and since Mr. Cromwell said he'd return the marriage paper to you there's no need to contract another marriage because of the child."

"No," I agreed, and turned away to hide the tears in my eyes. I would trade both the Jaubert fortune and the one Papa had made for Sebastian, I thought, with or without Rohann Textiles behind him.

When Tom came to the house to see Phoebe, he was both horrified and fascinated by her recitation of the chain of events since his last visit.

When I asked him, ever so casually, if he had seen Mr. Rohann, he shook his head.

"I heard, though, that he was in a bar on the waterfront, drinking as if he intended to make it his life's work. He's well thought of here, and there was them that shook their heads over that. But he's a good man, he'll come out of it, miss."

No doubt he would. I wondered if I would be so fortunate. I even looked at Belle's brandy bottle and wondered if there were really any solace to be found in it, and knew, of course, that there was not. Perhaps there would never be any solace, anywhere, again for me.

When Dodie had been dispatched to her new position in a handsome carriage with the young man who was, Phoebe observed, quite unremarkable, and Aunt Pity had moved to Belle's room on the second floor, handy to the bathroom, and the bewildered old men had been informed that this would no longer be a rooming house once they had located new quarters, I went upstairs and flung myself across the bed. I was dry-eyed, but I'd never felt more full of tears in my life.

Twilight threw shadows across the beautiful room, the room Papa had created especially for me, and then darkness came, and I must have fallen asleep.

I woke some time later, disoriented, thinking at first that the nightmare of the previous night had been just that, the figment of a tormented mind. But no, Francis had been here, Francis who had not loved me at all, Francis who had wanted only to use me for his own purposes, Francis who was now dead.

I heard a step in the hallway and sat up, groping for the lamp. No doubt Phoebe had thought it best to let me sleep through dinner but was now becoming concerned enough to bring me something to eat.

The lamp sent a pleasant glow over the room, and I caught a glimpse of myself in the big mirror. Hair disheveled, bruises showing on my throat from the hands that would have throttled me, face pale and wan.

I picked up a brush to draw it through my hair, then turned as the door swung inward. "I'm not hungry, Phoebe, really I'm . . ."

The brush slid out of my hand onto the carpet, unnoticed, for it was not Phoebe who stood in the doorway.

It was Sebastian.

He looked terrible. He wore the same clothes he'd worn . . . when? Eons ago, when he left the house in a rage, vowing never to return. His eyes were bloodshot, his beard showed in a dark stubble, and he reeked of spirits.

I stared at him, unable to speak, unable to move.

"Saunielle . . ." His voice cracked, and he tried again. "I . . . I tried to get drunk, drunk enough to pass out, but the more I drank the more sober I got. I kept seeing your face . . . your lovely, lovely face . . . and I tried to hate you, but that didn't work, either."

When I had allowed myself to imagine his return, I had pictured myself rushing to him, begging him to hear my explanations, begging him to understand that things were not as they had seemed. Yet now that he was here, I could do nothing. I was as if turned to stone, except for the ache that was growing in my chest.

"I love you," he said, and despite his appearance I could not doubt that he was, indeed, sober. "That's all that matters . . . I love you."

He had not had a message from me. He knew nothing of Francis nor Papa nor any of the events of the past few days. Yet he had come back.

Our eyes locked, and held, and then without even being aware that I was moving I took a hesitant step toward him.

A moment later I was locked in his arms, in an embrace that sent fire searing the wound on my shoulder and blood thundering in my ears. The painful abrasion from his beard was as nothing, the stink of brandy of no matter, the bruising of my mouth sweet beyond anything I had ever known.

I drew enough breath to speak. "It wasn't the way you thought, Sebastian, I can explain . . ."

"It doesn't matter. It doesn't matter," he said, and once more his mouth claimed mine. I closed my eyes and wondered how long my ribs could stand the pressure from his arms, and then I decided that that didn't matter, either.

All that mattered was that Sebastian had come home.